Don't miss TIMESHARE—the first novel in the "thrilling"* time-travel series by Joshua Dann...

"Good escapist fun."

—*Kliatt*

"An action novel, a thriller with great good humor . . . with an underlying and thought-provoking current about what is happening to our social fabric."

—*Internet Book Reviews*

"A lot of fun with an occasional touch of high romance."

—*Locus*

"Funny, entertaining and thrilling . . . with style, sensitivity, and good writing."

—**The Midwest Review of Books*

Ace Books by Joshua Dann

TIMESHARE
TIMESHARE: SECOND TIME AROUND

TIMESHARE:
SECOND TIME AROUND

JOSHUA DANN

ACE BOOKS, NEW YORK

This book is an Ace original edition,
and has never been previously published.

TIMESHARE: SECOND TIME AROUND

An Ace Book / published by arrangement with
the author

PRINTING HISTORY
Ace edition / October 1998

The Penguin Putnam Inc. World Wide Web site address is
http://www.penguinputnam.com

Check out the Ace Science Fiction/Fantasy
newsletter, and much more at Club PPI!

ISBN: 0-441-00567-5

ACE®
Ace Books are published by The Berkley Publishing Group,
a member of Penguin Putnam Inc.,
375 Hudson Street, New York, NY 10014.
ACE and the "A" design are trademarks
belonging to Charter Communications, Inc.

PRINTED IN THE UNITED STATES OF AMERICA

10 9 8 7 6 5 4 3 2 1

"The twenties have lent themselves to extravagant foreshortening since they are years set off on one side by the first of world wars and on the other by the greatest of American depressions. The decade has seemed a sort of accidental pause in history, much of which will be remembered as if it were a willful, elegant sport of time."

—Elizabeth Stevenson,
Babbits & Bohemians, The American 1920s

PROLOGUE

11 MARCH 1926—WASHINGTON, D.C.

THE WAVES OF TRANSPARENT BLUE WATER KISSED THE silky beach, the gentle sun was warm on my skin, my hand was chilled by a tall cool drink with an umbrella, and Althea, looking delectable in a bikini, was snuggled against me. It was delightful.

Unfortunately, it wasn't reality.

I was freezing my butt off on a bench in front of the Lincoln Memorial. It was a chilly midnight in March of 1926. Our client, Mitchell I. Levitan, was pacing in front of the Memorial with Althea on his arm. Terry Rappaport stood at the top of the steps, keeping a careful watch. Mitch had arranged this meeting, and we were there to back him up.

I knew in my gut that things were going to fall apart at any moment. We had chased Mitch all the way across the country, but once we found him, he was determined to see this through whether we liked it or not. He was the customer, after all, which left us little choice but to see to it that he came through unscathed.

But the mark was late. We were beginning to lose the fine edge our careful preparation had given us. We had staked out the Memorial for more than an hour, and fatigue was beginning to set in. Mitch and Althea's practiced stroll became less natural, I began to drift in and out of my park-bench drunk character, and Terry's patrol became more impatient.

Finally, Terry signalled us to meet him at the top of the steps.

"What do you think?" I asked him.

"Let's blow it off," he replied decisively. "He's not coming."

"Or else he smells a rat."

"Oh, yes," came a voice from behind us. "I certainly do smell a rat. A big, fat rat."

In the dim light I squinted, more from disbelief than poor night vision.

We were being held at gunpoint by J. Edgar Hoover.

ONE

THE TROUBLE WITH HAPPILY EVER AFTER IS THAT IT HAS nothing whatsoever to do with getting down to the business of living your life. Even Sleeping Beauty and Prince Charming must've arrived at a point where she wasn't in the mood and he was comatose on the sofa with a beer in one hand and the remote in the other. Eventually, real life intrudes.

Things were going so well for me that I was becoming downright suspicious. I had rescued the love of my life from certain death in World War II. In fact, I had changed history. Althea was destined to die in an air attack on Manston Airfield in Southeastern England in 1940, and I had saved her. I had brought her back here to the year 2007, where we could begin our idyllic life together. But we had a small problem.

She *hated* 2007.

I wasn't that crazy about my home era, either, but then, I hadn't been uprooted from 1940. Doc Harvey, our resident sawbones-*cum*-headshrinker here at Timeshare, called

it a combination of post-traumatic stress syndrome and
something that, well, hadn't been invented yet. Some of
our customers had elected to remain back in the past, which
was fine with all of them, apparently. Unless you've recently gone through the California public school system,
you should possess an average knowledge of history that
can make the past both livable and profitable.

But coming straight from a World War II battlefield to
sixty-seven years in the future had to be a bit unnerving,
to say the least. Admittedly, I hadn't thought of that. You
never think of those things—or anything reality-based—
when love is new.

Althea was a real trouper. Here was a woman who had
burned up the screen with Bogart and Gable—she had even
copped two supporting actress Oscar nominations—and
was well on her way to becoming a major star. And then,
in 1940, she had turned down the lead in the *Maltese Fal-
con* to join the Royal Air Force. John Huston had been livid
about the whole thing. He begged me to make her reconsider. He even suggested that I shoot off her trigger finger
or something to render her unfit for military service. But
nothing could stop her. Her role went to Mary Astor, who
made film history. Althea, meanwhile, arrived in Britain
just before the blitzkrieg in Western Europe began in ear-
nest. The first time around, she was killed in a Luftwaffe
attack on Manston Airfield in Kent. I wasn't about to let
that happen again.

She was now safely in the present with me, and the music was supposed to swell and the end credits should have
been ready to roll. But there was a great deal for her to
overcome. Her kid brother, who was seven years old the
last time they had been together, was now seventy-four
years old. Her parents and all of her friends were dead. The
world had changed beyond all recognition. And there was
practically nowhere on earth where she was allowed to light
a cigarette.

She put up a good front, though. She didn't complain or

mope about it. The only giveaway was that although most of our music was incomprehensible to her, there was a song from the late eighties that caught her attention: "My Brave Face" by Sir Paul McCartney. As we relaxed around the pool here at La Quinta or just walked or played tennis, she kept humming the chorus. That had to tell me something.

We had debriefed her for three weeks at our Timeshare headquarters high above Mulholland Drive. Doc Harvey had pronounced her a woman of robust physical health, even though she was about ten pounds underweight and stressed out from the war. Her emotional health was equally good. However, he was quick to add, there were two serious hurdles. One, she had just been in a war, which in itself requires a mental adjustment. Secondly, she was the first person ever to migrate from the past to the future, which had to be somewhat disorienting, to say the least. Her assimilation had to be gradual and extremely gentle. The worst parts of the history of the last sixty-seven years had to be kept from her, at least for now. In other words, because we honestly didn't know with what we were dealing, we had to take it painfully slow.

So, after her debriefing, we drove out here to La Quinta. The temporal culture shock would not be as profound here, since the resort had been a favorite of Hollywood types since its Mexican-style villas had first sprung up from the desert floor in 1926. Located about twenty miles south of Palm Springs, only a two-hour drive from L.A., La Quinta had been my getaway spot for years. The look of the place hardly ever changed—although comforts and conveniences had kept up with the changing times—so I figured it would be easier on Althea.

I went all out and got us a private cottage with its own pool and Jacuzzi. It cost just a bit less than a shuttle launch, but it was worth it. The curative desert air and the lap of luxury can relax even the most intense of personalities.

Althea sat at the edge of the pool with her feet dangling in the water. She wore a lime-green bikini, and she looked great in it—still a little thin, thanks to her spartan wartime diet, but she wanted to keep the weight off after seeing the competition in 2007. This was over my strenuous objections. She was slender by 1940 standards anyway, and I had always preferred curves to sharp corners. But Althea was determined to fit in, no matter what it took.

"What movies are you going to rent for tonight?" she asked.

I chuckled. It was pretty funny hearing a forties girl ask me about renting a video. I was helping her to catch up with sixty-seven years of film and theatre that she had missed. It was a delicate process. I had so far avoided filling her in on the events that she had bypassed: the rest of World War II, the Cold War, Vietnam, and other historical milestones. Doc Harvey believed that she wasn't ready, and I agreed with him. But there were many wonderful films and plays that she had missed out on, and I enjoyed introducing her to them. The night before, we had seen two absolute winners: *All About Eve* and *The Odd Couple*. She practically kicked herself for missing her chance to be in *Eve*, and she was helpless with laughter at Neil Simon's timeless classic.

"I haven't decided," I replied. "Any suggestions?"

"Who was that utter doll we saw in *Hamlet*?" Her very first videos had been Shakespeare. I figured it would give her an emotional anchor to first see something familiar, albeit with a slightly different slant, so I had rented *The Taming of the Shrew* and *Hamlet*.

"Mel Gibson?"

"That's the one. Be still, my heart."

"Well, he won a best director Oscar about ten years ago—"

"He did? Oh, how wonderful for him! Can we see that?"

"*Braveheart*? I don't know, honey. It's a great movie, hell, it won the Oscar, but some of the battle scenes . . . well—"

She shivered slightly. "I think I've seen enough battle scenes in real life to hold me for a while," she said, lighting a cigarette. I disapproved, but I wasn't about to force her to go through the stress of quitting just yet. After all, just a few weeks before, she had lived in a world where the majority of people smoked. I had, however, insisted that she trade in her Camels for the lowest-tar filters available.

"By the way, there's something I've been meaning to ask you," she said.

"Fire away."

"When am I going to find out about the war?"

"Soon," I promised.

"When?"

"Look, we won, didn't we? You don't see the swastika flag over any countries, do you? We kicked their asses but good."

"But—"

"Honey, I give you my word. When you're ready, I'll give you the whole century."

"I trust you won't make me wait until the end of *this* century."

"Would I do that?"

She was about to reply when the air near the pool suddenly shifted. It was hardly noticeable at first, but then a certain spot near the Jacuzzi began to acquire the look of transparent camouflage.

"Ah," I murmured, "we're about to have a visitor."

"I wish people would knock," Althea remarked.

Our visitor materialized. He wore a ten-gallon hat, black leather chaps, boots, and a cowhide vest. There was a Bisley .45 Long Colt revolver on each hip. The entire ensemble was covered with dust and a horsey aroma was unpleasantly evident.

"Terry, yew ol' hound dawg," I called.

It was my assistant, Terry Rappaport. A former cop like me, he was now making exploratory visits to the Old West for our new Cimarron Central division. Terry was an enthusiast of the Wild West, but I had a feeling that its nos-

talgic study and its gritty reality were two vastly different
things.

"Howdy, Boss. Miss Rowland. I'm sorry to interrupt
your vacation, John, but we've got a problem."

"What else is new?" I asked lightly, but I could tell that
this was going to be serious. They wouldn't recall us both
without a damned good reason.

"What's the problem, Terry?"

"In a nutshell? The problem is Mitchell I. Levitan."

"The studio head-director-writer-hyphenate?"

"The same. God, it's hot."

"You're in La Quinta in April, Terry."

"It's late February in 1895, sport." He stripped off his
vest and began to work on removing the chaps.

"Who is Mitchell I. Levitan?" Althea asked.

"If you decide to go back into the movies, probably your
next boss. He's twenty-eight years old, and his movies have
already grossed over $2 billion."

"God," she gasped. "Would it bother you if I slept with
him?"

"You can sleep with him," I replied. "Just don't have
sex. Terry, what happened?"

"He's missing."

"What do you mean, missing?"

"We got a flatline on his Decacom signal."

"Oh, my God." I could feel myself going pale. The Decacom was the lifeline for anyone going back into the past.
Press the red button, and you instantly return to Timeshare
headquarters here in 2007. But without it, you were lost.
Since the Decacom could not be turned off, and its battery
lasted a month, the only way for the signal to flatline was
if the device was destroyed.

"Where is he?" I asked Terry.

"He's in 1926. He wanted to meet Valentino just before
he croaked. I think he was researching a new movie. Anyway, he's gone."

I looked at Althea. "Well, it was a nice vacation while it lasted."

"Hello." She nudged me. She had picked up the "hello" habit from me. It usually cracked me up, but not this time.

"Hello, what?"

"I'm coming with you."

"Yeah, sure you are."

"You're not leaving me in 2007 by myself. I'll get thrown in jail for smoking or eating a cheeseburger."

"Darling," I said, "may I remind you that as a former detective of the LAPD Fugitive Squad, this is my particular *oeuvre*?"

"And may I remind you, *oeuvre* your objections, that unlike you, I was *alive* in 1926?"

I always knew that only a woman who was as much of a wiseass as I could ever make me truly happy. I was currently delirious.

"She's right, John. Maybe she could help," Terry said.

"No. It's too dangerous."

"It wasn't too dangerous for me the first time around," Althea insisted. "Besides, I could show you around. It might really help. Anyway, I'm not staying here without you."

"Ah, you just want to meet Mitchell I. Levitan. He's an old movie buff—"

"Old? Well, I like that!"

"—and you know he'll go nuts when he meets you. I knew I shouldn't have let you see *All About Eve*."

" 'What a body,' " Terry quoted, " 'what a voice.' "

" 'Ah, men,' " Althea came back. Needless to say, her imitation was perfect. Bette Davis had been a good friend.

"Before we go," Terry said, "can I use your shower?"

"Please do," I replied. "How was the Wild West, anyway?"

Terry had been riding the Silverado Trail, searching for Wyatt Earp and his wife, Josephine Marcus. Cimarron Central had a business proposition for the two of them; we wanted them to run a sort of Western resort town for us. We figured they would be a big draw, and according to history, they needed the money.

Terry snorted derisively. "Full of dust, horse manure, morons and drunks. I only got into about a dozen fist-fights."

Since Terry had never lost a fistfight in his life, I figured they were probably one-punch affairs. But I also wondered if his romance with the Old West had paled.

"Did you have to draw with anybody at high noon?"

"Pure fantasy. I saw one gunfight. It took place in a saloon, at a distance of about five feet, and they both missed. The sheriff was right there and he conked them both on the noggin with his six-gun before either of them could get off another round."

"How will we find Mitchell I. Levitan?" Althea asked me.

"It won't be as tough as you'd think," I replied. As it turned out, I was half right. It was tougher.

TWO

"WHAT I WOULD LIKE TO KNOW," I SAID AS I SWUNG MY feet onto the conference table, "is how the hell he got past the lie detector."

My boss, Cornelia Hazelhof, aka Herself, gave me her trademark glare. "Apparently," she said, "the primary briefer forgot to turn it on. What kind of training are you giving these people, John?"

"All they have to do is flip a switch. These people are college postgrads in the sciences, Cornelia. I didn't think it would require all that much brainwork."

"All right." Felice Link, my other boss, took her usual role as mediator. "What's done is done. I can't say I blame the tech who's responsible. Interviewing the most successful movie producer in the world, I can see how it might rattle a young kid."

The lie detector was actually my idea. It was built right into the chair, and we used it to protect ourselves. Let's say someone wanted to go back in time and kill a guy who grew up to beat him out for a promotion, or a discovery, or a girl. How are we supposed to know? With the lie detector, although it isn't perfect, at least we know when a prospective Tourist is hiding something. We can either turn them away or keep them under strict surveillance.

"You're right," I told Felice. "Okay, first things first. When is he, and why?"

Cornelia peered through half-moon specs at Mitchell I. Levitan's file. "He's in late February 1926. Oh, this guy's good. Listen to this transcript: 'I'm tired of people telling me that it was my dad's money that got me where I am. I want to go back and just see if I can get into a studio and sell a screenplay, or even just a scenario. I want to prove I can do it on my own.' "

"What makes you think he was lying?" I asked her.

"What makes you think he wasn't?" she shot back.

"He's not lying. He's just not telling us everything."

"John's right," Felice said. "It's common knowledge that Mitchell I. Levitan's father bankrolled his first movie. And we're not talking about $35,000 for a UCLA Film School student project, either. Not even a low-budget sleeper. His father got him a $40 million line of credit from the biggest bank in California.

"Even then, he played it smart," Felice added. "He spent half the money on making the film and the other half generating publicity. Soon the project was getting so much play that a studio stepped in and snapped it up before the answer print was completed."

"With that kind of momentum, he had a megabucks hit on his hands before the film even opened," I said. "Smart. And rare—an artist and a good businessman. A killer combination."

"With all that going for him, why would he disappear into 1926?" Felice asked.

"Hmmm. Is he married?" I asked.

"No," Felice replied. "By his own admission, he was kind of a geek in high school and college. Now that he's on top, he has all these beautiful girls chasing him, but he isn't having any."

"Is he gay?"

"Probably not. But whether he's gay or straight, news of any sort of romantic involvement would get around, especially in this town.

"You know what I think," Felice added, snapping her fingers. "Yes, of course! What was that, in his transcript— 'I want to prove I can do it on my own.' " She laughed at the sudden realization. "My goodness, it's . . . it's the sweetest thing I've ever heard of!"

Cornelia looked at her with amusement. Felice was the only person in the entire world for whom she softened her manner. If it were me, or Terry, or anyone else, she would have said, "Yeah, well, spit it out, already." But she let Felice enjoy her triumph in solving the mystery. "I'm really curious now, Felice," she said softly.

"It's wonderful!" Felice cried. "Think about it. You grow up in Beverly Hills, a rich kid. Your dad is Edward C. Levitan. The man is worth hundreds of millions. Got his start in the eighties, typical merger king of that decade. Bought companies and sold them piecemeal. Made even more money on all those real estate deals with the Japanese back then. Remember, they bought every property they could get their hands on at wildly inflated prices? Then, in the nineties, they had to dump them for peanuts. Eddie-baby just bought them back. And he's handsome, a real ladies' man. Still carrying a torch for his late wife, who died when Mitch was four. But that doesn't stop Ed Levitan from bedding the most beautiful and desirable women on the globe.

"But, with our Mitchell, the apple didn't just fall far from the tree; someone took it and blew it into the next county. Ed Levitan is charming, outgoing, a real Lothario. He loves his son, sure, but he doesn't know what to make of him. He gives the kid everything, including love, but he can't help thinking, 'Is this really my kid? How did this happen?'

"Well, poor Mitch can't help but infer this from his dad's attitude—even if it's only subconscious. And he hasn't got a mother to dote on him and build his self-esteem. He's got nobody, really. Just his old grandfather—a screenwriter who never quite made it, who died when Mitch was a teenager. He was really alone then. And because he's kind of a clod, the girls just shine him on. Until he hits it big—until he becomes the most powerful man in the movie biz."

"So, what are you getting at, Felice?" I asked. I was really interested.

She looked at me as if I were an imbecile. "He wants a *girl*, John. God, it's so simple! Look, he's one of the most famous men in the world. Everyone knows who he is. Everyone knows what he's worth. And in Hollywood, every time he goes near an actress, it must be like swimming in shark-infested waters with a pocketful of ground beef."

"He can't trust anyone," I said.

"That's right. 'I want to prove I can do it on my own.' He's not just talking about the movies. He's talking about . . . love."

Cornelia looked at me with raised eyebrows. "Jesus," she whispered. "But why 1926?"

"Oh, no," I sighed, envisioning the work I had ahead of me. "Felice, if you're right—and I believe that you are—this could take a while."

"Why?" Cornelia asked me.

"Because he's not just looking for *a* girl. He's looking for *the* girl."

"But who is she?"

"Damned if I know," I replied. "But I'd better get busy and find out."

•   •   •

I put in a call to Terry Rappaport, asking him to meet me at Mitchell I. Levitan's house in Beverly Hills. It would not be easy to get past the security detail, but I wasn't worried. I had scammed my way through more challenging barricades.

Mitchell's house was part of a new development of mansions higher up in the canyon. A private patrol car fell in behind me and followed me all the way to Levitan's house, a twenty-five-room replica of a Victorian country estate. When I got to the front gate, Terry was swapping laughs with Levitan's chief guard. He waved me over.

"John, this guy says he knows you."

I peered out my car window at the security man. Those guys all look alike. Grey flannel pants and a blue sports jacket with a gun bulge; muscles and a mustache. There was a word we had for it: security-faced. I shrugged. I didn't know the guy from Adam.

"Hey, John," the private cop greeted me. "Remember me? Bud Richter, Rampart Division Motors?"

"Oh, sure," I lied. Actually, I did remember the brawny ex-motorcycle cop slightly, but we had never been more than nodding acquaintances. Motor cops and detectives are usually diametrically opposed personalities. "How've you been? When did you pull the pin?"

"Two years ago. Put in my twenty and vamoosed. Thought about moving it on north to Oregon or Montana, then I thought, what the hell for? It's not like I drive a pickup. When this came along, I jumped at it. I've never had it so good."

"I'm glad you're doing well, Bud. How's the wife?" I was taking a chance here, not knowing his marital status, but I figured it was worth the risk.

His smile widened. "I made parole last year. She's in Arizona with her new guy. Tell you the truth, we never got along so well until now. I got somebody, she's got somebody—at least, now it's official. We might even have kids."

"That's great," Terry said. "Bud, we've got to go inside," he said, abruptly switching gears.

The smile darkened under the mustache. "I can't."

"Oh, sure you can."

"Hey, John, this guy's no cheapskate. I like this job. And if I had to live on just my pension—"

"We'd give you a job with us," I finished for him. "Look, Bud, your boss might be in trouble. We just need to look through his room, his personal office. You can watch us like a hawk, if you want. We won't take anything out of the house, we won't snap any photos—we just need to get a handle on him."

"What kind of trouble?" Bud paled, envisioning his cake job going up in smoke.

"We can't tell you. But you know you can trust us, Bud. Where're you living now?"

He gave me a bewildered look. "Calabasas Park. Why?"

"Nice house? Pool? Got a little boat in the driveway? I bet you've got a room set up that's all yours, pool table, dartboard, big wall screen TV, and a bar with a real beer draft. All your police citations framed on the wall. You've been waiting your whole life for a room like that. I'd like to go over there some night, play a little poker or catch a ball game. Smoke some really good cigars. Yeah, sounds real nice."

"It is real nice," he replied dully.

"You know what else?" I continued dreamily. "It's not just the house and the great rec room, and the pool. It's your new wife. Am I right? All the things that you and your first wife went to war over, none of that even bothers her. You want to disappear into your rec room after work, drink a few beers, watch all five ESPN channels at once, hey, that's fine with her. I'll bet she doesn't even make you debrief after a hard day's work: 'Honey, the car . . . the plumbing . . . the lawn . . . our relationship . . .' She doesn't bug you with that crap. You go home, you hit your den, and just kick back. She knows that's your place, your little den, and she respects that. I'll bet that when she talks about it to her friends, she has this really indulgent, affectionate sort of smile on her face. The kind that says, 'Yeah, he's just a little boy, aren't they all?' And that suits her just fine.''

"Of course," Terry picked up, "this job is making it all possible. Ooh, Bud, you'd have to sell the house, move into some real dump, living on just your pension. Maybe get another job, door-shaking at eight bucks an hour in some refinery—wearing one of those dopey uniforms with a square badge and contrasting pocket-flaps. Or maybe bored out of your skull working midnights behind a console at an insurance office."

"And you had it so good," I added. "You really want to move back to Eagle Rock? On that pension? The only house you could afford would be on wheels and springs."

"All right!" he shouted. "If it'll help Mr. Levitan . . ."

"I knew we could count on you, Bud," I said. "After all, we're cops, right?"

"Were," he said.

"You never really stop, Bud," said Terry.

Bud straightened up. "Just do what you gotta do. And make it quick," he snapped. "And after this, you *owe* me."

"Of course we do." I smiled. Terry and I followed him through the gate.

"Must be a heavy mortgage, Calabasas," Terry whispered as we walked through.

"Let's check it out when we get back. Take care of his payments for the next few months. After all, he was a cop for twenty years. You ever hear of a cop who doesn't live beyond his means?"

I never could understand why rich guys who live alone buy these monstrous-sized digs that they couldn't possibly enjoy by themselves. In my experience, a guy like Levitan, or any filthy-rich loner, only uses three rooms in the house, no matter how big it is. There's usually a bedroom that is connected to a sitting room and a bathroom with an Olympic-sized bathtub—a bathtub which, since most guys just shower, anyway, is only used on particularly romantic dates. Then there's the guy's office or library, which is really where he spends most of his time. Sometimes, there's also a den, much like Bud Richter's beloved little hideaway, where a guy might just want to relax. The rest of the house, in my opinion, is useless, just more work for the staff.

Mitchell I. Levitan's domicile was no exception. There were seven bedrooms and nine bathrooms. Two broad circular staircases, and at the middle of each one was a balcony that looked out on the pool and tennis court beyond. There was a gorgeously furnished living room and a dining room with a table for twenty. But none of these rooms showed any real use. It was as though Mitch had handed a decorator half a mil and told her to go to town. The place looked hardly lived in.

I asked Bud where Mitch spent most of his time.

"Just the library," he said. "He never even went into the kitchen. If he wanted anything, like a sandwich, or some coffee, or even popcorn, he'd ring up the cook."

"What about his bedroom?"

"Sleeps there, that's about it."

"What about the pool, or the tennis court?"

"Nah. We use it more'n he does. There is an exercise room. He's in there for an hour every day after he gets up."

"What's in there?"

"Just a treadmill and a Nautilus machine. Oh, and a TV with a DVD. He usually watches movies when he works out. He told me otherwise it would bore him to death."

"Okay, Bud, show us the library."

We walked toward the rear of the house. "This is his favorite room," Bud said. "Matter of fact, I think it's the only room in the whole place he even likes."

I could see why. It was a wonderful room, done exactly

the way I'd have wanted it if it were mine. It was large, almost as big as the living room. The walls were lined with bookshelves that reached to the ceiling; there was even a ladder on a track. There was a small lounge area with a comfortable recliner and black leather couch; a good place to read or watch a little television.

The desk was a work of art, solid mahogany with a glass top. The kind of desk anyone would look at and say, "You don't see craftsmanship like this anymore." The desk was clear, except for a blotter, a pen set, a calendar, and a humidor filled with expensive cigars.

"He only smokes cigars once in a while," Bud said. "Like if there's another movie guy who smokes them. Not usually by himself."

"Who's this?" I asked, motioning to a framed photograph on the one shelf that wasn't crammed with books. It was an old black-and-white photograph, but professionally done, and obviously given a place of honor. The subject was a middle-aged man whose expression was somewhere between defiance and defeat. Next to the picture was a framed case filled with an impressive array of military medals and a pair of faded oak leaves.

"That was his grandfather," Bud said. "His dad's dad. He wrote a couple of movies in the thirties and a book after the war. He was some kind of war hero, too. Flew against the Nazis in the Spanish Civil War, and later joined the Flying Tigers in China. They were really close, but he died when Mr. Levitan was a kid."

I nodded, and made a mental note to keep the grandfather in mind.

"I can't get over these books," Terry said. "First editions—the real thing, not that fake crap you can order on TV. *Tom Brown's School Days. Sister Carrie.* Whole sets of Dickens, Balzac, Poe, Baudelaire—wow! Check out these anthologies! Clifton Fadiman! Jesus, I bet no one remembers *him* anymore. The plays of Clifford Odets, everything by Shaw, Ibsen, the Shakemeister, Molière—hey,

Bud? Was this guy really a reader, or is this just show time?''

"He reads," Bud replied gravely. I noticed that Bud was beginning to take on a proprietary air when speaking about his boss. "All the time, everything. His grandfather taught him before he even started school. He's even got me doing it. Said it's the secret of his success."

That struck me. "Really? Did he elaborate on that?" I was beginning to get the feeling that the ex-motor cop was Mitch's only confidant.

His face colored. "Well, yeah. See, I was askin' him about all these books once, and he turned around and said flat out that anyone in the business who doesn't read, well, he doesn't have much respect for their intelligence. He said he would still be just a producer instead of the head of his own studio if it wasn't for reading."

"Why?"

"He told me that after he started making some good movies, the studio—the one he owns now—the bosses there started telling him what kind of movies to make, what stars to write for, what the kids would go to see. He said he told 'em their ideas sucked, they'd all been done before, and who cared. 'Oh, yeah?' they said, and he said, 'Yeah.' ''

"Well, that sure told them," Terry remarked.

"No," Bud said, "that's not all. He sat down and wrote out a check for a million bucks, made it out to the studio. He said, 'If I can't come up with fifty good ideas right off the top a my head right *now*, you can keep it.'

"Well, hell, he's read every book in this room and more all the time. It was nothing for him. Nothing at all."

That somehow didn't surprise me. Like pretty much everyone else in the world, I was a fan of Levitan's movies, and now I understood why. He didn't go just for the safe, formula blockbusters. He was willing to give small films and new talent a chance, and his fearlessness and vision usually paid off handsomely.

Terry snapped his fingers. "Hey, when was that? I mean, what was his first movie after he took over the studio, the one that copped the Globe and the Oscar?"

"It was, uh . . . yeah, it was the end of '01, early '02. Came out just in time for the nominations."

I racked my brain. I was still on the Fugitive Squad at that time, and didn't get out to the movies very often. "Something with a divorce," I said. "Yeah, the guy's a real wimp, his wife dumps him, he goes off to Africa or someplace, comes back all buffed out—a real macho man. His wife doesn't recognize him, and falls for him all over again."

Terry flipped through some books on the nearest shelf. He pulled out a Guy de Maupassant anthology and turned to the table of contents. "Hah! I knew it," he shouted triumphantly. "*The Sequel to a Divorce*. Good story. Good movie. Yeah, this guy reads, John."

"Bud?" I had a sudden thought. "What was his next project going to be?"

"I'm not sure. I think it was going to be about his grandfather. He had a pretty interesting life, from what he told me."

Again the grandfather. I made another mental note.

I sat down behind the desk and absently opened the middle drawer. Pens, paper clips. A Beretta .380; no surprise there. He had probably bought it, gone to the range a few times, and then forgot about it. Well, there were no kids in the house.

"Hey, what's this? A pack of Luckies? Without filters? What's the deal here, Bud?"

Bud looked embarrassed. "He said he was practicing," Bud muttered.

"Practicing? For what?"

"I dunno, maybe he was gonna be in one of his own movies."

"Wait—what the hell?"

"What've you got?" Terry asked.

"Son of a bitch. A Union Pacific Railroad schedule. *Effective 2-21-26*." I held up the faded and crumbling sheet of stiff paper. "Damn it! He blew town!"

"Where to?"

"What're you guys talkin' about?" Bud wanted to know.

"How should I know?" I replied to Terry. "He could be anywhere!"

"But where?"

"Chicago, New York, who knows?"

"Why would he take the train?" Bud asked. "What good is that schedule now?"

"Terry, we have a job ahead of us."

"No kidding."

"Will someone please tell me what's going on?" Bud pleaded.

"Bud, what was the last book he was reading?"

"How should I know?"

"Think!"

"Uh . . . this one. He usually kept the book he was reading right behind him in the shelf here."

Terry picked it up and examined it. "Trouble," he whispered. "*You Dirty Rat: The True Story of the Mob in the 1920s.*"

THREE

TERRY AND I OPENED THE DOOR TO MY APARTMENT ON the Golden Mile of Wilshire Boulevard and found Althea sitting on the living room floor, amid a pile of children's books by that eminent author, J. S. Devon. The books all starred the same character, a kid by the name of Danny Dreamer. Danny had a way of indulging in flights of fancy, daydreams that were so involved and detailed, it was hard to believe he hadn't actually experienced them. Which, of course, in a mystical way, he had.

Althea looked up at me with glistening eyes. She looked beautiful, sitting cross-legged in a pair of twenty-first-century designer jeans and an LAPD "Protect and Serve" T-shirt.

"I love you, Mr. Devon," she said softly.

What can I say? I'm a man of many talents. "I love you, too, dear. Come on, sweetums, action stations."

"We're going?" She brushed at her face with the back of her hand and shook off her emotions. It didn't surprise me; she had not only been a great actress, but until a few weeks ago, she had been an officer in the Royal Air Force. And Section Officer Althea Rowland, WAAF, took over immediately.

"Where and when?" she demanded.

"We'll start here," I said. "Los Angeles, late February, early March, 1926. We'll firm it up. Terry, you're on call in the Zoom Room. We get in a jam, one of us'll give you three short bursts on the Decacom. You come in ready to rock and roll."

"Rock and roll?" Althea asked.

"It's a long story, and we don't have time for it now. Terry, get on the horn and alert the wardrobe, medical, and currency teams. Two to go back, and you and your stuff standing by."

"Gotcha." He went for the phone and stopped. "Hey, John. The twenties could get a little hairy. What're you gonna use for self-defense?"

I considered this for a moment. I was strictly forbidden the use of deadly force, and usually carried only a Taser, a stun gun that could drop a two-hundred pound man at ten feet. But I didn't trust it completely and neither did Terry. When he had gone back into the 1890s, he had carried real ammo in his six-guns, but he was a good enough shot with a pistol to inflict minimal damage while still eliminating a threat. I was an expert marksman with a skeet gun, but my handgun shooting wasn't on Terry's level.

"I guess we're gonna have to break some rules, old buddy."

"Maybe not," said Terry. "Tell you what. Why don't you call the office and make the arrangements. I'll meet you there."

"Where're you going?"

"You'll see," he said, shutting the door behind him.

"Alone at last," I said to Althea. "Are you sure you're up for this? The doc doesn't recommend it."

She waved off my concern. "John, you have a beautiful apartment. Even if I can't figure out what anything is for or how to use it. But this place . . . this time . . . it gives me the willies. Sometimes I feel . . . like I don't even exist. I can't stay here alone. And I won't be cooped up at Time-share. Besides, you promised me we'd be doing everything together from now on. Remember? Remember when you told me that? At Manston?''

Of course I did, to a degree. I didn't have a perfect audio memory like hers. "Sure," I said. "I just don't want anything to happen to you, that's all.''

"I'll be fine," she insisted. "You're the stranger to 1926, not me.'' She had a sudden thought and shivered, then laughed. "I was twelve years old. What do I do if I run into myself?''

"Do what I always do," I replied.

"What's that?''

"Say hello. By the way, do you remember a screenwriter back in the thirties, a guy named Harry Levitan?''

"Harry? Related to Mitch?''

"His grampa.''

"I knew Harry. Not well, but he was in Bogie's crowd. Handsome.'' She smiled wickedly. "Very handsome, now that I think about it. In an Angry Young Man sort of way. He's in—he went to Spain to fight the Fascists. Is he all right?''

"I suppose we'll find out, one way or another.''

The Zoom Room, that is, the section around which our time-travelling apparatus was located, was bustling as usual before a trip. Cornelia was going through the checklist with a technician. Felice was overseeing our preparations.

I wore a dark wool suit with a heavily starched shirt and a silk tie. Felice handed me a straw boater and waited for my objections. My dislike of hats was legendary, but I placed it on my head without argument this time, feeling silly. I was going into the 1920s, when everybody, without exception, wore a hat, and I couldn't afford to stand out in a crowd. Althea came out of the changing room looking great, as usual. She wore a pleated skirt that reached just above her knees and a blouse with a sailor knot.

Felice handed us our personal items. My identification papers included an ID card from U.S. Naval Intelligence, which was supposed to keep me out of any legal difficulty that might crop up. Sometimes, it even worked.

Terry rushed into the Zoom Room and waved me over to a corner. He pressed a small fanny pack into my hands.

"Put that with your luggage," he said, "and don't let the boss see it."

I unzipped the bag and peeked inside. "Terry, this is a .45. I can't—"

"It's all right. I've been reloading this ammo for a while, and it works. It's a low-grain load, the round comes out and hits you maybe as hard as a shot from a BB pistol. The kicker is, they're charged."

"Charged? Like electric?"

"Yeah, it gives the bad guy a nice enough shock to knock him down. It's better than the Taser. I gave you five mags worth."

I turned away from the room and attached the bag to my waist. "You're a buddy."

"Just stay out of trouble. And if you can't, you know where to find me."

Felice walked over and handed me a stack of bills in an envelope. "I figured you'd be back there for a while," she said. "Here's twenty-five thousand. That ought to hold you till the job's done."

"I can always wait until October and bet on the Series," I said. "Yankees, right?" Terry, a New Yorker, was the resident Yankee fan and baseball expert.

Terry rolled his eyes. "Shmuck! Cardinals! The Cards beat the Yankees that year. Grover Cleveland Alexander comes in to pitch in the seventh, hungover out of his gourd? Strikes out Tony Lazzeri on three pitches?"

"Sorry," I said, reddening. "I should have remembered that."

"Just don't bet on any ball games."

We went over to where Doc Harvey was giving Althea a final checkup. "Watch her diet, John. She's hardly had time to get used to our century, and now she's going back to that crap." He drew some pills out of his medical bag. "Give her one of these a day until they run out. Absolutely no dairy. And stay away from bathtub gin."

"Yes, Mother," I said. "Are you ready?"

"God, yes," Althea said. "Back to civilization. Let's go."

"And no smoking," said the doc. Althea turned, walked back to him, and gave him a light kiss on the cheek.

"You *must* be out of your mind," she whispered to him.

We stepped into the Zoom chamber, which in politically correct terms was known as the Temporal Transference Unit, or TTU. Naturally, only new employees called it that, and not for very long.

"John," Cornelia said, "per your instructions, we're dropping you at exactly the point where we lost contact with Mitchell I. Levitan's Decacom unit."

"Where is that?"

"Santa Monica Boulevard, west of Beverly Hills. That's about as exact as I can make it."

"Okay. Let's do it to it."

Althea took my hand. "This is one hell of a surprise, the way things turned out," she said.

"What do you mean?"

"I mean that when I first saw you walk into that party in Cole Porter's bungalow, I thought you might be an interesting man. How little I knew."

The chamber began to hum. "Godspeed, John Surrey," Terry called. There was no religious connotation involved. It was after the style of Alan Shepard, who had given John Glenn the same benediction when he blasted off in *Friendship 7*. It had become a tradition between Terry and me; after all, we were explorers, too.

•   •   •

28 FEBRUARY 1926—SANTA MONICA
BOULEVARD, WEST LOS ANGELES

A quick phone call—in a real phone booth, with a speaker-horn, which only cost one buffalo nickel—to the brand-spanking-new Beverly Hills Hotel revealed to us what we already suspected: Mitchell I. Levitan had never checked in.

I was a little bit too preoccupied to fully appreciate my first minutes in 1926. Other than the rattle of automobiles on spoked wheels, and the occasional *awooga* of the car horns—followed then, as now, by an "Aaah, blow it out your ass!"—the aura of a strange decade was lost on me. This was my ninety-seventh trip back to the past, and my mind already had its own temporal adjustment shorthand: The cars were different, the people dressed funny, the buildings were smaller but more solidly constructed, yadda, yadda, yadda. I wasn't being blasé, it's just that I was in a hurry. The main reason for my reluctance in rose-smelling was that I had long since passed that particular hump of the novice—the belief that the folks who live in the era you are visiting actually give a damn one way or another. The clock doesn't stop just because *you* show up. People still have their own lives to live, jobs to do, meals to cook, kids to raise. There's an odd feeling for the inexperienced time traveller that all these people are wearing idiotic suits, driving old cars, and demanding, "Say, what's the big idea?" just for your benefit. They're not; they're living their lives according to their times. It's still fun, mind you, and there are an awful lot of laughs to be provided, but then, as now, you have to learn how to stay out of people's way.

Althea was still new at the game, however, and drank in everything as though it were part of an elaborate surprise party laid on just for her.

"Nice to be back?" I asked her.

"You couldn't possibly imagine," she replied. "What are we doing?"

"We're trying to figure out why Mitchell I. Levitan broke off contact on this spot. There's nothing here but the Mormon Temple. He's not a Mormon."

She turned around and I saw her do a slight double take. She tapped me on the shoulder. "Neither are they," she observed.

She was right. We weren't looking at the Mormon Temple. What we were looking at was Sister Aimee Semple McPherson's Foursquare Gospel Church.

"Come along, my dear," I said, taking her arm. "I think it's time we were saved."

Ever since a Chicago White Sox infielder named Billy Sunday hung up his spikes and traded in his glove for a Bible, there has been a long procession of so-called evangelists who specialize in separating impressionable people from their money in the name of God. Sunday, a recovering alcoholic, used to visit the back room where the money was counted, wanting to know, "How much did we take the suckers for tonight?"

Others followed. Some never became more than tent show hosts in the Bible Belt. Others went no farther than their own storefronts. But until the age of television, no one could even approach the level of success enjoyed by one Sister Aimee Semple McPherson.

Aimee was, for lack of a better word, a true artist. Her act boasted a mixture of sex, fear, and old-time religion. When she touched a bum leg and pronounced it cured, no one was going to argue. Not in front of four hundred tear-streaked, adoring worshippers. And after a while, the guy with the leg would start to think, hey, maybe it doesn't hurt so much anymore at that—the way a sick person starts to feel a little better just waiting in the doctor's office.

We took the rearmost pew but had no trouble hearing

Aimee. She was suffused with an angelic glow from a
follow-spot—one that became considerably brighter by
contrast after a few "praise Jesuses."

I spotted at least ten shills spread out among the faithful.
They weren't any too subtle; whenever Aimee would ask
for a "praise Jesus," or any other sort of validation, the
shills were quick to nudge their neighbors and jump to their
feet in an almost orgiastic response. The real giveaway was
when the clothesline came around.

Your average church, I'm sure you're aware, has what
is known as the collection plate, which is usually passed
around midway through the service. It might be a straw
basket attached to a long wooden rod. Whatever it is, it is
an efficient enough receptacle for coins and paper.

Well, a collection plate wasn't going to do it for good
old Aimee. After all, people might get the wrong idea and
give her coins. To avoid any confusion at all, instead of a
collection plate, two deacons stood at opposite ends of the
pew holding a clothesline. Attached to this clothesline, at
approximate pew-seat intervals, were golden safety pins.
You didn't have to be a genius to figure out that only paper
money could be attached to those safety pins. Which was
how, in a few short years, Sister Aimee had been able to
build a magnificent church with its own powerful radio station.

Anyway, when the clothesline came around, Aimee's
shills made a huge show of pulling out a ten or twenty and
pinning it to the clothesline—which, in turn, made the poor
suckers sitting next to them rethink that one-dollar dona-
tion, making it a two- or even five-dollar gift.

When the clothesline approached us, I took out two fifties, and attached them to the pins in front of us. Then I
motioned to the nearest deacon, who saw my generosity
and hurried over. I handed him a twenty.

"I'd like to visit with Sister Aimee for a moment," I
whispered.

"I'm afraid that'll be impossible." He shook his head.

"We're in the house of the Lord," I replied, slipping him another twenty, "nothing is impossible."

He went over to the other deacon and they whispered a few words back and forth. The second deacon came over to us.

"I'd like to help, but—" He shrugged helplessly.

I rolled my eyes and took out another twenty, which he pocketed with almost comic nonchalance. "Another fifty each, after we see Sister," I said.

He half-bowed. "Follow me, please."

He led us out a side door through a narrow corridor to the vestry room. "Sister will join you in a moment," he whispered in reverential tones.

Althea gave me a wide-eyed look. "I don't know why I'm nervous," she said. "She was such a fake."

"You're in the presence of greatness," I said. "A con artist, but a great one."

The door opened and Sister Aimee Semple McPherson slipped into the room, quietly shutting the door behind her. Her manner was surprisingly modest, as though she was sorry to have disturbed us.

"Hello," she said shyly. "I'm Sister Aimee." She still wore the cross-spangled cloak in which she had run the service. Her blond hair was spit-curled; her eyes were a startling blue. Her face was not what could be called attractive—in truth, I unapologetically state that she brought to mind a handsome, show-quality Airedale—but it was an arresting face that could not be ignored. And when that face turned its attention on me, it was difficult to dismiss the pure sexual current that bore at me right through her eyes.

"Sister?" Althea spoke first. Aimee's face, in one glance, spoke volumes.

Althea fell to her knees. "Oh, Sister, oh, Sister," she sobbed, kissing her hand. "You're the only one who can help my . . . brother and me! Please, Sister!"

At the word "brother," Aimee's face relaxed instantly.

Her manner became soothing almost at once. "Now, there, it's all right, child. Sister will help you."

"Oh, Sister," Althea blubbered, "I know you can! The way you heal all those people."

"Now, now," Aimee replied, gently chastising her, "I don't do the healing. Jesus does the healing. I'm just the li'l office girl who opens the door and says, 'Come in.' "

Aimee helped Althea to her feet. "How can I help you, child?"

"It's m-m-my fiancé, Mitchell. We were supposed to g-get married, but he said he wouldn't unless you said it was the right thing to do. He *adores* you so," she cried. "Oh, Sister! Whatever shall I do?"

It occurred to me that right now I was witnessing perhaps the greatest scene ever played between two consummate actresses—and the world would never know it.

What impressed me even more was the way Althea instinctively knew Aimee would be threatened by her looks, and she undertook to work sexual competition out of the equation by making me her brother.

Aimee took ahold of Althea's hand and mine, immediately beginning to caress me with her thumb.

I drew Mitchell's head shot out of my pocket. "Have you seen this man, Sister? He answers to the name of Levitan—Mitchell I. Levitan."

"Why . . . yes," she said, but she was looking in my eyes, and not at the photo.

"Did he say anything? Like, where he might be heading. It's life and death for my sister, Sister."

"Oh, you can call me plain old Aimee. All my friends do," she added significantly.

"He seemed like a nice young man," she said, biting the inside of her lip. "Even though he was in that den of iniquity, the movies."

"Oh, Sister!" Althea shrieked. "I tried to keep him from the movies! It's the Devil's business!" She betrayed a slight lip curl that only I could see. "Tell me you made him stop!"

"Only Jesus could do that, child." She let go of Althea, a gesture almost rudely dismissive, and took both of my hands. "He didn't tell me much," she said. "Only that he had always wanted to meet me and he had a train to catch."

"Where to?"

She put my hand on her breast. "What's your hurry?"

I gave her the flirtiest grin I could summon. "Sis. It's driving her nuts. But I can always come back later."

"My last sermon's at eleven," she whispered.

"I'll be there, Sister," I whispered back.

"Did he say where he was going?" Althea wailed.

"Yes, child, I remember now," Aimee said through her teeth. "Chicago. And"—she bit the inside of her lip again—"Dixon, Illinois." She gave Althea a glance that I could swear was malicious. "He said he was looking for a lifeguard in Dixon, Illinois. You sure about him, honey?"

"I suppose we'll find out when we get there," I said. Come on, *Sis*."

"Oh, thank you . . . thank you, Sister," Althea whined tearfully.

"Not at all, honey," Aimee sang. "Midnight?" she mouthed at me.

I gave her a wink and a nod. With any luck, I'd be on a train rolling eastward past Needles by then. No hard feelings, though; we both ran a pretty good con.

I had never been aboard a train in my life, so when we got to Union Station I gave Althea some money and told her to get us the best accomodations available. I wasn't disappointed. The conductor showed us to something called a "drawing room," which had all of the appointments one would find in a good hotel, including, I was gratified to see, a nice big bed.

The rails were king in America at this time, and would continue their reign until the late fifties, when air travel became advanced enough for the middle class to afford it.

The train crews were strictly divided along racial lines. The engineers, brakemen, and conductors were all white. The cooks, porters, and waiters were all black. Yet all were part of an aristocracy of travel. Once the conductor showed you to your drawing room, you were handed over to the careful ministrations of the porters, for whom your comfort was a matter of professional pride. A steady job with the railroad was pretty much the best career a black man could hope for in the 1920s, and not one of them took it for granted. When you left your shoes outside your door at night, they were returned the next morning as shiny as patent leather. If there was one speck of dust on your coat, someone was there with a brush before you even knew it. If you wanted your morning coffee at precisely 9:01, a porter was at your drawing room door with a tray at 9:01 on the dot. All of these services were performed with cheerful dignity and solicitousness by men who took pride in their work. Through far hindsight these men have been considered by some to be Uncle Toms, but having experienced rail travel in the 1920s, I can attest to the unfairness of such a sweeping generalization. These men were professionals who made the best of an unacceptable situation.

Our porter, a stocky man in his sixties named Greene, committed our names and our tastes to memory within seconds of meeting us. Over the next four days, my coffee arrived light and sweet, and Althea's, black with one lump. Greene took great pride in his ability. "You on'y has to tell Greene wunst, Mist' Surrey," he pronounced, and I believed him. I never saw him write anything down—I later found out that he was barely literate—and yet he never got a single order wrong in four days.

"You're awfully quiet," Althea said as we rolled through a small town in Iowa. "You haven't said much since we left Los Angeles."

"I'm not used to doing nothing for this long at a stretch."

"How long would this trip take in your time?"

"Three, maybe four hours by plane. A workaholic like Mitchell I. Levitan must have gone loony on this trip. And, of course, he didn't have you to help the time go by."

"That's not what's bothering you, is it?"

"No, it isn't. To tell you the truth, I was thinking about Greene. This guy must have an IQ of about 812. He works twenty hours a day, never screws up an order, always makes you feel like you're the only passenger on the train. Yet this is as high as he can go in life. And this is the best he can hope for, for his kids."

"I didn't get out much in 2007," Althea said. "Is it very different?"

"Oh, you still have problems. Hell, when we're all wearing space suits and living in domes, we'll still have problems. But somebody like Greene could be whatever he wants to work at becoming.

"You know, it's a problem we've had at Timeshare. We have clients who happen to be black, and they want to go back in time and visit old neighborhoods and witness family milestones, just like anybody else. You know how rotten it makes me feel to tell them that if they go back far enough in time, they can't stay at the same hotels or eat in the same restaurants as our white clients? And what makes me feel even crappier is that they all understand. They expect it; they don't even hold us responsible. And we hate it—we feel like we're part of the problem."

"It's not your fault, John. It would just cause trouble for everyone if you tried to fight it."

"It still stinks," I muttered.

On the last night of our trip, I went into the men's restroom and found Greene sitting on the radiator, reading a book.

"Hello, Greene," I said. "What are you reading?"

"Tryin' to," he said. "My daughter been teachin' me." He showed me the cover; it was an elementary school primer. "I figure it's never too late to take up schoolin'."

"You figured right," I said. "I'm sorry you had to wait this long."

"I ain't complainin'. I done good, considerin' I was born a slave in Mis'sippi."

I was taken aback. Although I had travelled through time, and farther back than the twenties, I had never met anyone who had actually been a slave. I had always taken the attitude that it wasn't my fault, no one in my family had ever been a slaveholder—but when confronted with an actual victim, I was struck dumb. The simple fact remained: If I had been born at the same time as Greene, he would still have been a slave and I would have been free.

"I was two years old when the war ended, an' I was free, so I didn't have much time t'get used to bein' a slave," Greene said. He put down his book and drew a flask out of his pocket.

"It's the real thing," he said. "Green River." He took two paper cups out of the dispenser over the sink, and poured us each a shot.

"Thanks," I said. "To better times."

"Oh, they'll get better," Greene nodded. "After I'm dead, maybe, but they'll get better. I was talkin' to a white man on the Chicago run las' week . . ." He trailed off and shook his head at the memory. "No disrespec', but he wuh little crazy."

The hair on my neck stood up.

Greene looked around, as though checking for eavesdroppers. "He said it's all gonna happen. Colored gonna vote, eat where they want, sleep where they want, git jobs, go to college. Be movie stars." He laughed. "Hoo-wee, colored movie star! That Greene gotta see!"

"He's right," I said. "Who was this guy, Greene?"

"He called me *Mist'* Greene. He tol' me to call him Mitchell. I tol' him that wouldn't be fittin'. So we compromised. I called him Mr. Mitchell, an' he call me . . . he din' call me nothin' after that. Called me 'uhhh.' "

"Mitchell?" I asked.

"Mitchell I. Levitan," he said. "Greene don't forget a name like that. Got off at Dixon."

I kept my self-congratulations inside.

"Mist' Surrey," Greene asked me thoughtfully, "was Mitchell I. Levitan right? It's gonna happen? For my chillen?"

"Yes," I said, "but even more for their children."

He straightened on his perch, setting his face as though posing for a statue. "Good," he said. " 'cause every last one of 'em goes to college. When the time comes, Greene's kids gon' be right out front."

2 MARCH 1926—DIXON, ILLINOIS

"Your bags'll be at the station in Chicago," Greene told me. "I'll look after it personal."

"I wouldn't trust anybody else, Greene," I said. The train was slowing as it reached the outskirts of Dixon. I handed him an envelope with a thousand dollars inside. He pocketed it without looking. I was sorry I would miss the chance to see his face when he counted up my contribution to the Children of Greene Educational Fund.

"It's been a pleasure, Mist' Surrey, ma'am."

I put out my hand. He looked surprised, then smiled and gave me a firm clasp. "Good stuff startin' already," he said. "Thanks, Mist' Surrey."

"That's *John* to you, *Mister* Greene."

Greene laughed and shook his head. "World ain't ready for that, *John*." He shook his head again. "Nope. Ain't *quite* ready for that."

So far, in my four days of experience in 1926, I had yet to witness any of the so-called prosperity of the 1920s. Our trip had taken us through desolate western towns and parched looking Midwestern farming communities, the latter of which enjoyed none of the benefits of a skyrocketing stock market. The twenties were not good times for rural America. There were droughts, price-fixing, and fixing of the price-fixing. Foreclosures were already becoming the order of the day by 1926, and the mass exodus to places like California had already begun.

Dixon, Illinois, was an unremarkable little town, almost indistinguishable from any other of its size. Like many small towns I had been through, this one gave me the impression that the current generation had pretty much given up hope and were sacrificing everything for their children. The kids were doing their part, as well. Kids of all ages made deliveries for local stores, labored on farms, picked up odd jobs wherever they could—all the while staying in school and keeping up their grades so that they could someday go to college and break the endless, joyless cycle.

I'm a California boy, and western Illinois in March was a bit much for my thinned-out blood. I was freezing and I said as much to Althea, who told me to stop being an old nance, whatever that meant. She had grown up in northern California and England, where freezing one's butt off was an inherent skill.

"Mind telling me what we're doing here?" she asked.

"We're looking for Mitchell I. Levitan's lifeguard."

"Where do you expect to find a lifeguard in winter?"

"I'll find him, don't worry. Fortune favors the brave."

"Do you know who he is?"

"I have a feeling I do."

"Would I know him?"

"As a matter of fact, you might."

"And what do you expect to find out?"

I turned to her. "Althea, this is what a detective does, especially when you're chasing a fugitive. You find out where he's been and talk to the people who've seen him. Look, we spoke with Aimee, who put us onto his trail right here in Dixon. Her statement was corroborated by Greene. Now we're going to talk to the lifeguard, and he'll tell us about his conversation with Mitch, and maybe give us a little more information. Probably not much, but maybe enough to put us onto where he's going next.''

"I can see where this can get awfully dull.''

We walked through the center of town toward the local high school. "It's repetitive, and sometimes tedious, but hardly ever dull. Look, sweetie, I was a detective for eight years and never once did I stand in a crowded parlor and announce, 'The murderer is right here in this room,' or 'Stabbed, Colonel? I never said the fellow was stabbed. Just how did you know that, sir?' ''

It was after three o'clock, and most of the kids had already left school for the day. I was about to curse my luck when a tall, well-built, bespectacled kid wearing a letter sweater stepped out from the main entrance. I waved to the kid, and he pointed questioningly to himself. I nodded, and saw him look at me, then Althea, and then remove his glasses.

"I know him!" Althea whispered excitedly. "He's an— he'll be an actor!''

"That ain't all he'll be," I replied.

The young man approached us. Even at that young age, he had his trademark engaging smile. "Well," he said, "this is my week for strangers.''

"Mr. P—'' I stopped myself and cleared my throat. "Dutch?''

"That's right. Dutch Reagan. Who're you?''

"I'm John, and this is Althea. Can we talk a minute?''

"I've got to get to work, if you don't mind walking with me.''

"Dutch, did a man named Mitch Levitan pay you a visit last week?''

"Yep, sure did. Why, who is he?''

"He's a friend. He got lost. What did he talk to you about?''

"Nothing, really. He said he was on his way to Chicago and wanted to stop off and see a real American town. Just sorta ran into me and struck up a conversation.'' He smiled.

"He told me I had a bright future ahead of me," Reagan said happily. "I sure hope he's right."

"He is," I said. "Did he say anything else? It's very important, Dutch."

"Well, I'm sure he was kidding."

"Kidding about what?"

"He said he was on his way to Chicago. Wanted to have lunch—no, wait a minute, he said 'take lunch'—no, that's not right, either. Ah! He said he wanted to 'do lunch' with Al Capone. Well, gee! How do you 'do' lunch?"

"With Al Capone?" I asked.

"Well, everybody who's heading for Chicago says that. It's just a joke."

We stopped in front of a drugstore. "I've gotta go. Will you folks be around?"

"No, we're on the next train."

"Aw, too bad. Well, nice meeting you."

"Dutch," said Althea, speaking for the first time.

"Yes, ma'am?"

"Ever consider, when you get out of school, going into the movies?"

"Me? Are you kidding? Thanks for the compliment, though." And with that, he was gone.

"*Now* I'm starting to enjoy this," Althea said smugly.

3 MARCH 1926—CHICAGO

My first thought upon entering the city of Chicago was, wow, this town is *alive*. Carl Sandburg called it the "city of the big shoulders," and I can't imagine a more accurate description, especially in the 1920s.

There were massive, stately buildings lording it over a broad river that ran right through downtown. I have never been so struck by the mere presence of a city. The very physicality of the place seemed to boast, "Hey! I'm Chicago! You got a problem with that? *Loser*?"

This was no city with an inferiority complex, no "second city." There was a certain confidence with which her citizens promenaded down her streets, as though their town was the center of the universe, and what kind of fool would even think of living anywhere else. The hell with New York, London, ancient Rome for that matter; this was what a city was supposed to be.

The people of Chicago, of all races and economic classes, strode through the streets as if they owned them. And it was here that I first began to witness the salad days of the Roaring Twenties. Store windows were filled with merchandise, street vendors lustily hawked their wares, and restaurants and hotels boomed with land-office business. Endless queues of shiny automobiles choked the wide boulevards; bright-colored taxis discharged their fares and quickly boarded new ones.

It was a town built for good times, and Chicago was having one now.

We checked into the Blackstone as Mr. and Mrs. Surrey, in deference to the morality of the times. I figured that we might as well get used to it, anyway. I don't know if it was the pulse of the city, or the effects of time travel, or even the idea of being man and wife, but for whatever reason, Althea and I both became horny beyond all sensibility. As we rode up in the elevator, accompanied only by an elevator boy with his back to us, Althea began caressing the front of my pants. She leaned over and kissed my ear, whispering a line that would set men on fire even eighty years later: "I'm not wearing any underwear." When we left the elevator, I had to carry my coat in front of me to avoid embarrassment. We both stood quivering in our suite while the bellman situated our luggage, opened window shades, turned on the light in the bathroom . . . Frankly, I thought the little bastard would never leave. I finally gave him a five-dollar bill and practically threw him out of the room. We jumped each other the second the door closed. We didn't even bother taking our clothes off. We didn't have to; she really wasn't wearing underwear.

Then the phone rang.

"Nooo!" we both groaned together. I picked up the phone and shouted, "Call back in a half hour, goddammit!"

A little later—certainly not, as you might have expected, a half-hour later—we were lying spent across the living room sofa. I was nodding off to sleep, when it hit me. Who the hell even knew we were here? I opened my eyes and saw that Althea was smoking and staring right at me.

"Who knows we're here?" she asked me.

"Who in the entire world?" I replied. We both thought and came up with the answer at exactly the same time.

"Mitchell I. Levitan," we said together.

"Christ!" I said. "And we missed him."

Althea looked at me miserably. "It's my fault . . ."

I grabbed her and covered her with kisses. "Oh, no, no, of course not. Don't *ever* apologize for that. That was worth anything. Anyway, like my uncle Jack always says—and probably in the same situation—'If it's really important, they'll call back.' "

The phone rang again. "Hello."

"Heh-heh-heh. That's some swell dish. All done now, Mr. Surrey?"

"You want a rap in the mouth?"

"Ooh, temper, tem-per."

"Who the hell is this?"

"Oh, sorry. Jake Lingle, Mr. Surrey, of the *Chicago Tribune*. I understand we have a friend in common. A friend of mine said he knew you'd be showing up. I been staking out all the class hotels in town for the last week."

"When did you see him?"

"Why don't we meet for a drink, Johnny. Mitch told me all about you. Okay if I call you Johnny?"

"No. When and where?"

"There's a speakeroo down the street. Smoky's. Just take

a left outside the lobby and it's right on the next block. You can't miss it. Bring the cutie.''

"I'll see you in twenty minutes.''

"Don't you want to know how to recognize me?''

"I can always spot an asshole," I said, and hung up.

"Who was it?" Althea asked.

I smiled. "If I can't get information out of this twerp, you can take away my Decacom. Son of a bitch. Jake Lingle.''

"Why does that name sound familiar?''

"He's a reporter. Actually, what they called a 'legman' in those—these days.''

"A legman? Sounds like you.''

"Not that kind of legman, sweetie. Old Jake couldn't write to save his life, but he was good at gathering info. He'd call in everything he knew to the rewrite man, who would put together the actual story. Of course, part of what made him such a storehouse of knowledge was—is—that he's on Capone's payroll. I sure hope he enjoys himself for the next five years.''

"Why five years?''

"That's all the time he's got. In 1931, Capone'll be fed up with him. Playing both ends against the middle and all that. You don't do that with Capone.''

Althea ran her hand up my thigh and shivered. "What *is* it about the 1920s?" she asked.

"I said I'd meet him in twenty minutes," I whispered, sliding her onto my lap.

"You'll be late," she breathed into my ear.

"He can wait." For a girl from the 1940s, who was currently visiting the 1920s, she sure did one hell of a twenty-first-century lap dance.

Lingle was easy to spot, although it was hard to get used to seeing him upright. History usually portrayed him as a dead body on a sidewalk. He was an unremarkable-looking man who was rapidly surrendering his youth to excess. His face was already bloating from liquor and his middle was beginning to thicken. He looked like a kid dressed up in his father's suit and hat, who had also spent a little too much time in Dad's liquor cabinet. However, unlike my home era, where reporters jog and drink Perrier so that they can pick up scoops from sources who also jog and drink Perrier, this was a time when newsmen and the people they wrote about all drank, smoked, and gambled.

"Lingle," I said, coming up behind him.

He turned around. He was already half lit up. "Johnny! The hell are ya!" He pumped my hand vigorously. He gestured around the room, a dull little bar whose only distinction was that it was illegal. "Let's siddown."

I ordered a beer, which Lingle warned me would be thinner than baby piss, while he ordered Scotch and bring the bottle.

"When did you see Mitch?" I asked him.

"Whoa, whoa, hold yer horses. Let's negotiate. This is Chicago, pally. I got something you want, what are you gonna give me for it?"

I considered this for a moment. "How's this? You tell me everything I want to know, and I won't beat the crap out of you. Fair?"

"Hey, you can't talk to me like that. I got friends."

"All right, Jake," I said tiredly. "How much?"

"A grand."

"Bye, Jake."

"Wait, for chrissakes, siddown. A c-note, okay? I got bills."

"Okay, a c-note. After we talk."

"Fifty up front."

"Don't piss me off, Jake." But I handed him the money.

He snatched the fifty and looked around for eavesdroppers. "Your friend looked me up when he hit town. Said he always wanted to meet me. That kinda gave me the creeps—I don't know why, but it did. I mean, yeah, people know me in Chicago, but L.A.? Anyway, he told me he wanted me to set up a meeting with the Boss. Just wanted to meet him.''

"The Boss?'' I asked, thinking, *Springsteen?*

"*Capone*, ya moron,'' he whispered bitingly. "Well, sure, everyone wants to meet him, and the Boss don't mind. Makes him feel respectable.''

"So? Did you?''

"Yeah. I brought him to the Lexington, ya know, the Boss's place. And they had a drink and shot the breeze— tell ya the truth, I think the Boss liked him. They laughed a lot. I was outside, but as Mitch was leavin', the Boss had an arm on his shoulder and said, 'I hope it works out wit' that dame.' ''

"Dame? What dame?''

"I dunno.''

"Well, is she from around here? Chicago?''

"I don't know.''

"Does the Boss?''

"How should I know?''

"Well, then, set up a meeting for me.''

"Are you nuts?''

"Five hundred, Jake.''

"I'll call you tomorrow.''

I leaned back and took a sip from my beer glass. Lingle had been right; it *was* thinner than baby piss.

Harold Lloyd was hanging from a clock.

Practically no one outside the film industry remembers him anymore, but in the 1920s, Harold Lloyd was a huge star, right up there with Charlie Chaplin and Buster Keaton. However, it was 1926, the last full year of film without sound, and Lloyd had gone about as far as he could go.

We had a night to kill, and Althea had insisted that we take in a movie. I went with some ambivalence because I had found that most silent films did not translate well into my era. To tell you the truth, silent movies usually bored me. I had always considered Charlie Chaplin brilliant and imaginative, but he had never made me roar with laughter as had the audiences of his heyday. I was spoiled, I guess. I needed verbal as well as visual humor for a real hoot.

But sitting in the crowded theatre, surrounded by an audience deeply involved in the story, I was beginning to enjoy the experience. I gasped along with the audience as Lloyd clung desperately to the giant minute hand, feeling the tension mount as his hand slipped, bringing him ever closer to certain death on the pavement of Cahuenga Boulevard far below. Of course, I had seen a documentary on PBS about Lloyd, and knew for a fact that there was a huge mattress spread out just beneath the shot.

Finally, though, I just gave in and had fun like everyone else. I began to appreciate Lloyd's skill in communicating a story, and it soon became much the same as watching a foreign movie with subtitles.

"What do you want to do now?" I asked as we strolled out of the theatre.

"It's 1926, darling," she said. "What do you think I want to do? The Charleston, of course."

Ten minutes later, we were in an elegant speakeasy on Lakeshore Drive. There was no little slot on the door opened by a gangsterish-looking guy demanding a password. Instead, we walked into a small lobby where a maître d' sat like a lordly concierge. He sized us up and nodded, then escorted us into an ornately furnished restaurant, one that looked much like a grand salon on an ocean liner. It was crowded, but we were given a pretty good table near the band.

I ordered us some champagne and a late supper. I felt a little underdressed, wearing only a suit while most men wore tuxedoes, but the feeling soon passed.

The band was all black, led by an energetic young man with long slicked hair that flew around his head, almost in perfect sync with the music. He had a powerful tenor voice and an incredible facility with lyrics, trilling up and down the scale with unbelievable accuracy. He was so gifted, and so charismatic, that I found myself wondering who he was. I furiously searched the vast corridors of my brain for his identity.

Althea, as always, had read my mind. "Do you know who that is?" she shouted over the din, smiling.

"I should," I shouted back. "Damn it! It's driving me nuts!"

"Is he the greatest?"

"I swear to God, he must be the coolest man alive," I replied earnestly.

The marvelous bandleader jumped and danced across the stage, belting out a song flawlessly all the while. Once or twice he looked directly at us and winked, and I noticed that this little piece of stage business had to be a major reason—in addition to his prodigious talent—why he was so successful. In one wink, he was able to create a conspiracy that said, "Hey, you're my *real* audience, I'm just giving the rest of these stiffs their money's worth."

"Whoever he is," I said, "he's going places."

"Darling, he's already there."

Suddenly, he let out a magnificent whoop, and the mystery vanished. I knew exactly who he was, and I exploded with laughter at my good fortune.

He whooped again, and the audience took the hint and replied lustily in kind.

"HIDY-HIDY-HIDY-HO!"

Cab Calloway led us through a thunderous repetition of his musical gymnastics, and although no one could match his skill, everyone certainly had as much fun. I know I did.

The band took a breather. They needed it, and so did we. Singing along with Cab took a lot of energy, and the room had grown hot and sweaty with the effort. Which was fine with the management; it also made everyone thirsty.

I figured the hell with it and caught Cab's eye. He nodded and leaped athletically off the bandstand.

I stood and held out my hand. "John Surrey, Mr. Calloway, and this is Althea Rowland. It's a real pleasure."

He shook my hand and bowed low to Althea. "Thank you, Mr. Surrey, I'm glad you enjoyed it."

"Won't you join us, Mr. Calloway?"

His engaging smile vanished. I wondered what I had said, what gaffe I had committed.

"We're not allowed to sit with the guests, Mr. Surrey."

I felt sick. I also began to feel exceedingly pissed. This man's ability paid the rent on this place and he couldn't even sit with an appreciative member of his audience? They could stick Jim Crow sideways.

"If you'll excuse me . . ." he began.

"Wait," I said, rising to my feet again, "if you can't sit with us . . . can you *stand* with us?"

Althea stood up. "Nothing wrong with that, Mr. Calloway, is there?"

He looked at us and slowly nodded. "Nope," he said, his winning smile once again crossing his face, "nothing wrong with that at all."

I stole a downturned glass from a neighboring table and poured us each some champagne. "How long are you going to be in town?" I asked him.

"New York after tomorrow night," he said.

"No kidding," I replied. "The Cotton Club?"

He nodded. "Harlem, baby. Where it all begins. If you're in town, I hope you'll come see me."

"Try and keep us away," Althea said.

"Are you in show biz, Miss Rowland? Don't take this the wrong way, but you look like an actress."

"Why, thank you. No, I'm not, but my father is."

"Oh, yeah," Cab said. "Angus Rowland, the set designer, right?"

"That's right."

"I've seen your dad's work in London, ma'am. He's a genius."

"So are you, Mr. Calloway."

"Just a bandleader. Whoa. I gotta get back to work."

"If we get to New York, we'll definitely see you," I

said. I held out my hand. "You've got a great career ahead, Cab. Think of your wildest dreams, and then double them."

He looked at me with a slightly bewildered glance. Then he smiled. "I don't know about that," he said. "My wildest dreams can get pretty wild."

FOUR

4 MARCH 1926—CHICAGO

THE RINGING OF THE TELEPHONE WOKE ME UP AND I WAS instantly sorry. Whoever said champagne doesn't give you a hangover never got loaded with Cab Calloway in 1926. He had joined us several more times for some stand-up drinks, and for the rest of the night directed many of his jokes toward us.

Subsequent conversation had also determined that he was an acquaintance of Greene's, which further validated us as trustworthy people in his eyes.

Althea, as it turned out, danced a pretty good Charleston. I couldn't do it worth a damn. It was a complicated dance; you had to twist your feet while doing a timestep, plus a few other complicated moves that were beyond me. I did manage the doo-wacka-doo trick with my knees, but that was the limit of my terpsichorean skills. Anyway, after all the champagne we drank, about half of which was Cab's treat, my coordination was shot. Also, I hesitate to reveal, once or twice I had snuck into the alley on Cab's invitation, and along with a few other band members, partook in a few inhalations of that evil marijuana weed. I guess musicians were a bad influence on me. The last time I had ever smoked dope was in 1966 with Jim Morrison at the Whisky A Go Go.

In other words, the night had been one to remember, although Althea later told me that it was forgettable in one aspect—which I made up for as soon as I regained my sobriety.

Anyway, I was pretty hungover when I picked up the phone.

"Johnny? It's Lingle."

"Yeah. What time is it?"

"Nine-thirty. Put on your best dress, sonnyboy, you're havin' lunch with the Boss."

"I am? When?"

"One o'clock. You know where the Lex is?"

"I can find it."

"Meet me in the lobby at one. Come alone."

"Count on it."

Althea rolled into my arms. "What're we doing today?" she yawned.

"You're going shopping. I'm having lunch with Al Capone."

Althea and I almost had a fight—our first—when I told her that she wasn't coming with me. She wanted to meet Al Capone, damn it, and who was I to stop her? I had to make her understand that I had been a cop, after all, and I was going to meet the biggest crook on the planet. He wasn't cute, he wasn't lovable, he wasn't a curiosity—he was a cold-blooded killer, and I wasn't going to let her anywhere near him. I eventually won the argument, but I found myself hoping against hope that it wouldn't turn out to be a Pyrrhic victory.

The Lexington had a lobby covered with lush red carpeting, broad staircases, and high columns. It reminded me somewhat of the great movie palaces of the 1930s. Lingle met me at the bottom of the stairs. I immediately noticed a change in his demeanor. The wisecracking squirt act was gone. He spoke in hushed tones, as if he were in church.

In other words, he was scared shitless, and probably with good reason.

"Just go straight up the stairs," he whispered.

"Straight up the stairs," I replied, a little loudly to see if it would shake him up. I wasn't disappointed.

"Just go on," he muttered, wincing. "That's McGurn up there. He'll bring you in."

"Thanks, Jake," I replied in the same tone, and smacked him on the shoulder, hard. I took the stairs two at a time and was met by a well-built young man, a very handsome guy with a large nose. I recalled from my studies that he was Vicente DeMora, later known as Machine-Gun Jack McGurn. The nickname didn't come from his mob activities—he was known to prefer a .45 automatic—but rather from his days as a boxer.

McGurn nodded for me to follow him. He took me through a set of double doors into an outer office, where I was met by another mug. This worthy was a heavyset guy with a cratered face. He gave off an aura of quiet danger, and I knew right away that he was Al Capone's big brother, Ralph. He frisked me somewhat rudely.

"You Surrey?"

"That's my name," I replied breezily. For some reason, Ralph's quiet intensity didn't scare me. In fact, it had the opposite effect. Having been a cop, I supposed, and having been accustomed to showing no fear around crooks, I felt more than anything else a sense of coming home.

Ralph gave me a penetrating glare, expecting me to shrivel. I returned it nonchalantly. Ralph might have been a big guy, and a tough one, but unlike me he had never been a Marine. Or a cop. I was one hundred percent positive I could kick his ornery ass for him in about thirty seconds. Of course, that was still no guarantee that I would leave the place alive.

The door to the inner office flew open and out stepped my host.

Al Capone was wearing a nauseatingly colored suit that looked like a thousand hot dogs had been scraped of mustard for its hue. He was shorter than I thought he would be, only about five ten, but he looked bigger. He was heavy like his brother, and he looked very strong. Like the city he virtually owned, he had presence.

In every movie I had ever seen about him, he was played as a man in his comfortable, late forties, but in fact he was only twenty-eight years old. He looked a little older because he partied so hard, but in person he seemed like the young man that he was. He had a pleasant, almost cherubic side-of-the-mouth smile, but his brown eyes, like the eyes of many bad men, were dead. The scar on the left side of his face, the one that had earned him the nickname no one dared call him, was more livid than in photographs.

Al Capone was a scary guy, so naturally I acted as though I was meeting an old school chum.

"John Surrey, Mr. Capone," I greeted him heartily. "Thanks for your time."

He shook my hand. His grip was surprisingly fishlike. "Al Capone." He held on to my hand like an old grandpa and sat us down on a nearby couch.

"You want some coffee, Mr. Surrey? It's good coffee." His solicitousness almost made me laugh outright.

"I would love some coffee, Mr. Capone."

He nodded his head at McGurn, who left the room.

"You know, it's funny, Mr. Surrey, but you look to me like a cop. Sorry if you take that wrongly."

This time, I did chuckle. "Oh, well, you got me, Al," I confessed cheerfully, throwing up my hands in surrender. "Twelve years with the Los Angeles Police Department."

"You mean, you ain't a cop no more?"

"In L.A., we call it 'fuzz that was.' "

He looked at Ralph, who blew out his lips and shrugged. "What that what?"

"Fuzz that was. It's an L.A. thing, I guess. Anyway, I'm retired. Just a businessman now."

"Just a businessman, huh? What kinda business?"

"Travel," I said. "I'm a travel agent. It's not as exciting—well, sometimes it is—but it's a lot safer."

McGurn came back in, followed by a liveried waiter with a silver coffee service. We were quiet as the waiter poured us coffee and uncovered a plate of watercress sandwiches. That disappointed me. I was kind of hoping for a really good feed, but I supposed that Al ordered the watercress sandwiches because that's the way the upper *clahses* did it—and Al was the ultimate blue-blood wanna-be.

"Oh, good!" I exclaimed. "Watercress. I'm starved!"

Capone stared at me. I stared back. Then we both broke into raucous laughter that started as between-the-lips raspberries and ended, for him anyway, as a bronchial spasm.

"Hey!" he called to the waiter when he recovered. "Take this sissy shit away and bring us something for *men*!"

Capone predictably wore his napkin around his neck, but other than that, his table manners were surprisingly good. We had tucked into a mammoth lunch of pork chops, baked potatoes, and a ton of vegetables swimming in butter. Doc Harvey would have had apoplexy if he saw what was on that table, but it was a great meal and I consumed it with gusto.

"Whatcha gotta understand," Capone was telling me, "is that ya got different types a people come from different places, and that's what makes the way they do business. I'm a Neopolitan, see, I don't do shit exactly the way Cholly Luciano does, 'cause he's a Sicilian. Then ya got—ya had—Dion O'Bannion. He was a crazy mick. He'd sing that too-ra-loo-ra-loo-ra shit wid ya one minute, and then ventilate your brains in the next, then go to his shop and weep while he did the flowers for your funeral."

"What about somebody like Bugs Moran?" I asked,

chewing the last of a chop. I was enjoying both the food and Al's sociology lesson. After we had established that I had been a cop, he seemed to relax, enjoying a truce with an enemy who wanted nothing of him.

"Moran," he sneered. "He ain't even Irish. He's a Polack. And he does things like a Polack. But ya gotta give 'im credit. He don't have just Polacks workin' for 'im, just like I don't have only wops. We all got somethin' in common—wops, Polacks, micks, hebes—and don't take this personal, but we all hate cops. Because where we all come from, the government uses the cops to keep people down, take away their manhood."

It was a pretty cogent statement from a supposedly illiterate gangster, and I have to admit that I was impressed.

The phone rang. Ralph answered and then handed it to Al. "Maxie Eisen," he said.

Al held the speaker over his chest and said, "Then ya got hebes, like this guy. I like hebes. You can trust 'em. They're like wops who can do arithmetic. Yeah, Maxie? What horse, the eighth at Aurora? Dragon Lady? Eight to one? Yeah, I'll go half. If we win."

He hung up. "Where was I?"

"You like 'hebes,' " I replied.

"Yeah. Lepke? Schultz? Tough guys, good business heads. Lansky? That kid's a friggin' genius. He oughta be at friggin' Harvard, teach those nancy-boys a thing or two."

"What about Hymie Weiss?" I asked, curious about Bugs Moran's fiery-tempered lieutenant.

Capone shook his head dismissively. "Polack. Ain't even his real name. Can't figure why the hell somebody'd change their name to Hymie Weiss, unless maybe it's one a them Polack names sounds like milk bottles fallin' off a truck."

Ralph was staring at Al and tapping on his wristwatch. I took the hint and stood up.

"It's been fun, Al."

He stood up, put his arm around my shoulder, and walked me toward the door. "You're all right, Johnny. You need a job or anything?"

I couldn't help it, but I was slightly touched. "That's nice of you, Al, but I'm doing okay."

"Well, anything you need while you're in town . . ."

I stopped. "There is one thing . . ."

Ralph rolled his eyes, as if to say, here it comes.

"I'm trying to catch up with a friend of mine, and I understand he met with you last week. Mitch Levitan?"

Ralph blinked, obviously surprised that my request was such a minor one. "I remember him," Ralph volunteered. "That tall, skinny guy from L.A.? Wanted to make a movie about you?"

Capone thought for a minute, then chuckled. "Oh, yeah, sure. I remember him. Nice kid." His eyes narrowed. "He's not in any trouble, is he?"

"Not at all. He has an important message from the studio, and we're trying to track him down."

"Yeah," said Al. "There's a broad in New York he was moonin' about. I told him I'd fix him up right here—ya know, I c'n do that—but he said, no, he wanted this girl."

"He didn't say who she was?"

"Nah. Just that he'd find her in New York."

"And that's where he is?"

"No-o," he said slowly. "He asked me if I knew anyone in New Orleans. He needed a favor, had to get a copy of a police report down there."

New Orleans? A police report, I thought. Jesus, what the hell was going on? "So he's in New Orleans?"

"Yeah, then he's goin' to New York."

"Al," I said. "Thank you. You're a prince."

"Hah! Hear that, Ralphie, cop calls me a prince. And he don't even want any money. I tell ya, it's a crazy world."

FIVE

MISSION REVIEW—LOS ANGELES

MY PARENTS, ALONG WITH MY SISTER AND HER TWO KIDS, live half the year in New Zealand, and the other half in the canyons above Beverly Hills. They had moved to New Zealand when things started getting irretrievably awful in Los Angeles around the turn of the century.

But they were true Angelenos and couldn't stay away for long. To them, the city was like an incorrigible kid who raised your blood pressure to dangerous heights but was in the long run bighearted enough to be worth all of the effort. Also, my sister's long-estranged putz husband had begun making certain noises about turning over a new leaf— among other such reconciliatory mewling—which could no longer be ignored. So the folks had just bought a new Mitchell I. Levitan–type domicile in Beverly Canyon, where they stayed during the social season.

It was great having them back. I'm a family-oriented guy, and I love the aroma of a backyard barbecue and the sound of the laughter of relatives on a Sunday afternoon. I have also reached the point in my life where I depend upon my family's advice because, God damn it, it turns out that they *are* usually right, just like they always said they were.

I bring this up because, in addition to the official reports of my debriefings at Timeshare, I have gotten into the habit of keeping a meticulous journal of each trip I have ever undertaken. I keep copies of the journal on disk and in my safety deposit box, but I also send or fax a copy to the family as soon as I complete an entry. It provides them with a few laughs and, occasionally, a good fright, like the time I was kidnapped by Nazi spies in 1940. My mom went nuts after that one, as you might suspect.

However, it was my sister who brought up a point that I believe should be addressed before I go any further.

"I don't get it," she said. "Everybody *likes* you. Not"— she was quick to add—"that you're not a charming man-about-town, but let's face it: You walk right into a meeting with *Al Capone*, and after a few minutes, he's offering you a *job*? I mean, *hellooo . . .*"

As usual, she had a point, and I think it's one I should clarify right here.

Being an L.A. native, I naturally have many friends who have gone into the movies. My alma mater, Chatsworth High, has a drama department that is to aspiring actors what Notre Dame and Penn State are to young football players. There's also Althea, who was a film legend and a good enough actress to deserve the title. Even my grandpa Joe was a stuntman for a while. So we can assume as a given that I understand theatre. And anyone with the slightest grasp of theatre will be acquainted with the term *subtext*. Subtext is not just the thought behind the spoken line of dialogue; it is also *who* that person is who is speaking that line of dialogue.

Well, when I go back in time, I am always armed with powerful subtext. When I meet historical figures, I often know more about them than they know about themselves. I certainly know what life holds in store for them. It's an almost unfair advantage. Sometimes, it seems like it's too easy.

That subtext affects my demeanor. Add on the fact that I was a cop, and that knowing how to get people to open up was my stock-in-trade, and it's much the same as the salesman who easily gets in to see prospects while others spend their careers on fruitless cold calls.

But, I hasten to add, this does not mean that I am universally adored, or that all of my trips go off without a hitch. Many of them have their problems, and 1926 was no exception.

4 MARCH 1926—CHICAGO

I emerged from the Lexington Hotel feeling pretty smug. It was a clear, chilly afternoon, with a fierce wind blowing in off Lake Michigan, but for once I found the cold bracing instead of torturous. I had decided that I would stop at the next jewelry store and buy Althea a little gift, and quickened my pace. But I wasn't fast enough. A Chevy coupe piled onto the curb in front of me and screeched to a halt. Two big guys got out, followed by a skinny little fellow in wire-rimmed glasses. The skinny guy had a permanent scowl on his face and looked like a refugee from Rent-a-Psycho.

None of them were armed—at least, none were brandishing any weapons—but I was sure they were packing heat somewhere. The only thing that kept me from running or making a move right then was that I was curious. I wondered who they were and what they wanted of me.

"Get'na f'ck'n car," the little wacko hissed.

I shrugged and did as I was told. I still wasn't scared—not just yet. But I *was* interested. And no one had pulled a piece on me.

"So, what do I call you?" I asked the little guy conversationally.

He leaned over the front seat and stared at me. He was consumed with hatred, this creep, and I figured if a bullet didn't get him, hypertension would.

"What d'you call me? What d'you call *me*?" He nudged the driver. "He wantsa know what does he call me. I'll tell you what you call me, shithead. You c'n call me, 'please, mister, don't kill me,' how about that?"

"It's original," I remarked, knowing that I was casting pearls and would be given pain for my pains.

He leaned over and punched me in the face. I turned my head to avoid a broken nose and received what would probably cause a black eye instead. I tried to swing, but the guy sitting next to me blocked me with his arm. I could tell from his look—and here's subtext again—that he was protecting me as much as the little guy. Wherever I was being taken, it was obvious that I was wanted there in one piece—although I questioned the wisdom of whoever picked this little nutcase for the job.

"I ain't done wit' you," the little guy warned me, but that seemed to mollify him. He turned around in his seat and ignored me for the rest of the trip.

We pulled into a warehouse on the Near North Side. Someone rolled down the steel door as soon as we were inside.

The little guy skipped out of the car before it was halted and ran into the office. My two escorts shoved me out of the automobile and stood on either side of me. Both of them now had .45 automatics in plain view.

The little guy returned, followed by a very stocky, jowly guy with piercing blue eyes and a Kirk Douglas buttonhole in his chin.

"Tie him up," the stocky guy grunted. The little guy smiled, and I didn't like that smile one damn bit. Before anything else could happen, I felt the outside of my right front trouser pocket and hit the Decacom button three times. I was too far from L.A. to be transported back, but there was a slim chance that my danger signal might be received.

"Would you mind telling me who you guys are and what it is you want?" I said.

The little hump came toward me with a rope. "I'm Hymie Weiss," he said, "and I want your balls."

The near future didn't seem too promising. I couldn't make a move for my Taser because it would look like I was going for a gun, and those two guys could easily shoot me down before the stun gun cleared my pocket. The piece Terry had given me was back at the hotel. I had left it there on purpose because I knew I couldn't have brought it to a meeting with Capone. So I was helpless.

Hymie Weiss packed a good punch for a little guy. He smashed me in the solar plexus, knocking the wind out of me. While I was doubled over and gasping for breath, I was roughly pushed into a chair. My hands were tied behind me.

The stocky guy ambled over to where I was trussed up and gave me a slap on the head. Not hard, really, just enough to let me know where I stood. Or sat.

"Let me take care of him, George," Weiss said.

George, I thought, George *Moran*. Old Bugs himself.

When I'm really scared, I turn into a wiseass—or, perhaps I should say, a bigger wiseass than I usually am. It's simply my reaction to fear. Some guys shake or shiver, some guys pee their pants, some guys just get tougher. For me, whether it's Iraqi fire in Desert Storm, or a shoot-out with drug dealers, whatever the situation, I just get more sarcastic and irritating. Which relieves my own tension, but also gets my opponents even more pissed.

I have always believed that everyone has at least one annoying aspect to their personality, and that just happens to be mine.

So it was completely in character for me to regard Moran for a moment and then say, "Bugs! How the hell are ya?"

I think I was unconscious for at least three minutes after Moran belted me on the jaw. When I came to, my mouth was full of blood, but I still had all my teeth, and my mandible seemed to be working.

"Call him that again," Hymie Weiss said. "Go ahead, you dumb shit."

It's pretty much out of use today, but for the first half of the last century, the only character who enjoyed being called Bugs had rabbit ears and a cottontail. Calling someone "Bugs" was not something you did to anyone's face. The term *bugs* was a profoundly serious insult meaning bats, wacko, loony, or certifiable—it was not an insult accepted gracefully or in kidding. Mental illness was considered a personal failing, not a treatable disease. Come to think of it, it would have been a more fitting nickname for Hymie Weiss.

"I don't like dat," Moran said. He spoke with a slight Polish accent. "Don' say dat again."

"Sorry to have taken the liberty," I replied. Moran must have picked up on my tone, but he let it slide.

"I know your name is Surrey, and you come from L.A.," he said.

"You do your homework, B—Mr. Moran."

"Dat's why I'm still alive," he said. "Now, who da hell are you? I heard you was a cop."

"I was a cop." I nodded.

"I ain't never done a cop," Weiss said happily. "This'll be fun."

"*Was* a cop, you little dipshit," I snapped. "Pay attention."

One of my guards suppressed a chuckle. Weiss took a step toward me, but Moran held him back.

"Later," he said. "Siddown and shuddup." He smiled at me approvingly. "You're a real fuggin' wise guy, hah? You don' scare easy, I like dat." He lit a cigarette. "You wanna zhmoke?"

"Don't smoke," I said.

"It figures," Weiss sneered. "California queerbait."

"I said shuddup, Hymie. I ain't sayin' it again." He

turned back to me. "What kind cop was you? You look too zhmart for a dopey flatfoot. Was you a big shot?"

"Detective lieutenant," I replied. Actually, I was a detective three—technically a senior-grade sergeant—but I was on the lieutenant's list when I quit the force. Anyway, it wasn't as though they were going to check.

"Why you quit?"

"I had a better offer."

"From Capone?"

"No," I said. "I'm legit. I'm just a travel agent."

"Why was you wit' Capone, then? He plannin' a vacation? Back to Guinealand?"

"No, nothing like that. I'm trying to track down a friend of mine, and I heard that he met Capone last week."

"Dis friend do business with Capone?"

"No. He's in the movies."

"Who is he," Weiss interjected, "Buster Keaton? Charlie Chaplin?"

"Theda Bara," I shot back.

"Hymie," Moran waved him off disgustedly, "I'm tryna tink here. What's dis movie guy want with Capone?"

"I don't know. Maybe he wants to make a movie about him."

"A movie about Scarface Al?" Weiss said incredulously. "What the hell for? Who'd pay to see him?"

"Who'd pay to see you?" I replied. Weiss balled his fist at me. "Mr. Moran, I'm just trying to find my friend. That's all there is to it."

"Okay." Moran shrugged. "You can go."

"Really, Boss?" one of the torpedoes asked.

"Nah," he said with a slight chuckle. "Just kidding." I might have been wrong about Moran. Maybe he did merit his nickname after all.

"Look," he said a little sadly, "we gonna have ta get rid of you. Sorry, but you know, dat's how we do tings aroun' here."

"I wish you'd reconsider," I said, trying not to sound

as though I was pleading, which I was. "Capone won't like it."

"I thought you din't do no business with Capone."

"I didn't, but he liked me."

Moran shook his head dubiously. "I don' tink Capone'll go to war over you, Lieutenant Surrey. If you was still a cop, maybe we'd tink about it, but youse retired."

"I'm still a cop," I said quickly.

Moran looked at Weiss, who made an autoerotic gesture with his hand.

"Dat's da ball game," Moran said. "You'll go to heaven," he added consolingly, "it won' be so bad. We'll do it quick."

"The hell we will," Weiss protested.

"Shuddup, Hymie. He ain't a bad guy." He nodded to my two guards, but the one on my right keeled over, unconscious. He was immediately followed by the one on my left, who fell across my lap.

It happened so fast that neither Hymie nor Moran had time to react. Something hit Moran, and his eyes rolled up into his head. His legs gave out and he fell in an almost comical heap.

Weiss's gun cleared his shoulder holster.

"Drop the piece, shrimp," Terry Rappaport's voice ordered. Hymie put his hands up and the revolver clattered to the floor.

"You okay, John?" Terry asked me as he shoved the unconscious torpedo off my lap and loosened the rope around my hands.

"I've been better," I said, "but am I glad to see you. I didn't think you got my signal."

"We were lucky. Atmospheric conditions made it possible."

"Who the hell are you?" Weiss demanded.

"Just somebody who can kick your pygmy ass," Terry replied with a grin. "Keep your hands where I can see them. John," he said, "do I detect the urge to play catch-up?"

I stood up and rubbed my sore wrists. "Why, Terry, I'm shocked. Shocked, do you hear? How can you even *think* a gentleman like myself would react in such a way?"

He bowed. "You have my apology, sir."

I turned to Hymie Weiss and tried to think of a decent quip. Unable to come up with one, I settled for throwing a haymaker that sent him sprawling over a table and somersaulting into an unconscious heap.

"That wasn't nice," Terry said.

"I'm letting him off easy," I replied. "Someone else can have the pleasure."

Althea and I had our second fight when Terry and I went back to the hotel to pick her up. At first, she was predictably alarmed by my condition; I had the beginnings of a black eye, a split lip, and a swollen jaw. But that issue was quickly tabled when I told her that we were going back to 2007 to regroup for a little while.

"I'm not going back," she said flatly.

"Althea, I can't leave you here alone."

"Why not? I've been here before without you."

"Because it's dangerous. Jesus Christ, Bugs Moran and Hymie Weiss were about to take me for a ride."

"They don't know anything about me. Besides, I won't have anything to do with them. I'll go on to New York and see what I can find out there."

"I can't allow it," I said, and immediately regretted it.

"You can't *allow* it? Who the hell are you to allow me to do anything?"

"I know, I'm sorry. It came out the wrong way. But I don't want anything to happen to you."

"John, I can't handle 2007 just now. I just can't."

She sank down onto the couch and tried not to weep.

Terry looked at his watch. "Goodness," he exclaimed.

"I have to run out and get my dog groomed! I'll be down-stairs."

"Everyone I've ever loved is alive right now," she said after Terry left. "When we go back, they'll all be gone and Tony'll be an old man And I don't know anything about 2007. It frightens me."

It was news to me that anything frightened her at all, and I said as much.

"Oh, I'm scared, all right. Jesus, even the kids look dan-gerous. What is it you call them—'gangbangers'? You can't eat a steak or add real cream to your coffee. And God help you if you light a cigarette."

"Cigarettes kill," I said.

"I don't care!" she exploded. "I'm on borrowed time, anyway. I was supposed to die in the Battle of Britain, remember?"

"I remember," I said softly.

"Anyway, that's not the point. I'm useless in 2007. All right, I'll go back with you when this mission is over. We'll live together in your beautiful, confusing apartment. I'll quit smoking and eating things that taste good, and watch every-thing I say because I can get sued if someone takes it the wrong way. I'll carry a water bottle everywhere I go, like some Bedouin. I'll go back to where cops can't keep the streets safe because they'll get fired if they arrest anybody. I'll go live in your ridiculous, intrusive decade, and I won't say a word against it. I promise. But please, don't make me go back now!"

I took her in my arms. The doctor had been right; she was in a fragile state. But she was also very strong, and very, very determined. "Doc Harvey is going to kill me," I whispered to the top of her head.

"Thanks, John."

I stood up, went over to my suitcase, and took out the rest of our expense money. "This ought to tide you over until I get back. I want you to stay at the Plaza. That way, I'll be able to keep track of you. *Always* leave a message when you go out, so if I show up when you're gone, I'll know where you are. Can you handle the .45?''

"No."

I gave her my Taser. "It's no good past ten feet. Just point it and shoot. And shoot first and ask questions when the guy wakes up. If anyone makes you feel the least bit uneasy, blast him. Don't wait.''

"I'll be fine, John.''

I looked down and scratched at the carpet with my shoe. "I didn't realize you hated my time so much. I'm sorry.''

"Oh, John, it isn't that. I'm overcome with happiness at having found you. But you and the doctor both said it; bringing someone into the future has never been done before. There's sure to be some problems adjusting. Well, I'm having them now. But I'll be fine.''

"I can't help but feel—'' I began miserably.

"It's not your fault,'' she cut me off. "Now, come over here.''

"Now? Terry's waiting downstairs.''

"Terry's a sweet man. He'll understand.''

"Well, all right,'' I said, going to her.

"What *is* it about the twenties?'' she wondered aloud.

SIX

"WE HAVE GOT TO DO SOMETHING ABOUT TRANSPORTA-
tion back there," Terry said as we stepped out of the
Zoomer. "I mean, rail travel is very relaxing, and they treat
you like royalty, but man, it's boring!"

We were lucky enough to land Greene's return route, and
he and Terry had hit it off as I had expected they would.
Greene had also given me regards from Cab Calloway, who
was looking forward to seeing Althea and me in New York.
But Terry was right. Crossing the country in days instead
of hours was time-consuming, and being cooped up on a
train took away our fine edge.

"Where's Miss Rowland?" Doc Harvey demanded.

"She elected to go on to New York," I replied.

"Are you out of your mind?" he fairly shouted. "Are
you nuts?"

"She is one determined lady," I said. "And I used my
prerogative as mission leader. She didn't want to come back
just now, and when Althea says she wants something . . ."

"Face it, Doc," Terry chimed in, "she was a movie star. Having her own way is in her blood."

The doc gave us a disgusted wave and walked away.

Everyone was grouped around the television, including Cornelia and Felice. "Anybody home?" I shouted.

One of the technicians shushed us without turning around.

"What's going on?" I asked no one in particular. Standing on tiptoes, I could only glimpse an ocean of protestors in front of a governmental-looking building. Many of them were carrying signs. One of them said, "GIVE US NEW JOBS THEN, OR SHUT THE HELL UP." Another said, "OF COURSE TOFU IS OKAY WITH YOU GUYS; IT TASTES LIKE SHIT."

Felice turned to me. "It's the Dairy Farmers' Association. A few of them have taken over the Surgeon General's Office and the rest of them are outside."

"Why?"

"They're demanding that the Surgeon General revise his study on dairy products. Apparently, so many people have stopped drinking milk, eating cheese, and buying real ice cream that it's causing a depression in the industry. They're tired of it, and they want the Surgeon General to find every one of them new jobs that will equal their previous incomes."

Terry and I looked at each other and started to laugh.

"It isn't funny, John," Felice cautioned me. "The Cattle Ranchers' Association has thrown them their support. So has the Tobacco Institute. It's a mess!"

"Thank God," I said fervently.

"Thank God what?"

"Thank God Althea isn't here to see this. I'd never live it down."

Felice turned her attention away from the television. "Are you all right, John? You look awful."

"I ran afoul of some famous gangsters," I said. "But

I'm okay now. I've got some work to do.''

"Will you be needing my help?"

"In a day or two I'll be going back, so I'll need some more dough. But—"

"Oh, wait a second, John," she interrupted. "There's an urgent message for you." She handed me a pink memo sheet.

I pocketed the memo without looking at it. "I'll take care of it." Felice nodded and rejoined the crowd around the television. "Terry, did you ever have any contacts in the New Orleans Police Department?"

Terry smiled. "Oh, yeah. We made a few cooperative drug busts down there. Steve Fortescue runs the Narco Division now, I think he finally made captain. What do you need?"

"It's long shot, and I doubt they updated their records from that far back when they went on computers, but see if he can help you find anything from early 1926—any famous guy who got pinched for anything."

He whistled. "That's a tough one, John."

"If that doesn't work, go to the FBI. You worked the mob, you must know a couple of Feds."

"More than a couple. Okay, you've got it."

When Terry left me, I took the memo out of my pocket. My eyes popped when I read it.

> Drop by my office at your earliest convenience.
>   Edwin Blaine
>   Chief, LAPD

5 APRIL 2007—LAPD HEADQUARTERS, PARKER CENTER, LOS ANGELES

It was good to be back.

I hadn't been to Parker Center since putting in my papers

two years before, and the place still felt and smelled exactly the same—like home. The little newsstand in the lobby was still there, doing a bang-up business from uniformed and plainclothes cops alike. Bearded and scraggly haired undercover guys with badges or ID cards hanging from ragged jeans and army jackets shed their street characters and strolled the hallways proudly, secure on their own turf for at least a little while. There were even pale and nervous-looking police officer candidates scattered in small whispering groups, waiting for their background investigation interviews and endless rounds of entry-level paperwork.

I took the slow elevator to the Administrative floor, where I had never been before and, quite frankly, had always worked to avoid. My good friend and former watch commander, Randolph Dickinson, had just been made assistant chief and was waiting for Blaine, the ineffectual interim successor of an even less competent chief, to retire and clear the way for his own accession to the throne.

I had never met Acting Chief Blaine. He was not widely known throughout the Department. Blaine was a pure pogue, a guy who got himself promoted off the street as soon as he became eligible, and had immediately latched on to the coattails of his predecessor, a bloodless, bean-counting Yuppie paper-pusher named Spier. Spier had been widely hated throughout the Department and loved by the politicians. He never supported the men in a crisis and could be counted on to go at the departmental budget like a sushi chef. Fortunately, he could only serve two five-year terms, the second of which had expired a month before.

Chief Blaine was an enigma. No one knew who he was or what he stood for, nor had anyone bothered to find out. Frankly, some people are born to play second fiddle, and he seemed to be at the top of that particular list.

I stopped by Randy Dickinson's office to congratulate him on his new status as heir apparent, but there was no one in his office. I went to the end of the hall, to the hallowed office once occupied by the man for whom this building was named. I entered a reception area and found no one there. I was about to leave when the inner office door opened.

"My secretary quit," a voice said. "Her thirty was up last week and she was off to Hesperia the next day."

I turned toward the voice. Its owner was a small man wearing a cardigan sweater, loose gabardine slacks, and to complete the odd ensemble, slippers.

"Chief Blaine," I said. "John Surrey."

He came toward me and shook my hand warmly. "Randy Dickinson has always spoken highly of you, Detective Surrey. It's a pleasure to finally meet you. Won't you come in?"

I followed him into his office. There were boxes all over the place and bare walls with clean paint outlines where pictures had hung for years.

"I haven't really moved in yet," he said apologetically, "and I don't know if I should bother. I'll have forty years in next November, and I may just turn the whole mess over to Randy at that time instead of finishing my term."

I was taken aback by this confidence and didn't know how to respond. I stared at a picture on his desk, an old photograph of a tough-looking cop in a woolen uniform and Sam Browne belt.

"My dad." He nodded. "The original hard-nosed Irish copper. He was one of Chief Parker's favorites, could have beaten out Davis or Gates easily. He drove Parker nuts because he wouldn't leave the streets."

"He must have been proud of you," I offered.

Blaine laughed but the irony in his voice was evident. "When I made sergeant, he treated me like a traitor. The higher up I went, the more he seemed to disapprove."

"Maybe . . . it just seemed that way," I ventured.

Blaine leaned back in his roomy swivel chair. He seemed grateful for the chance to talk to somebody—anybody. "My dad was all cop. When somebody committed a crime on his beat, he took it personally. He was a mean and bigoted son of a bitch, but that went out the window when it came to protecting the people on his beat. Somebody got robbed or beaten or raped, no matter what color or nationality they were, when he found the creep who did it, he came down on them *hard*.''

"Well," I said carefully, "he still must have been proud of you." I didn't know what the hell to say to this surprisingly lonely, wistful man.

"He was a prick," the chief said decisively, "and he hated me."

I wasn't going to touch *that* one, so I just sat there wondering what he wanted from me.

He reached into his desk and took out a beautiful, gleaming lieutenant's shield. He slid it across the desk toward me.

"It's yours if you want it," he said. "You can take over the Fugitive Squad tomorrow."

"Did Randy Dickinson put you up to this?" I asked him.

"Yes. But after he told me about you, I was convinced that he was right. We've been losing officers, Surrey, good cops. All of our best guys are now chiefs of police in little tank towns all across the Northwest. They put in their twenty and can't wait to get out. We need our good officers back."

"Do I have to decide now?"

"I checked your file. You have a month left until the two-year cutoff. After that, you lose your seniority, and you'd have to come back in as a basic police officer."

"Not likely," I said.

"I didn't think so. But in the short time I have left, I'd like to make my mark by bringing this department back. I want it to be the kind of department that once made this city proud. That starts with men like you."

There wasn't much I could say to that, so I waited for him to continue.

"Tell me," he said. "What do you think is the biggest problem we, as cops, are facing today?"

"The same problem we've had for the last twenty years. Gangs."

"What would you say if I told you that I had an idea that might just get rid of them, once and for all?"

"Have you got a hundred thousand jobs?"

"No. But I'm a police officer, not the mayor. My concern is crime. What would you say if I told you I had a plan?"

"I'd say, 'Good luck.' "

"If you thought it was a good plan, would you consider coming back?"

"Maybe. I'd have to hear the plan first."

My cellular phone rang.

"I'm sorry, Chief. I have to take this call. They wouldn't bother me if it wasn't important."

"That's okay." He nodded. "Would you like some privacy?"

"That's kind of you, but I'll be okay. Excuse me." I flipped the phone on.

"John?"

"Yeah, Terry. Go ahead."

"I called Steve Fortescue at New Orleans PD. He said the only way we could find out about anything in the 1920s would be to fly down there and go through their archives."

"Screw that. It would take days."

"No kidding. I'd have to sift through a whole mountain of old files. I'll do it if I have to, but it might be for nothing."

"What do you mean, for nothing?"

"Well, after I got off the phone with Steve, I called Herb Villaverde at the FBI office in New York. He kicked me over to their guy at the NCIC. What a character. A really old bastard. You know how the FBI used to have mandatory retirement at fifty, then all those age-discrimination suits made them get rid of it?"

"Yeah."

"Well, this old guy has been with the Bureau for more

than fifty years. He was really helpful at first. We were talking shop, getting along like a house afire. Then, when I mentioned New Orleans in the 1920s, he came down on me like a fucking anvil.''

"What do you mean?''

"He clammed up. Then he got real abusive, said shit like 'Who are you again?' 'Whom do you represent?' He started screaming at me because I wasn't an official representative of a law enforcement agency and asked me for my name so he could sic the IRS on me. Naturally, I hung up on the old fart.''

"Hmmm,'' I said. "Interesting.''

"Yeah,'' he replied, "but not real effective.''

"Okay,'' I said. "You did your best. We'll just have to try another approach.''

"I'm sorry, John.''

"Don't worry about it. I'll be back at the barn in an hour.''

I snapped the phone shut. "A problem?'' the chief asked.

"Sort of,'' I replied.

"Can I be of any help?''

I regarded the chief with surprise. "Chief, your time must be very valuable . . .''

"I can spare a few minutes,'' he replied sardonically.

"Okay,'' I said. "Chief, you are now a consultant to Timeshare.''

"I'm honored,'' he replied. "Actually, I may need the work someday soon. How can I help?''

"You can't ask me any questions.''

"I like it already. Papa *would* be proud.''

"In 1926, a famous person was either busted or written up in an incident report in New Orleans. We don't know who he or she was, or the charge, but we have to find out somehow. The FBI won't help us, and NOPD says we'd have to go into their archives and look at every single report from that year. We don't have the time or the personnel to do that.''

"I think I can save you the trouble," Chief Blaine said.

"Really."

"I'm not sure," he began, a slow smile crossing his face, "but I think I might have an idea. Let me make a few calls."

"Are you sure it's no trouble?"

"Mr. Surrey," he said, assuming dignity in his manner for the first time, "I'm a pencil-pusher. That's what I do well. I promise you, I'll have some results for you quite soon."

"All right, Chief," I said, getting up. "I appreciate the effort."

"Forget it," he said. He held up the lieutenant's badge. "And give this a little thought, won't you? Randy Dickinson may work for me, but that still doesn't mean I'd want him mad at me."

I returned to Timeshare feeling pretty good about the way things were turning out. The chief had turned out to be an interesting guy, and I looked forward to meeting with him again.

"How'd it go?" Terry asked me.

"Surprising. Anyway, the chief might be able to help us with our New Orleans problem. He said he'd get right to work on it."

Terry's face clouded and he motioned his head toward the TV screen. "He might be delayed," Terry said. "The Department just went on tactical alert."

Tactical alert meant that all leaves and days off were cancelled in anticipation of a civil disturbance. The normal three-shift rotation was cut down to two twelve-hour tours until the alert was cancelled. It also meant that Blaine, in his first major test as chief, would hardly have the time to go to the john, much less handle our inquiry.

"What's the alert for?" I asked Terry.

"All hell's breaking loose. The Dairy Farmers thing?

They're marching on every Federal building in every major city. This could get really ugly."

I had to see this. I suddenly felt myself worrying about Chief Blaine, wondering how he would handle it. But I had to put such curiosity aside and concentrate on the mission.

"Terry," I said, "how much do you know about the twenties?"

"I'm a Wild West man," he said. "You're the twentieth-century guy."

"Do what you can. Let's sit down and write out everything we can remember about that era. Mitch is visiting everyone he can think of. Look, he knew President Reagan was a kid in Illinois, and he stopped off to see him, didn't he? Well, now he's in New York. He knows who's famous, and who's going to be famous. He wants to meet everybody."

"I thought he was just looking for the gorilla his dreams."

"He is. But he's a writer. Everyone he meets goes into that creative bank—his imagination. Say you're writing a movie about a historical figure. Wouldn't you be able to do a better job of writing about someone if you actually met them?"

"Sounds good to me," he replied.

"All right, then let's get to it."

"The twenties," Terry began. "Who do I know in the twenties? Babe Ruth. Lou Gehrig."

"Not just baseball," I said. "Anyway, it's March back there. The Yankees'll be in spring training in Florida."

"Spoilsport. Okay, Ernest Hemingway. Scott Fitzgerald. Ring Lardner."

"Now, we're getting somewhere," I said.

"Yeah," he snorted, "but we're getting there awfully slow."

"I think we have enough," I said an hour later. My list was ten pages long. Terry's was about seven, which wasn't bad considering that his expertise wasn't in that era. I had a sudden brainstorm and made a mental note to find out everything I could about Harry Levitan, Mitchell's grandfather. Maybe that would shed some light on Mitchell's motive. It was a reach, but I needed all the help I could get.

I picked up the remote and turned on the television. "Let's see how the Dairy Farmers are doing."

The Federal Building was surrounded by an angry mob. They weren't doing anything destructive, at least not yet, but their mood was getting uglier and uglier. It was just a matter of time before someone or something set them off.

There was a ring of cops in riot gear surrounding the crowd. Terry and I, who had both been there and done that, knew exactly the sick feeling they each must have had. Riot duty was the worst. A lot of cops I worked with always felt that there was something intrinsically un-American about it, that it made them seem like the goon squad of a banana republic. Most people who attended protests such as this were not there to cause trouble—they were there to be heard. It was usually a handful of self-aggrandizing low-lifes who set them off for their own ends and ruined everything for everyone. The protests had already degenerated into riots all across the country. Terry and I fervently hoped it wouldn't happen here, but given L.A.'s recent history, the chances of a peaceful outcome seemed remote.

I was curious as to how Chief Blaine would handle it. Would he just turn the whole problem over to Randy or one of the deputy chiefs with expert credentials in crowd control? As much as I wanted Randy to become chief, I also wanted to see Blaine succeed.

As it was, I didn't have long to wait. The crowd parted— rather unenthusiastically, I thought, and two figures walked to the front steps of the building, where the leaders of the protest had set up their podium. The head protestor had his face set in an almost Hymie Weiss–type of scowl.

"Are they going to tell them to disperse?" Terry wondered aloud.

"They haven't got a permit to assemble," I replied. "Shades of the Rodney King verdict."

The cameras zoomed in. The two figures were Randy Dickinson, a six-foot-seven giant in riot gear, and Ed Blaine, five-eight in his slippers and cardigan. Blaine handed a sheet of paper to the riot leader, who snatched it impatiently.

I wished I could see the expression on Randy Dickinson's face, but it was obscured by his tactical headgear. I couldn't help but notice, however, that his attention was riveted on Chief Blaine. I could tell from his demeanor, though, that he was probably thinking his world-famous "Boy, you crazy." He had said that to me often enough when he was my boss on the Fugitive Squad, and I recognized his posture.

But Chief Blaine looked unconcerned as he watched the Dairy Farmers spokesman read the slip of paper. The spokesman suddenly looked up, and stared at Blaine. Blaine shrugged and then nodded.

And then a strange thing happened. The spokesman reached into a beer cooler and took out a single-serving container of milk. He handed it to Blaine, who opened it, raised it in salute to the entire assemblage, and then tipped it back and chugged down the entire contents. Then Blaine and Dickinson turned and walked back through the crowd. And as they did so, the crowd applauded. Wildly. Some protesters even patted them on the shoulder as they went by.

I turned up the volume as a reporter caught up with them.

"Chief Blaine," the reporter asked as he struggled to keep up with them, "are you going to disperse the crowd?"

"No need," Blaine said.

"But they don't have a permit."

"They do now," he replied firmly.

"Chief Dickinson, the Farmers have already rioted in other cities. Aren't you afraid that could happen here at any moment?"

Dickinson pulled off his helmet for the cameras, but Blaine stopped and turned to face the reporter. "I'll answer that. These people have a permit to assemble. As long as they are not breaking any laws, and I have their assurance that they won't, they are exercising their right to protest as guaranteed by the law of our land. It's our job to uphold that law."

"Then why are the police on tactical alert?"

"I'll leave you in Chief Dickinson's most capable hands," Blaine said, getting into his car. On Randy Dickinson's face was the most reluctant look of admiration I have ever seen.

"We're here to protect the crowd as much as anyone else," Randy said. "We expect no trouble. This is a peaceful demonstration. Now if you'll excuse me."

I turned off the TV. "Wow," I said.

"You said it." Terry nodded. "The guy may look like Perry Como, but inside, he's Niccolo Machiavelli. You're lucky to have a chief like that."

"I feel bad for Randy, though."

"How come?"

"If I know Randy Dickinson, he just found out something about Chief Blaine that he absolutely did not want to know."

"What's that?"

"He likes him."

SEVEN

I MIGHT HAVE DONE SOMETHING MORE STUPID IN MY LIFE than parachuting from a jet over water in the early evening, but try as I may, I just can't seem to come up with anything.

The Mitchell I. Levitan situation had become too critical to waste five days crossing the country by train, and striking the whole Zoom Room and moving it to the East Coast was not a viable alternative. So, a moron named John Surrey opened his mouth and said, "Why don't we fly cross-country in the company Gulfstream IV?"

Timeshare's own private jet was a perk that Felice and Cornelia added on when we started doing business beyond our wildest hopes. Our customers came from all over the country, and flying them in free of charge was an added feature to the Timeshare package. Felice, our resident financial genius, had even figured out how to depreciate the operating costs into a virtual profit.

Our pilot was a retired Naval Aviator who had flown sorties over Vietnam with my uncle Jack. He was a short, bald-headed guy who had been a real hot dog in his Navy days. He missed the action but was happy to still be flying for a living—and anyone who worked for us made a damned good one.

The idea was to zoom the jet back into 1926. That wasn't a problem; the Zoomer had a fifty-mile range and could even transport the plane while it was airborne, although the turbulence it created was a little on the scary side. The difficulty was that in 1926, there wasn't anywhere on the globe where a large, twin-engined business jet could land. First of all, we didn't want anyone in 1926 to see the plane, and secondly, there were no concrete runways for the jet's sensitive landing gear. Air travel in 1926 was still primitive by our standards; all planes were tail-draggers and all airports were grassland.

It was Terry, my good friend and assistant, who unknowingly got me into the whole mess. He actually volunteered, not realizing that I was the one who had to go.

"Kirk," he asked the pilot, "would it be possible for you to drop down to about seven thousand feet, depressurize the cabin, and cut the throttles all the way back?"

"Sure," Kirk said, chewing on the end of an unlit pipe. "Why would I want to?"

"So I could jump."

"The hell you say."

"Come on, Kirk, I was Airborne. The good old 101st. I know my way around a chute."

"The engines are on the tail. You'll get turned into hamburger."

"Not if you cut the throttles and dip your wing; I'll free-fall right out, and my chute'll open at fifteen hundred feet."

"If I cut the throttles and dip my wing, I'll hit the goddamned ground before you do."

Terry slapped his shoulder. "Not you, sport. You're too good a pilot."

"Forget it, Terry," he said.

"What's the matter, you can't do it?" Terry needled him. "I thought you Navy pilots—sorry, Naval *Aviators*—

were such hot shit. Christ, I've met *Coast Guard* pilots with more balls.''

Kirk reddened. "Don't even go there, Dogface.''

Terry looked at me appealingly. "Come on, John. Talk some sense into him.''

I didn't like it, but I was out of options. "What's your plan, Terry?''

"You got any maps of the New York area?'' he asked Kirk.

"I think I can scrape one up,'' Kirk replied edgily. He reached into his Jeppeson case and pulled out a chart of the tristate area.

Terry flipped through the pages quickly. "There,'' he said.

"That's Connecticut,'' I said.

"Right. Here we go.'' He nodded to Kirk. "You take the northern route, over the Canadian border. Make sure you've got all the fuel you can carry.''

"The G-IV has a good enough range to go there and back,'' Kirk said, "but we could fill up the auxiliary wing tanks just to be sure.''

"Okay. Now, you maintain altitude until you hit Boston. Then you start losing height over the Atlantic. You make a slow, descending circle to the southwest. Then you slide right in over the Sound between Long Island and Connecticut.''

"I can do that,'' Kirk said thoughtfully. "It'd take some navigation, though, you want to do it at night.''

"Sunset is good enough. The point here is that you don't want to be visible, that's why I don't want you to drop altitude until you're feet wet past Boston. By the time you turn west, the sun'll be setting. You keep all your nav lights off and no one'll see us coming out of the east.''

I nodded my approval. "You've thought of everything, Terry,'' I said. "Where's the jump site?''

"Compo Beach, Westport, Connecticut. I know the place, my aunt and uncle live there. It's a good-sized drop zone, the area won't be heavily populated, and there's a train station less than two miles away."

"Was the station there in 1926?"

He nodded quickly. "It was built in 1918 for the troops going off to World War I. I jump at around six, I can make the 6:38 to Grand Central, no problem. Be in the city by eight."

Kirk flicked a paper clip at the no smoking sign and lit his pipe. "And how do I find this lovely garden spot?"

Terry pointed to the map. "You see this little U-shaped island about a mile and a half offshore? That's Cockenoe Island. About forty years ago they were gonna stick a nuclear reactor plant there; the town went batshit. So, it's uninhabited."

"What about in 1926?"

"Same deal. Anyway, who cares? No one'll see me. So, Kirk, my drop zone is this point just across from the island. I'll bring a little entrenching tool, bury the chute on the beach, and before anyone knows what's happened, I'll be in the bar car on the 6:38. What do you think?"

"It's a good plan, Terry," I said.

He grinned hugely.

"However, you're not going."

His smile froze. "What the hell do you mean, I'm not going? Who is?"

I swallowed painfully. "I am."

"Jesus H. Christ, John!" he exploded. "I've made over two hundred jumps."

"Yeah," I said. "That was before you got a metal shinbone working the mob undercover."

He looked insulted. "So what? I can handle it."

"I can't risk you, old pal."

"You weren't a paratrooper, John."

"I got my wings," I said.

"How many jumps?" he challenged me.

I mumbled an answer.

"How many?"

I cleared my throat. "Six."

"Oh, so you qualified and never jumped again. John, you'll kill yourself."

"I'll be fine. You're gonna be jumpmaster."

"John—"

"Terry, it's a good plan. But it's my party. Can I count on your help?"

He fumed. "Yeah," he breathed.

I was afraid that selling the plan to Cornelia and Felice was going to be difficult; in fact, I had thought that the two of them would veto it outright. It turned out to be not only difficult to sell the plan, but just as much of an effort to convince them that I hadn't lost my marbles.

"Are you nuts?" Cornelia demanded.

"Have you gone round the twist?" Felice wanted to know.

"Five more days on the train?" I retorted. "*That's* crazy. It's a waste of time and energy."

"Oh, I'm sorry to hear that," Cornelia shot back. "You can't stand being cooped up for five days, so let's risk your life, Terry's life, and Kirk's. Oh, and lest we forget, how about a $27 million aircraft?"

"Look, I can do this," I insisted, although I was far from sure about it.

"I'm sure you can," Cornelia said. "But you're not."

"Oh, come on, Boss . . ."

"And after the three of you get killed in a fiery wreck, what do I tell Kirk's wife? Althea? Your uncle Jack?"

"Oh, yes, John, your uncle Jack would *really* take this well," Felice added. " 'Well, you see, Admiral Surrey, John assured us that he would be all right. So, based on that, we let him parachute out of a business jet flown by one pilot with no relief from all the way across the continent—in other words, the longest airborne mission since Entebbe.' I don't think so, John."

"Look, I'll handle Uncle Jack."

"John, the answer is no."

"Are you going to give in? I don't have the time to argue anymore, and I'm going to do it anyway. So here's my offer. Either give me your blessing, or I'll sell you back my shares in Timeshare, plus make you the beneficiary of all my insurance policies."

Cornelia and Felice glanced at each other.

"Oh, Christ," sighed Cornelia, "he's getting like *that* again."

"He's in martyr mode," she agreed, "there's no stopping him."

"I hate it when he bluffs like that," Cornelia said. "Someday I'm going to have to call him on it. Just to see what happens."

I ran off to make preparations for the trip before they changed their minds. Currency, medical, wardrobe—all teams had to be put on full alert. The debriefing room had to be set up for our return. Finally, and perhaps most importantly, Levitan's bill had to be totalled up. Timeshare would be lucky to be on the receiving end of that particular check.

It would be Kirk, our pilot, who would have to work the hardest this trip. He would have to fly cross-country from Van Nuys to Cape Cod and then back again—without one single stop. His skills as both pilot and navigator would be tested to the limit. Not to mention his stamina.

"I need a weather report," Kirk said as I joined him and Terry in the briefing room.

"For Connecticut?"

"For Connecticut on March 7, 1926. Not to mention the rest of the country. John, I have to know what altitudes to use. Which route to take—"

"Well, at least you won't have to worry about air traffic," Terry remarked.

"Maybe. But I won't have any air traffic *control*, either.

No weather updates, no wind speed and direction changes. And no Global Positioning Satellite.''

"I'm beginning to see your problem," I said.

Kirk stared at me frankly. "I don't think you are. Look, John, you're a pilot. Maybe just a weekend Cessna jockey, but you still fly. You know all about filing a flight plan, getting help from the flight service center, even making use of pireps. But we're in the dark right now."

"All right then. What can I do?"

"I need the most exact weather data for 7 March '26 that you can get me. I'll tell you why: I have to calibrate the flight computer, the Loran—every goddamned needle and dial I've got. You want me to get you there, I can. But I also want to get back in one piece. The autopilot can save me a hell of a lot of work, but I have to feed in the correct information to begin with."

"Okay. Say no more. I think I can solve your problem. Just sit tight."

"Admiral Surrey's office."

"R. B.? Is that you?"

"Big John! How the hell are ya, kiddo?"

Master Chief Rodney Bates had been with my uncle in one capacity or another since Jack's return to full flight duty after his return from captivity in the Hanoi Hilton. R. B. had been the maintenance crew chief of every aircraft Jack had flown from then on. Later, when Jack rose to command of an aircraft carrier and then to flag rank, he took R. B. with him as his administrative assistant. I had known R. B. since I was five years old.

"Still working on that novel, R. B.?"

"It's done and five publishers have already rejected it," he announced proudly. R. B. had spent the last three years working on what he firmly believed was going to be the biggest Navy novel since *The Sand Pebbles*.

"Keep plugging, R. B."

"Is my middle name 'Quit'? What can I do you for, John?"

"Is Himself around?"

"He's on leave, John. He should be out your way. Didn't he call you?"

"No," I answered, surprised. Jack was not merely my uncle, he was my best friend. It wasn't like him not to call when he was in from Washington. That had me worried, and it made me feel guilty because I didn't have the time to think about it.

"R. B.," I said quickly, "I need a favor, a huge one, and I need it yesterday."

"Ask and ye shall receive," he pronounced.

"I need the weather records for 6 March through 8 March 1926, for the entire country. Conditions, winds, whatever."

"It would be pointless of me to ask what this is for, wouldn't it?"

"Pretty useless, yeah."

"Well, even if Jack were here, he'd kick it back to me anyway. If it weren't for us chiefs, our damn boats would still run on coal."

"Do you think you'd have those records somewhere?"

"I'm sure I know someone over at Met. Gimme your fax number and stand by."

"You're a buddy, R. B."

"Anything for Jack. Now stand by. Your fax is gonna start singin' like Pavarotti."

R. B. was as good as his word. Within twenty minutes the fax was spitting out page upon page of charts, meteorological data, and other facts vital to our flight. The information was so complete it almost evinced a grin from Kirk.

"This is good." He nodded approvingly. "Maybe we *won't* die. I'll be at the airport."

"Wheels up in ninety minutes," I said.

"You hope," he grunted.

After he left, Terry gave me a crash-refresher course in parachuting. His mood had mysteriously changed from disappointment to enthusiasm, but then Terry had always been a team player.

"Okay, I saw on the charts that the only wind is going to be a very light offshore breeze. You'll hardly have to steer at all. But you know how, right?"

"I qualified, didn't I?"

"Yeah, but what do I know about *Marine* Airborne qualification? It's common knowledge that you jarheads are much more at home with your schlongs in the mud."

"That's only because Congress gives all the money to you dogfaces."

"Right," he replied, rolling his eyes. "Now when you hit the ground, tuck and roll. Don't try anything fancy. You try to come down standing up, as if you were, well . . . *me*, or something, you'll probably break your legs."

"I'll be careful."

"Good. Now, I've got to ask you one more time: Are you sure you want to do this? You have to be a hundred percent."

"I'm sure," I replied, although I wasn't.

"Great," he answered sarcastically. "Hit your Decacom when you land, once for okay, three times for trouble."

"There won't be any trouble, Terry."

"There'd better not be."

Terry went ahead to the airport to help get things ready. He had also insisted upon packing my chute himself.

"John?" Felice caught me on the way to the parking lot. "This fax just came in for you."

I stuck it into my pocket without looking at it. "Thanks, Felice. By the way, tell the techies to be precise when they zoom the plane back in. It can't go off the radar screen for even a second. It's got to come back exactly the instant that it disappears."

"I'll take care of it." She nodded. "John. Please be careful." She gave me a tight hug.

"I will," I promised, kissing her cheek.

"You know, Cornelia can be pretty tough," she began.

"But inside she's hard as nails," I finished for her.

She grinned. "True. But when she really cares about someone—"

"Like you."

"And like you. She's worried about you."

"I'll be fine. One long blast on the Decacom to Kirk, when he gets back you'll know I'm okay."

"John, you don't have to do this."

I kissed her again. "Of course I do."

I was pretty shaky when I climbed aboard the jet at Van Nuys. I took one last look around the airport and spotted my little Cessna at its tie-down near the 94th Aero Squadron, wondering if I'd see it again. To tell you the truth, jumping from an airplane scared the hell out of me. But the Marines had taught me how to deal with fear: I was more afraid of looking scared or chickening out than I was of the consequences of my actions. The Airborne Rangers had probably taught Terry the same thing.

"You're scared to death." Terry grinned.

"You got that right."

He slapped me on the shoulder. "Enjoy it. That's the fun! Being scared shitless and defeating it."

"Terry, did anyone ever tell you that you're a total and utter psychopath?"

"*Moi?*"

"Doesn't anything frighten you?"

"Just one thing."

"Oh, yeah? What's that?"

"Marriage."

Terry went forward to the control cabin and reappeared almost immediately. "Let's belt up," he said, pushing the button that automatically shut the cabin door and locked it.

The starboard engine kicked in, setting off an army of

butterflies in my stomach. The effect was doubled as the port engine turned over.

I looked around the jet and noticed how different it was from the last plane out of which I had jumped. In the Marines we had leaped out of the rear end of a gigantic, noisy, and spartan C-130 Hercules. The Gulfstream, on the other hand, was carpeted and luxuriously appointed. There were plush recliners, a couch that folded into a bed, a bar, a fully stocked galley, and a bathroom with small shower. Not the sort of aircraft one would think of as an airborne platform.

There was a loud hiss as the intercom went on. *"Gentlemen,"* Kirk's voice blared out at us, *"we have received clearance to taxi and hold short of the runway. We are currently number three for takeoff. Please fasten your safety belts, and stay the hell out of my cockpit. Except when I ask one of you to bring me coffee."*

We began a brisk taxi across the tarmac. A little too brisk, I thought, but I wasn't the pilot. Terry was staring pensively out the window. He looked over at me and winked. I burrowed into my impossibly comfortable seat and tried not to think about plummeting to my death in the icy Atlantic.

We swung onto the runway, and, without stopping, Kirk goosed the engines all the way forward. Our speed increased fivefold almost immediately.

In another instant, we were airborne, and I could feel the gear retracting and the flaps returning to zero degrees.

"Gentlemen," Kirk's voice interrupted my thoughts, *"prepare for time travel. In five, four, three, two, one— zoom."*

The turbulence was terrifying.

The plane bucked and buffeted, the nose pitching up, and just as suddenly, the tail. The wings dipped on their axes. I could imagine Kirk up forward, fighting the control yoke with every ounce of his strength. Terry, I noticed with some triumph, looked a little green around the gills.

"What the hell," he said with a weak smile, "I like jumpin' out of 'em, not the flying part."

All at once, the turbulence ceased. The plane continued its climb smoothly and with the slightest bump. A brilliant sun shone in through the windows.

"Okay, guys," said Kirk over the loudspeaker, *"unless somebody's really screwed the pooch, we are now in 1926. So, boop-boop-be-do, everybody."*

Terry breathed a sigh of relief and reached into his pocket. He flashed a deck of cards at me.

"Go Fish, anyone?"

EIGHT

THE PITCH OF THE ENGINES CHANGED EVER SO SLIGHTLY.

"*Gentlemen,*" Kirk's voice said over the intercom, "*we are beginning our gradual descent.*"

"Let's get you ready," Terry said. "First, put on your jumpsuit. It should fit right over your clothes. Then we'll hook you up."

"Terry," I asked, struck by a sudden and perhaps belated curiosity, "why did you become a cop?"

"My dad was a cop," he replied, straightening my jump suit. "He's one hell of a guy, my old man. You ought to see him. He's big, like your pal Randy Dickinson. No one knows where he got it from, either—his folks were tiny."

"Why'd he become a cop?"

Terry attached my supply bag to my ankle. "It's actually not a bad story. My grandparents came over from Russia, you know, they got burned out by Cossacks and all that *Fiddler on the Roof* kind of stuff. Well, they worked their asses off, my grandma got sweated in the garment shops and Grampa busted his hump hauling ice. Just a couple of hardworking immigrants who didn't ask much from life and didn't get much back, either. But they grew tired of working for other people, so they saved for years and years—my dad was a midlife baby—and they finally scraped up enough money to open a little soda fountain. You know, one of those places with the green signs that said 'Lunch-eonette'? Maybe you *wouldn't* know, I guess they didn't have them in California. Anyhow, just a little place; you could get an egg cream or a sundae, newspapers, candy, cigarettes, that kind of thing. It made them a living—not much more than that, but at least they were working for themselves and not some slave-driving son of a bitch. And then my dad came along—long after they gave up on the idea of ever having any children—and they knew that they'd be able to send him to college. Maybe not Harvard, but at least he'd be able to take time out from helping support the family to go to CCNY. Break the cycle of poverty, or 'get off the schneid,' as Gramps used to say.

"Anyway, they run this little soda fountain. And once a week this police sergeant comes in. Big Irish guy—this was in the days when Irish cops really were Irish, with the brogue and all. And the NYPD was about a hundred-and-twelve percent Irish back then. So, this sergeant comes in, and you have to understand the kind of presence this guy must have had. In those days, New York cops still wore the double-breasted tunics with the brass buttons and hook collars. And if you were a sergeant or above, you had all that gold braid to go with it. A cop *looked* like a cop in those days. When that sergeant walked into my grandparents' little store, he probably took up the entire place. Scared the hell out of them. After all, what did they know from cops?

"Well, the cop would smile—a patronizing smile, ask solicitously about their health, and then give them a dollar bill for a couple packs of Old Golds. He'd get his smokes, his dollar, plus his change . . . a ten-dollar bill. Every week.

You know what ten bucks was to my grandparents back then?''

"I can imagine," I said. Terry was damned good—I had forgotten how scared I was for just a little while.

"When my dad got old enough to understand what was going on," Terry continued, "to say that he was enraged would be an understatement. It grated on him until he became old enough to do something about it."

"I don't get it," I said. "If I had grown up in that kind of circumstance, I'd hate cops."

"He did. But not what they stood for. It occurred to him that while it was true that these cops took advantage of his parents, they also protected them. A guy tried to rob them once. Nothing really serious, he just shoved Gramps around a little. When the cops found out—well, let's put it this way, the guy took his act to another precinct after he got out of the hospital."

"They still shook down your grandparents."

"Yeah. And that's why my dad became a cop. He wanted to make lieutenant at least, preferably captain, because he wanted guys like that big sergeant afraid of *him*."

"Did he make it?"

"He retired as a full inspector. Yeah, he made it. He commanded a whole division. But he always says his happiest days were when he was a captain running a precinct. He ran a clean precinct, too. He'd've thrown guys like that sergeant right out on their asses."

"Is that why you became a cop?"

He shook his head. "I love my dad," he said. "He's the greatest guy in the world, and I wanted to be just like him."

"I don't think he was disappointed," I said.

Terry shrugged. "I know he'd like grandchildren, but you know how it is, working undercover. Not good for relationships, not good at all."

"What does your mom think?"

He laughed. "She made me take piano lessons."

"You play the piano?"

"A little. Mom wanted me to be another Glenn Gould. I wanted to be Eliot Ness. Who do you think won?"

"Gentlemen," Kirk said over the loudspeaker, *"our altitude is now seventeen thousand feet. We are just passing Boston, feet wet and about to commence our turn southwest. Please make your departure preparations."*

I looked out the window and was just able to make out the Cape Cod curve below. The left wing rose slowly, and soon I could see nothing but blue sky. I wondered if anyone below could see us, and if they could, what must they have thought?

Terry motioned for me to stand up. He buckled me into my chute like a squire armoring a knight before a joust. Then he began changing into a jumpsuit of his own.

"Terry? What the hell do you think you're doing?"

"Excuse me?" he replied. "I'm sorry, you must have forgotten what kind of aircraft this is. Is it a C-130?"

"No, but—"

"Is it a C-5 Galaxy?"

"What are you getting at?"

"Is it even a Globemaster, or a DC-3?"

"No."

"Did you happen to notice any ramps in the aft section of the plane?"

"Terry—"

"Was this plane designed for airborne operations?"

"No."

"Tell me, John, do you see, anywhere at all on this aircraft, any sort of safety tether to which I can attach myself as I bid you a fond farewell?"

"Oh, I get it."

"Wonderful. Therefore, what do you suppose would happen if I foolishly slipped or tripped or, yeah, even stumbled from this aircraft without the benefit of a large canopy—not to be confused with the sort beneath which those of my creed exchange nuptial vows—to retard my speed as I plummet earthward?"

I nodded my head in surrender. "That last foot would be a killer," I recited.

"Right you are, sport. Help me with this chute."

I buckled Terry into his own rig. Then he attached a large nylon bag to his ankle. "If I fall out, I want to be prepared," he said.

The engines softened to a dull roar as Kirk throttled back and bled off airspeed.

"Gentlemen, we are passing through eleven thousand feet," Kirk announced over the loudspeaker. *"Prepare for cabin depressurization."*

In another instant, my ears started to pop and I began swallowing continuously for relief.

"Over New Bedford now, guys."

"Okay," Terry said, "you fall right out of the airplane. You remember what that's like. Try and spread your body out like you're a kid pretending to be an airplane. When you hit fifteen hundred, your chute'll open automatically, but don't take any chances. You start getting a little scared, forget the auto-open. Pull the ring and steer yourself right onto the beach. Remember to tuck and roll."

"I'll be fine, Terry."

"Okay."

He left me to my own thoughts for the next few minutes. I was so scared I thought I was going to vomit, but my Marine training had long since taken hold and I was able to put it aside.

"Okay, John, we're almost there. Seventy-five hundred feet, over Branford. I'm knocking the airspeed down to a deuce."

"Well," Terry said, "in the words of my old jumpmaster, STAND UP!"

I stood.

"CHECK EQUIPMENT!"

I felt around on various buckles and straps to make sure they were all attached.

"Three minutes. Opening cabin door."

The aircraft door slid up into the ceiling. A bone-chilling wind flooded the cabin.

"*AWOOGAH! AWOOOGAH!*" A warning siren erupted. On a business jet, it was often considered somewhat hazardous if the door opened in flight.

The aircraft jerked, and then righted itself. Kirk had left the intercom open, and I heard him gasp, "*Shit!*" followed by a sigh of relief as he shut down the port engine, increased power to the starboard, and trimmed the control surfaces to maintain proper flight attitude.

"*Stand by,*" Kirk said, much calmer than a moment before.

Terry stood up and held out his hand. As we shook, he shouted in my ear, "You can still change your mind."

"I'm okay," I shouted back.

We stood at the cabin door, to me, the edge of eternity. The blueness of the ocean in the last stages of the day, and the clarity of the land stretching beneath us made it seem as though it were summer on the ground below.

"There's Cockenoe Island," Terry said. "To the north— just across the bay—is your drop zone."

I nodded dumbly. Kirk gave the aircraft warning dip to the right. Terry stepped back away from the door, and I stood alone at the open hatch.

The aircraft slowly rolled to the left.

"*Good luck, John,*" Kirk called.

Terry gave me a thumbs-up, which I returned. Then the aircraft's roll to port became too steep for my feet to maintain their hold on the aircraft floor.

I slipped, regained my footing, and before I could change my mind, stepped from the aircraft into thin air.

7 MARCH 1926—COMPO BEACH, WESTPORT, CONNECTICUT

I was screaming. It may have been a drawn-out shriek of a profanity, or something completely unintelligible, but I was in the middle of a nightmare.

When I had qualified as an airborne Marine, there was always so much to do, so many others around from which to draw strength and dispel fear. But here I was alone.

I kept falling and falling, pitifully clawing at the sky, praying that I would awaken and find myself in bed, covered in sweat and breathing heavily, but no higher off the ground than my mattress.

Absurdly, I shouted, "HEEELLLPPP!"

"Spread your goddamned arms like I told you, for Christ's sake," came a voice directly above me.

I dared to open my eyes and saw Terry Rappaport directly over my position.

"Spread out! Arch your back!" Although I was still dropping like one of Galileo's rocks off the Tower of Pisa, I suddenly felt a little less, well, doomed. I did what I was told, glad for something to do.

In an instant almost too surreal to be really happening, Terry floated down from above me and took hold of my wrists. For a few endless seconds, we literally flew together. I looked down and saw that we had been placed perfectly within our drop zone. The flat-ended, U-shaped Cockenoe Island was directly behind us. Beneath my feet was the protruding finger of beach where we would land. There were not many houses in the area, although there were some farms and what appeared to be a golf course.

But there was something else, too.

"Here we go, champ!" called Terry. In another instant, my chute opened with a satisfying bang, resulting in perhaps the only kick in the balls I have ever received with appreciation. My fall slowed instantly, the parachute giving me a false but palpable sense of security.

I looked up and saw the jet slowly circling above. Kirk had secured the cabin door and was watching our descent.

"You're doing fine," Terry called. "It'll all be over in a minute."

Actually, I was beginning to enjoy myself. The steerable parachute gave me a sense of control, and I no longer felt helpless and afraid. In fact, I was beginning to understand why folks made a sport of skydiving in the first place.

However, I was troubled by the fact that when we landed on the beach, we weren't going to be alone. I could see a small motor launch grounded on the sand and a knot of about two or three dozen people standing around it. I was concerned that at any moment one of them would look up and easily spot us.

But I needn't have worried. In 1926, there wasn't much reason for anyone to look up at the sky. Airplanes were not common, and parachute jumping was in its infancy. No one would be looking for us.

But just to be sure, I motioned for Terry to follow me as I steered westward, away from the people on the beach. He nodded, and the ground began to appear closer and closer.

"Tuck and roll," Terry called, "tuck and roll."

I did exactly as I was repeatedly told. As the ground came up to meet me, I tucked my legs into my body. As I struck the ground—at a force akin to jumping off a garage roof—I rolled my body, allowing it to dissipate the impact.

I jumped up and immediately began hauling in the chute, before the wind could billow it. As I did so, Terry, working the cords expertly, fell toward me and hit the ground running, or limping, given his bad leg.

"Show-off," I sneered.

"That's the Airborne Way, old buddy. Have they seen us?"

"Apparently not. I wonder what's going on over there."

"We'll find out. First let's bury these chutes. Are you okay? No bones broken, no internal injuries?"

"No, I'm all right. Thanks to you. And by the way, if this were the Marines I'd court-martial you for insubordination. You were supposed to stay behind."

Terry looked at me archly.

"However," I continued, "thank God you didn't."

"Think nothing of it. Okay, Boss, you're in charge again."

I surveyed the beach. It was rockier than the smooth California beaches I was used to, more gravelly and full of sharp, broken shells. I wondered how people could walk here barefoot.

"Check this out," Terry said. We had landed near a mount of two big cannons. They had been filled in and were now, I supposed, a sort of monument. Terry looked for a plaque. "Well," he said, "it seems the British landed here in 1777."

"Oh? What happened?"

"I guess they bought up the place and enacted a two-acre zoning law."

I climbed onto one of the long guns and stood up. "What do you suppose is going on over there?"

Terry reached into his jump bag and took out a pair of small but powerful binoculars. He climbed up next to me and surveyed the beach. When he took the glasses from his eyes again, he was laughing.

"Bootleggers," he said.

"Really?"

He handed me the binoculars. "Take a look."

The scene going on over a hundred yards away jumped into focus. There was a group of men near the little launch, some dressed as workmen, others as white-collar types. One at a time, they handed a nattily dressed guy a bill or two. The guy would reach into the motorboat, pull out a burlap-wrapped object—a bottle, obviously—and hand it over. Oddly enough, order was being kept by a lone, uniformed state trooper.

"Leftovers," Terry said. "A case gets knocked over or something in transit, a couple of bottles get broken. You can't sell the case anymore. So the bootleggers get one of their peons to get rid of the rest of it. He probably sets it up with the state cop over there, keep things running smoothly. Not a bad little racket."

"Let's ask him for a ride," I said.

"Are you serious?"

"How far did you say it was to the train station?"

"Well, there're two: Saugatuck and Greens Farms. Both are about two miles away. Saugatuck's the better bet, the train always stops there."

"The hell with that," I said. "I'm not shlepping this bag two miles."

There was a huge roar from the sky as Kirk, having seen us land, returned his engines to full power. Down the beach, the bootlegger's customers looked around for the source of the noise, but not up, where Kirk flashed his nav lights in salute.

"I don't envy him the trip back," I said. "He must be whipped."

"So am I," Terry said. "You're right. Let's bum a ride off that flatfoot."

The walk toward the trooper's car gave me the chance to look around a bit. If this part of town were any indication at all, then Westport was a beautiful little place. It was far different than my own southern California seashore. Every acre of beachfront where I lived was completely utilized. Houses seemed to be built almost on top of one another, the business sections of towns inching right up to the sand.

Even allowing for the fact that it was 1926, Connecticut beaches were still entirely different. A small town on the seashore in Connecticut didn't seem reminiscent of Calcutta, like those with which I was familiar. There was a beach, a rich guy's property, then a farm, then another rich guy's property.

Terry explained to me that towns such as this took not only their zoning laws seriously, but their history, as well. By our time, many houses in Westport would be designated as historical landmarks: some were almost two hundred and fifty years old. I wondered if a single building in Chatsworth was even half that age.

"You should see this place in our time," Terry said. "Joggers, walkers, roller-bladers all over the place. I used to hang out at this beach when I came up to stay with my aunt and uncle during the summers. But it's still a beautiful place. Right where we're walking is now a one-way black-top, and there are more houses along here, but the place still has its character. Back over there, where we just came from, is where all the lockers are—you rent 'em for the season—and right next to it is the snack bar. On the other side of that is parking and the marina. My folks wanted to move here, but my dad didn't like the idea of an hour train ride every morning."

"Nothing personal, but he was nuts," I replied. "This place is great."

"Whoa! You mean the Original California Kid would actually consider a move eastward?"

"No, but if it did happen, like when hell freezes over, this town would be tops on my list."

We looked up at the gathering darkness and could just make out the Gulfstream as it streaked homeward.

"He told me he's going to put on the autopilot and just conk for a few hours," Terry said. "The weather picture looked smooth, and he's going to have tailwind."

"Good luck to him," I said. What Kirk had done—was doing—took courage. I would see to it that he was amply rewarded upon my return.

The knot of men was beginning to break up. Apparently, the bootlegger had sold most of his wares and was ready to head back to his boat, a cabin cruiser anchored a few miles offshore.

"The cop is probably starting to say stuff like, 'Aw right, break it up,' " Terry observed.

"No bets here," I replied.

"Aw right, aw right, let's break it up," we heard the state trooper say as we neared the group. We hung back as the bootlegger's customers began heading for their cars. There were mostly Chevy sedans and Model T's, but there was also a Duesenberg and a gorgeous Stutz Bearcat.

"I had one of those when I was a kid," Terry said, enviously regarding the princely two-seater. "No, not a real one," he added in response to my exceedingly dubious look, "a plastic one, ran on a big dry-cell battery. I was about five years old. You couldn't get me out of the thing. But I always wanted the real McCoy."

"What do you think that one goes for?" I asked, nodding toward the real one that was being driven away by a drunk-to-be.

"Three, maybe four grand. A steal."

The customers had all left and the cop was helping the vendor shove his launch back into the water. The bootlegger slipped the state trooper a couple of bills and hopped into the boat. The cop stood and watched as the smuggler tried to start the engine. Finally, after a few yanks on the starter cord, the engine caught and the bootlegger was on his way.

"Pardon me, Officer," Terry said to the cop, startling him.

"Hoo-aah!" The cop jumped about five feet backward.

"Glad to see the town is in such safe hands," Terry said to me. "Little burgs like these won't have their own police force until maybe ten or twenty years from now. This bozo is probably the sole law enforcement officer for miles."

"Who you callin' a bozo?" the cop demanded, recovering. He was a young guy with a huge overbite, full of himself and his uniform.

"Did I say that?" Terry replied innocently.

"I ain't deaf, fella." He gave us and our suitcases a suspicious leer. "Whattaya guys want around here?"

"We'd like a ride to the train station," I said politely.

"Do I look like a fuckin' taxicab? Go on, beat it, before I run ya in."

"Run us in? For what?"

"Because I says so. Go on, scram." He put a hand on his flap holster.

Terry reached into his pocket. The cop ripped open the flap on his holster. "Getcha hand outta there."

"Relax," Terry said. He pulled a gold New York City police captain's badge out of his pocket and showed it to the cop. I tried not to look flabbergasted.

"Aw, fer Christ's sake," the cop breathed heavily, "whyncha say you was onna job?"

"You didn't ask," Terry replied.

"What're you guys doin' aroun' here?" the cop asked, his manner becoming respectful in light of Terry's supposed rank.

"Oh, we just *dropped* in," Terry replied, winking at me. "What's your name?"

"Delinko, Richie Delinko."

"How long you been a trooper, Richie?"

"Almost a year," he answered proudly. Terry gave me a look; he obviously suspected, as did I, that "almost a year" was probably closer to three or four months. The Smokey the Bear hat looked too big, and the young cop seemed lost in the navy blue greatcoat, cinched into folds by the Sam Browne belt.

"Where're you headquartered?" Terry asked as we walked toward the trooper's car.

"Barracks G, do'n 'ere 'na Post Road," Richie replied. The local patois was unintelligible as far as I was concerned, but Terry seemed to have no trouble with it. In fact, he even began to lapse into it slightly.

"I understand," Terry said, "that you state boys get your own car and your own motorcycle."

"Yeah," the cop affirmed, "but this time a year it's too goddamned cold for the Harley. I'll take the Dodge any old day. You gotta live inna barracks, ya ain't married, an' it cramps yer style. Ya know what I mean," he added, with a ridiculous eyebrow raise.

"Dodge comes in handy for dates." Terry nodded.

"You said it! I get my share, bein' a cop 'n all."

Terry and I glared at each other, our telepathy remarking, probably *once* and not for free. We finally reached the Dodge sedan and thus commenced the longest five minutes of my life. Richie the Trooper became Richie the Tour Guide.

"Dis here's da Longshore Golf Club," he said. "Lotta fuckin' money there."

"It's public now," Terry whispered.

"Dis here's da Minuteman Statue," he narrated, as we passed a bronze rendering of a Colonial Westporter, kneeling, his musket at the ready.

"Over here's a Cromwell estate. Lotsa fuckin' money, 'n 'ey gotta daughter, wouldn't mind givin' her a ride inna backseat some night.

"Do'n 'ere'sa Wallingfords. Lotsa fuckin' money. 'Ey gotta son, a real drunken bastid. Goesta Harvard or Yale, or one a them pansy-ass places. Gonna be scrapin' him off the road some night, I just know it.

"'At big white house up 'ere'sa Van Hartogs—"

"Lotsa fuckin' money?" I suggested.

"You said it. This parta town's all rich humps. Udder parta town, across the Post Road there, just normal guys, go ta work onna train every day. Den ya got dis part we're comin' to near the train station, that's where alla hard-working folks like us come from."

"Is that where you come from, Richie?"

"Nah, I'm from Stamford," he replied, pronouncing it *S'damferd*.

We went over a swing bridge, beneath which a motley

fishing fleet lay in their moorings. Mercifully, I saw that the train station was within a hundred yards.

"Thanks, Richie," I said. "It's been swell."

"Think nothin' of it."

"If you ever get down to New York," Terry said, "look us up, me and . . . the lieutenant here."

"Sure," he replied enthusiastically, pleased to be welcomed into the fraternity. "Who do I ask for?"

"Captain . . . Lawrence Fishburne," Terry said.

"Lieutenant . . . Clint Eastwood," I added.

"I'll do that," Richie said. "It oughta be fun."

"I'm laughing already," I said.

The train ride was boring and uneventful. There was no bar car, as it was during Prohibition, just seats with hard cushions and lots of smoke. The whole train smelled like a urinal choked with cigarette butts. The train also stopped virtually everywhere. Terry told me that in our time, the New York, New Haven, and Hartford Line, now Metro North, ran express once you reached Stamford. Not so in 1926. If there was a station anywhere, we stopped. Not only that, traffic was worse than the 405 at rush hour before a holiday weekend. As soon as the engine picked up speed, there would be an irritating braking sensation and the train would cough to a halt.

"How do people do this every day?" I fumed.

"You still think my father was nuts?" Terry smiled.

"And I thought the freeways were a pain in the ass."

Terry nodded. "The train does suck, even more so eighty years from now, but it'll be worth it when we get into Grand Central. I'll show you what a real city is supposed to look like."

"I've been to New York, Terry."

"Not with me, you haven't."

NINE

IN EVERY TIME PERIOD I HAD EVER VISITED, THERE WAS always one social characteristic that powerfully demonstrated an era's differences from that of my own. On my first long trip back, to 1940, there was smoking. In the 1960s, there was drugs. In the fifties, there were huge, gas-guzzling automobiles.

In the 1920s, there was fur.

That was what I noticed first when we got off the train at Grand Central. Well, not first; the first difference I really noticed was the formality of the period. It was a little after eight o'clock at night, and everyone was dressed up. Nowadays, people dress comfortably for travel, or even after work. It's hardly a rare sight to see a fellow in a suit standing on line at the movies behind a couple in jeans and another in sweats.

Not so in 1926. When people left the house, they weren't wearing jeans or jogging shorts. They wore ties. The women wore dresses. Everyone wore a hat.

Grand Central, Terry informed me, was now a place

where people boarded their trains or alit from their trains and left immediately.

"It's a shithole," he said. "They've always tried to clean it up, but it's full of scumbags and pickpockets and muggers. And poor homeless bastards. I can't believe it was ever like this."

By "like this" Terry meant the scene before us now. The big clock opposite the gates was apparently a meeting landmark for many New Yorkers. Standing beneath it were well-dressed young men who constantly and sometimes impatiently glanced at their watches; fashionable young women in the same posture; and couples waiting for other couples.

And no one sat on the floor. Today, at crowded train stations and airports, you can always find more people seated Indian-style on the floor than on benches. There was none of that here.

"It's amazing," I told Terry, "a public place that the public can actually use."

It was March and it was cold. Consequently, women wore the warmest article of clothing they could find—fur. There were full-length mink, lynx, and fox coats. There were ermine stoles. There were what seemed to be stuffed whole dead animals thrown across women's shoulders. And there were men in racoon coats.

"Boola boola." I nudged Terry, as a racoon-coated guy strode past us.

"Icka-backa-soda-cracker-sis-boom-bah," he replied. "I'll bet he's got a flask in his pocket."

"I can't get over this fur," I marvelled. "The animal rights folks would go completely ripshit here."

"They'd get thrown in jail," he replied. "Come on, let's take a walk."

"Althea's at the Plaza," I said. "Can we walk there?"

"This is New York, John, not L.A. Fashionable guys like us walk everywhere."

•   •   •

In his enduring song "Night and Day," Cole Porter wrote a lyric describing "the roaring traffic's boom." Well, old Cole must've been in Manhattan when he wrote it. As soon as we stepped through the doors onto Forty-second Street, it was as though someone had turned up a compact disc of city noises to full blast.

They talk about traffic in L.A., but I never understood the meaning of the word until I set foot in Manhattan in 1926. There were headlights and taillights stretching across Forty-second Street in both directions as far as the eye could see. None of them moving, and all of them blasting away on their horns.

I stood at the corner of Vanderbilt waiting for the light to change.

"Got a problem?" Terry asked.

"No. Why?"

"You trying to grow into the sidewalk?"

"I'm waiting for the light to change."

Terry looked at me as if I were completely bonkers. "What the hell for? This is a side street."

"But the light's red. That'd be jaywalking!"

Terry rolled his eyes. "You're in New York, John. *Everybody* jaywalks on side streets."

"Oh." I followed him across the street. "Doesn't that traffic ever move?"

"Theatre and dinner hour traffic. You'd have to be a schmuck to drive anywhere this time of night."

We crossed Madison and continued up to Fifth, where we turned right and headed uptown.

"Wow!" Terry exclaimed. "Look—a double-decker bus! And the traffic goes both ways! I'd forgotten about that."

"Is it really that different?" I asked him.

"Yeah. I can hardly recognize it. No Duane Reade Drug every block and a half. No Benettons. No rip-off electronics stores. No Lotto signs. This place has class!"

"I'd like to see this place in daytime," I said. "Right

now it reminds me of the time I climbed the Cologne Dome in Germany. I went up these steps—ancient stone ones, uneven so you couldn't get a good rhythm going. A spiral staircase, but narrow. A new definition for claustrophobia. Took me forever. Then when I got to the top, with my tongue hanging down to my knees, I had no idea what the hell I was looking at."

"Well, neither do I," Terry said. "I'd say at least half the places I'm used to are gone—or not here yet." We crossed Fiftieth Street and Terry stopped suddenly. "Rockefeller Center!"

"Where?"

"That's just it. It isn't!"

"Welcome to the club," I said. "Now you know how I felt being on Sunset Boulevard back in the past. It's a bit disorienting, isn't it?"

"Just a bit. Oh, well," he observed with relief, "here's the Plaza. It doesn't look all that different."

The one thing that was different was the name Terry gave the desk clerk when he checked in. He had signed the register "Terence Portland."

"What's with the moniker?" I asked him as we walked to the elevator.

"This is 1926, John, and it's tough to tell where you stand. Give them a name like Rappaport and they might not do anything. *Or*, they might say, 'I'm terribly sorry, Mr. . . . Rappaport'—they always give you a pause of distaste when they say your name—'I'm afraid we have no reservation under that name. No, there's no mistake.' "

"Well, I'm glad you thought so quickly," I remarked. "I'd hate to have to spend my first night in New York in jail for beating the crap out of a hotel clerk."

The suite Althea had reserved overlooked Central Park— not that I spent too much time looking out the window. On the rare occasions when we got out of bed that first night, we had a lot to talk about. She had found Mitchell I. Levitan.

"Where is he?" I demanded.

"It's all right, John," she said. "He's not here yet. He's on his way back from New Orleans. He has a reservation at the Algonquin for tomorrow night."

"The Algonquin, huh? What else? Do we know what train he'll be on?"

She looked away guiltily. "Uh . . . I forgot."

"Don't worry about it. You're still a rookie detective, and rookies often miss the obvious."

"Did you?"

"Oh, God, yes. I remember once, just before I made detective, I was on loan to Robbery-Homicide, doing some peripheral legwork for the big boys. Some gangbanger drive-by in Rampart Division. They had me go talk to the suspect's mother. She told me he had taken her to the movies at the time of the shooting. I asked her which movie and what theatre. I thought that was enough. Apparently, it wasn't. What neither of us knew at the time was that the theatre she had mentioned had had a problem with its air-conditioning—smoke coming through the vents or something like that—and had closed down that night."

"Did you get in trouble?"

"Nah, a few ruffled feathers was all. Everybody on the squad had screwed up themselves at one time or another. So they just gave me their JAFR Award of the week."

"What's that?"

" 'Just Another Fucking Rookie.' "

"Do I get the JAFR Award this time?" she asked.

"Nope," I replied. "You've got too many friends downtown."

The next morning the three of us scattered. Terry went to Penn Station to check on the trains. I went to Grand Central, after lounging in bed for a while longer. I hadn't slept very well, as I kept dreaming about falling out of an airplane and waking with a thump. Althea went shopping.

"I'm in New York," she said. "The last time I was here I was in a show, and I didn't have time to do anything. Now, I'm going to shop—"

"Till you drop?" I finished for her.

"I like that. Yeah, 'shop till I drop.' That's *almost* clever. But, John, I also have an idea."

"Shoot."

"Why don't you and Terry meet me at Rudley's at three o'clock."

"Rudley's? What's that?"

"A coffee shop on Broadway near Times Square. You'll find it easily enough."

"A coffee shop? What the hell for? Don't you want to go to 21 or someplace like that?"

"Maybe later. Trust me. You'll like it."

There was an aroma in New York that was irresistible. Above the exhaust fumes, frankfurters, dog poop, and urine, there was a sweet but not cloying odor. It occurred to me that I had smelled that same aroma in downtown L.A. when I was a very small kid. Whatever it was, it was gone from the earth. I later discovered that it was grease, actually lard, used for cooking donuts. It was probably lethal, but in 1926 everybody ate donuts—or sinkers, as they were called, in 1926, because people dunked them in their coffee—all the time. I loved that smell. It became part of my emotional landscape for my entire stay in New York, and I would miss it when I returned to the low-fat days of my home era.

The trip to 1926 was also significant because that was when I bought Althea her official engagement ring. I stopped into Tiffany's and bought a pear-shaped, six-carat monstrosity with a platinum band. I spent two grand on it, a ring that would cost at least ten times as much in 2007. She wouldn't be able to wear it out when we returned to L.A., as a ring like that was a virtual engraved invitation to a mugger, but she would at least be able to enjoy it in 1926.

By the time the ring purchase had been completed, I headed over to Times Square. The whole area reminded me of Hollywood Boulevard—scumbag heaven. It didn't seem as bad as it would probably become later on, but it had that hard-core, Piccadilly Circus, dangerous carnival atmosphere. Like Hollywood Boulevard, it had garish shops and tourist traps, con artists and bumpkins. Not my kind of place, and from what I could see, not a favorite venue for native New Yorkers. If I were a cop here, I'd've had my work cut out for me. I shuddered as I imagined what the place was like in 2007.

Rudley's was, as Althea had said, just a coffee shop, no different from hundreds of others that I could see. However, as I entered the stuffy restaurant, I could understand her interest. Most of the patrons seemed relaxed and even a bit lethargic, as though they had nothing to do, but beneath that was a layer of intense hunger. They were scruffy without being lowlifes, and I realized, as the place was right near the theatre district, that this was a hangout for struggling actors playwrights, and directors.

Althea was involved in an animated discussion with two men at a table near the back of the shop. She looked up and waved me over, wearing the widest smile I had ever seen on her. Next to her was an intelligent-looking young man with a high hairline that tapered into a widow's peak. Across from them, with his back toward me, was a broad-shouldered guy with almost jet-black hair.

The black-haired guy looked up at me as I pulled out the chair next to him. When I saw who it was, I almost gasped in recognition, and Althea laughed outright at my reaction.

"John," she said, "I'd like you to meet the best writer I've ever met who hasn't made it yet, and the best actor, too." She pointed to the guy with the widow's peak. "John Surrey, Moss Hart."

I knew that Moss Hart was special to her because Althea's first professional role was a supporting part in *Merrily We Roll Along*, his second collaboration with George S. Kaufman. The play was not as successful as their other efforts, but it served as Althea's launching pad to Hollywood.

"Mr. Hart," I rasped, extending my hand to shake with a man who was living in terrible poverty at the moment, but in four years would be the toast of Broadway, and wealthy beyond even his own prodigious imagination.

"Moss, please," he said.

"And, John, this is—"

"Cary Grant!" I blurted. The handsome, dark-haired young man looked at me quizzically.

Althea grabbed my necktie and pulled me down to her. "Not for another five years, John," she hissed through her teeth.

"I'm sorry," I said, shaking hands. "My mistake."

"Archie Leach," the man said. "But if it'll get me an acting job, I'll be this Grant fellow all right."

"Archie hasn't worked in a while," Althea said sympathetically.

"That'll change," I replied.

"You think so?" Leach asked anxiously. "I keep tellin' Moss here to write something with a role in it for me."

"I have," Hart said. "If I could get someone to produce it."

"I don't know why we bother with theatre," Leach said. "It's like playing the Irish Sweepstakes."

"Because we're suckers," Hart said. "Sorry to be so glum," he added apologetically. "But on the bright side, I just got rehired by the Flagler Hotel for the summer. Social Director. I can kiss sleep good-bye from May to September."

"I've heard it's a lot of work," I said, having read in his autobiography that it was a season in hell.

"Oh, well," Hart replied with a shrug, "it beats slingin' hash."

"No, it don't," Leach said. His accent was less polished than it would be later on.

"He won't come up to work with me," Hart said, pointing at Leach.

"Not on your life," Leach replied breezily. "You never know what'll turn up. That's why I'm stayin' in New York."

"You got that right," I replied. "It's a place where anything can happen."

"As long as it happens to me," Hart said.

"It will," I assured him. "I don't think the name Moss Hart will languish in obscurity for very much longer. What kind of plays do you write, Mr. Hart?" I asked, as if I didn't know.

"Dramas. Good ones, too. At least *I* think so."

"You ever consider comedy?"

Grant laughed. "The next Eugene O'Neill here?"

" 'Dying is easy,' " Hart quoted, " 'comedy is hard.' Besides, I'm no good at it."

Oh, really, I thought. That's why Kaufman would later refer to this brilliant comedic mind as "Forked Lightning."

"What about the name Archibald Leach?" Grant asked. "You see any big future there?"

"I'm not sure about the name," I replied. "But I've got a pretty good idea that actor will do just fine."

I looked around for a waiter. Althea gave me a gigantic smirk and waved one down.

"Can I help you, sir?" The waiter was very young, probably no more than sixteen, but he was tall and very serious-looking.

"Harry," Moss Hart said, "get Mr. Surrey a coffee an', on me."

Knowing Hart's financial situation, I shook my head at the waiter and made a few other facial pantomimes to let him know that I was picking up the whole tab. It would probably set me back a dollar—nothing for me, but a big gesture for Hart and Grant.

I could tell Harry didn't need a diagram; he looked extremely intelligent and capable.

"Is he a struggling actor, too?" I asked them.

Althea winked at me and said, "Well, duh," in the style of a twenty-first-century teenager.

"Playwright," Hart said. "He's young, but he has talent."

"Harry," I said, thinking out loud. "Oh, for Christ sake!"

"You got it, sport," Althea said. Hart and Grant looked at the two of us as if we were escaped mental patients.

"I guess Harry will do okay, too?" Hart asked.

"I'm sure he will," I replied, but something about my tone made them doubt me. "You make it first, Moss. Then you can give him a helping hand."

Hart nodded. "What would be the point, otherwise?" he wondered.

That's one of the benefits of visiting the past. When you meet a couple of hardworking, ambitious, and deeply committed guys like Hart and Grant—guys who are at present full of self-doubt and wondering if they should just chuck the whole thing—it feels good to be able to buck them up when they need it the most. Both still had a long road ahead, particularly Hart, who was supporting a family just on the edge of survival. When you bring that subtext of definitive knowledge with you from the future, they can feel it. They don't know why, and perhaps it isn't even conscious, but there is something about your vote of confidence that gives them a boost. I had met both Grant and Hart in 1940—in fact, at the same party where I first saw Althea—and although both were at the height of their success, neither of them were smug about it. Grant was unaffected, and Hart's extraordinary generosity was legend. But I was glad to have run into them now, when they were struggling, and their strength of character and will were most apparent.

As for Harry—that is, of course, Harry Levitan, Mitch-ell's grandfather—maybe Moss Hart would help him out. And maybe he had.

We strolled down Broadway to Penn Station. I hadn't heard from Terry, which could only lead me to the conclusion that he was staking the place out and didn't want to leave.

"What are you going to say to Mitchell when you see him?" Althea wanted to know. "Are you going to handcuff him or anything?"

"I doubt that'll be necessary," I said. "All we really want to know is what's on his agenda. It's still his tour, he's paying the freight. We just want to make sure he stays in touch."

"Did you ever have to drag someone back?"

"Yeah. But I've also let people stay."

"You have?"

I nodded. "Oh, I check up on them now and then, but if someone is basically honest and not too greedy, and doesn't try to change history, why not? The twenty-first century sucks." I winced as soon as I said it.

"Oh, really. Then why do *I* have to be there?"

"Oh, look," I said, "Penn Station. They don't make terminals like this anymore, nosiree bob. You know, when I was taking French in high school, I used to get the word for train station, *gare*, mixed up with the word for war, which is *guerre*. For the longest time, I used to think that when people said, *c'est la guerre*, they were saying, 'That's the train station.' "

"You're avoiding the question."

"Oh, well . . . that's the train station."

"Anyone ever tell you you're a wiseass?"

"Almost everyone."

Terry was waving to us frantically as we entered the concourse of Penn Station. We followed him to Gate 6, where a locomotive was chuffing to a halt. The big steam engine seemed larger than life, with a huge chrome front-piece that immediately brought to mind an Agatha Christie story.

The train was not crowded, and passengers seemed to merely dribble from the exits. Levitan was easy to spot; he was a head taller than most of his fellow passengers. He looked pretty sporty in grey flannels with a beige driving cap. I also noted that he walked with a certain jauntiness that I hadn't expected; clearly, the 1920s agreed with him. I wondered idly if we had yet another candidate for temporal immigration.

"You two stay here," I said. "I'll go get him."

Although Levitan and I had never actually met, I purposely avoided his line of vision as I passed him. When I was a few yards behind him I reversed course and quickened my pace until I was walking in step beside him. He saw me and I gave him a nod, which he returned in the fashion of someone who doesn't want to appear rude but at the same time is avoiding any sort of approach from a stranger.

"I think Woody is a genius, don't you?" I said in a nasal and pedantic approximation of a film critic.

His double take was classic.

A look of abject terror crossed his face. He picked up his pace and immediately bumped smack into Terry.

"It's okay, Mitch," I told him. "No one is here to hurt you. I'm John Surrey and this is Terry Rappaport. We were worried about you, that's all. We lost your signal, for all we knew you could've been dead."

He dropped his suitcase and sat on it. "I'm not ready to go back yet," he sighed.

"No one said that you have to, Mitchell. We just need to know what you're up to. For your own protection. I mean, Mitch, lunch with Al Capone?"

"He's a nice guy—I mean, he was nice to me."

"He was nice to me, too," I agreed. "But Bugs Moran was less friendly."

"You met Bugs Moran!" he exclaimed. He stood up and

took a pad and a big red fountain pen from his pocket. "Tell me all about him!"

"Later," I said. "Come on, we'll take you to the Algonquin."

"How'd you know I was staying at the Algon—" He froze when he saw Althea, who had just caught up with us.

"But you're *dead*!" he cried. "And you're from nineteen-for—"

"Hello, Mr. Levitan," she said soothingly, taking his limp hand into her own. "I'm Althea Rowland. It's a pleasure to meet you."

"Soon to be Althea Surrey," I added.

"What's going on?" he asked, wilting quickly. "I'm all messed up."

"I don't blame him," Terry observed. "Imagine going back to the Civil War and bumping into Madonna."

"It's all right, we'll take care of you, Mr. Levitan." She took his arm and began walking with him. "Tell me, Mitchell—it's okay to call you Mitchell?—when you made *Sequel to a Divorce*, what made you choose that particular actress for the lead? I thought it was an inspired decision, a little bit against type, perhaps, but that's what made it work . . ."

8 MARCH 1926—NEW YORK CITY, THE ALGONQUIN HOTEL

We were all in various lounging postures in the living room of Levitan's suite.

"Mitchell, Mitchell," I chided him.

"All right, all right," he replied in annoyance. "It's not like I did anything wrong."

"Well, actually, you did," I chastised him gently. "You trashed your Decacom—"

"I'll pay for it, okay?"

"It's already on your bill. That's not the point. Look,

what we do is secret. A secret opened wider'n the Astro-
dome, to be sure, but still, a secret. Your last known
whereabouts in 2007 was at our headquarters on Mulholland Drive. Let's say you disappear so completely that not
even a couple of supremely talented ex-detectives like myself and Terry here can find you. Your friends and col-
leagues file your name with the cops at Missing Persons.
They come to see us. What are we supposed to tell them?''

"I said I was sorry."

" 'Sorry' won't get it, Mitchell. There's a reason why
we give you the Decacom. It's for your protection and ours.
How do I know I can trust you anymore?''

He shook his head. "Look. I won't do it again, okay?
But I'm not ready to go back."

"Why not?"

"Because I'm just not. I haven't . . . I just can't."

Althea got up from the morris chair on which she had
been lounging comfortably and sat down beside Mitch. She
took his hands in her own. She looked deeply into his eyes.

"Mitchell," she began.

He backed away from her. "You're good," he said. "No
wonder you were such a big star."

"Thank you," she replied.

"I've always been a big fan of yours. I was sorry that
you—I would have liked to have seen you go all the way."

"You can," I said. "Maybe when we all get back, you
can put her to work."

The frightened and confused kid gave way to the *enfant
terrible* studio head. "Could do business," he said, closing
one eye critically. "She's got it, all right."

"Well, I'm glad you agree," I replied, slightly irritated.

"Sshh," Althea hushed me. "Mitchell, we can discuss
all that later. What we need to know now, what we *must*
know now—"

"Yes?" Mitchell was spellbound.

"Who is she?"

He was flabbergasted. "How did you—" He stopped

and looked accusingly at all three of us. "I'm not telling you."

"Why not?" I demanded.

"Because—I'm just not."

"Will you tell me?" Althea asked.

"I—no. You'll tell them."

"They'll find out anyway. But I won't tell them. I promise I won't say a word."

"Mmmm," he wavered.

She held a finger to her ear. "Just whisper it like a sweet nothing, Mitchell. Please."

He clamped an arm on her shoulder and hissed something quickly, before he could change his mind.

I searched for a hint in Althea's face, but she gave nothing away. She merely said, "I thought so."

Mitchell balked. "What do you mean?"

"We'll discuss it later. Good choice, though, Mitchell. She's quite a woman. And a fine man like you, well, maybe you could make the difference in her life."

"You think so," he exclaimed happily.

"Oh, I'm sure of it."

"You're gonna be a big star." He grinned.

"She's already a big star," I argued, lest he forgot.

"Well, she's gonna be an even bigger star! You're gonna be in my next film!"

"We'll see," she said lightly. "But thank you."

"This is all very wonderful," Terry said, speaking up for the first time. "Althea, congratulations on your newly revitalized career. But as long as we're being mysterious, I have a question: Mitch, what the hell were you doing in New Orleans?"

Mitch froze. I walked over and patted him on the shoulder. "Don't worry about it," I said, shaking my head. "Now it's my turn to keep secrets. I know *exactly* what he was doing in New Orleans."

"You do?" All three of them asked at once.

"*How* do you know?" Mitchell asked. "There's no way for you to know."

"Mitch, we all three of us know you went there for a police report. When you visited Capone, you managed to ingratiate yourself. Not hard to do, really. With civilians like us, he can be charming and solicitous. You probably gave him a vague promise about the movies—he's enough of an egomaniac to take it seriously. Then he probably asked if there was anything he could do for you, and why not. Capone loves to do favors for people, because he knows that he'll always be owed a favor in return."

I could tell from Mitchell's face that I was right on the money.

"You wanted a copy of a police report. Capone must've thought, 'Christ, is that all?' A phone call to the Marcello family in New Orleans probably took care of it in five minutes. I'll bet a New Orleans cop was waiting for you on the station platform, a copy of the report in his hot little hand."

Levitan glanced up at the ceiling. "Go on," he breathed.

"Nope, that's it," I said cheerfully. "Although I do know who the arrestee in that report happens to be."

"Who, for God's sake?" Althea exploded.

"Are you going to give me the apple of Mitchell's eye?"

"Not on your life," she said firmly.

"Well, all right then," I said. "We'll just have to let the plot unfold of its own accord. By the way, Mitchell, did you run into anyone else in your travels? I have to know. Just in case you accidentally changed history beyond all recognition."

"Did you meet Huey Long while you were in New Orleans?" Terry wanted to know.

"Tried," Mitchell replied. "I called his office. He was out of town, so they said."

"How many times have *you* pulled that one?" Terry needled him.

"I never say I'm out of town. I always say I'm in a meeting."

"Anyone else?" I asked.

"Oh—in Peoria, Illinois."

"Who's in Peoria, Illinois? Apart from the Peorians, that is."

"Lindbergh."

"Charles A. Lindbergh? Lucky Lindy? The first guy to solo across the Atlantic?"

"Yeah."

"I didn't know you were an aviation buff, Mitchell."

"My grandfather taught me. He flew in Spain and in China during the war."

"My grandpa, too. He flew a bomber. Won the DFC in Ploesti. What was Lindbergh like?"

Levitan shrugged. "He was a putz."

"He was?"

"Bor-ing. You know, he's not making that flight until next year. Right now he's just shuttling mail back and forth in the Midwest. He's not exactly a personality boy. Kind of a tall, taciturn guy. Not stupid or anything, but not exactly a bundle of charm. A big lox. I was at the airport, I saw him—he's not all that difficult to spot—and I walked over and introduced myself. He was polite, but only *just*."

"Well, Mitch," I said, "he doesn't know he's going to be the most famous man in the world a year from now. Right now he's just a pilot trying to scratch out a living. He doesn't know you from Adam, why should he be polite?"

"Why shouldn't he?" Mitch insisted. "But he cracked me up."

"You just said he had no personality."

"It wasn't his wit, believe me. It was his voice. You know who he sounded like?"

"Not if you don't tell me."

"Remember that big murder trial we had about ten, twelve years ago?"

"The O. J. thing? He sounded like O. J.?"

"No—"

"Johnny Cochrane?"

"No. Remember the judge? Judge Ito?"

"Charles A. Lindbergh sounded like Judge Ito?" I tried not to yelp.

Mitchell shrugged. "It added spice to an otherwise dull afternoon." He went into a Judge Ito/Charles Lindbergh imitation. " 'It's nice to meet you, Mr. Levitan, but I have a schedule to keep.' " His imitation was a good one and I laughed appreciatively.

"You're pretty good, Mitchell. You ought to consider being in one of your own films."

"Me, *act*? I don't think so." He looked at his watch. "Anyway, I've got to go. I have a meeting."

"Mitch, what is this, the Viper Room? You can't blow *us* off like this."

"I'm not," he insisted. "I really do have a meeting."

"Mitch, do you really think we're going to let you out of our sight? After all we went through to catch up with you?"

He looked at Terry, whose face was impassive. Then he tried Althea, an easier mark. "Althea? Will you talk to him?"

"He's obviously got a hot date, John," she said.

"Ah, you're just sucking up to him for a part in his next movie."

"Damn right I am." She backhanded me on the shoulder. "John, don't be a drip. You're going to cramp his style."

"Terry?" He shrugged. "Oh, all right," I said. "But if you try and lose us again, your butt is on the next train west, and I'll sit or your head all the way to L.A. if I have to."

"You're getting into a weird area there, John," Mitch replied with distaste. "Okay, I give you my word. I'll even check in every few hours. Is that good enough?"

"It'll have to be. Just remember, Mitchell, I'll always find you."

" 'You can run, but you can't hide,' " Mitchell, Althea, and Terry all said together.

"And don't you forget it," I said, recalling that particular quote tacked on the wall in the squad room when I was a Fugitive cop.

"Okay, Mitch, put on your top hat, white tie, and your tails. We'll get out of your way. Just remember what I said."

"Yes, Mother."

Terry was staring at me somewhat archly as we rode down in the elevator with Althea. "That was way too easy, John," he said. "You're not really letting him go, are you?"

"Of course I am. I'm not letting him out of my sight. However, whether or not I'm in his sight is another issue entirely."

"Well, I'm not missing this," Althea said.

"Naturally not, my dearest one. Neither am I."

"You know where he's going, then?"

"I've got a pretty good idea."

Of course I knew where he was going. His choice of accommodations—the Algonquin Hotel—was not lost on any of us. And as we left the elevator and strolled toward the Oak Room—then called the Pergola Room—I felt a shot in my stomach akin to the sensation which struck me when I jumped from the G-IV. We were about to go swimming with sharks.

The Algonquin had always been a theatre and literati hotel. From the time it opened its doors in 1902 to the present of 1926 and for more than half a century in the future, it would be a second, and sometimes first home to actors, writers, producers, and editors. By 1926, the Algonquin provided the setting for the most famous, and frankly most vicious, group of overachievers ever gathered under one Scotch bottle. I couldn't wait to see the Algonquin Round Table in action, but I would have preferred to go up against Iraqi artillery or kick down a crackhouse door rather than try to approach it. Yet here it was, and I was irresistibly drawn to it.

It has long since been ingrained in all growing American boys that when you are confronted by a gang of bullies, and running away is no longer an option, pick out the biggest one and sock him as hard as you can. That way, if he beats you, no one will be surprised. And if you beat him, everyone will respect you and leave you alone. That was my attitude as we crossed the threshold from the Pergola Room into the Rose Room, where the Vicious Circle was already holding boisterous court. We stopped at the boundary to the Pantheon, a velvet rope. An impeccably polite man in a tuxedo, bald with a frosted white mustache, gave us a glance that spoke volumes. I recognized him immediately as Frank Case, the Algonquin manager—soon to be its owner.

"Can I help you?" he asked, obviously convinced that he couldn't.

"Just a moment with Mr. Woollcott, please," I said. "We won't be long."

Case sized us up and decided that it was our funeral. He lifted the rope and ushered us through.

Althea was in seventh heaven. She had grown up on the exploits of this very table, and its effect was powerful. I had never seen her stuck for words before.

Terry tapped me on the shoulder. "I'm going to stake out the lobby," he said.

"Why?" I asked. Terry had yet to meet the man who could frighten him, but he was uncharacteristically ambivalent about taking another step forward.

"I don't know much about these guys," he replied, "but what I do know is enough to scare the crap out of me. I'll stick to criminals, thank you." With that, he turned and walked away.

A mischievously handsome man with dark curly hair did a double take as he saw Althea. He got up from the Round Table and walked over to her, completely ignoring me.

"Didn't I used to moon over your picture in high school?" he asked her.

"I . . . hardly think so," Althea stammered.

"You knitted me a sweater during the war, right? That was your photograph, stuffed in there with all the wool balls?"

"I'm afraid not."

"We never met?"

"Not likely."

"Then . . . who the hell are you?"

"Who the hell are you?" she asked, although I was sure she knew.

"Everybody knows me." He laughed. "When I was in the war in France, I got a rifle butt in the face from a German *Feldwebel*, and after he saw who I was he said, 'Oh, sorry, *mein Freund*, didn't know it vass you.' I'm Charles MacArthur. Won't you join me, Miss—"

"Rowland, Althea Rowland. Won't your wife object?"

"Object to what?"

Althea shrugged and took the proffered seat at the Round Table. Her face was glowing. I didn't feel too comfortable about her falling under the spell of that famous playwright and ladies' man, but I had other business to which to attend.

There were six other men at the Round Table, all of whom were pointedly ignoring me. Alexander Woollcott, who was talking to the famously unkempt Heywood Broun; Marc Connelly, who was in conference with his collaborator, George S. Kaufman, the most commercially successful playwright in Broadway history until the advent of Neil Simon; and the six-foot-seven Robert Sherwood, who was arguing animatedly with Harold Ross, the publisher of the *New Yorker*.

I stood behind Woollcott and Broun, afraid to say anything. Both were heavy men. Broun resembled a redneck
sheriff, and Woollcott, without his spectacles and tiny mustache, would have looked perfect if he were wrapped in a
diaper and given a bow and a quiver of arrows.

I could somehow tell from Woollcott's broad back that
my presence was beginning to annoy him. It would be just
another moment before I would be the target of a razor-
sharp barb. But I had to go after the biggest bully of them
all.

Finally, he turned around. "Is today Monday?" he demanded.

"Er, no," I replied.

"Do you see any laundry around you?"

"No."

"Then why are you here?" With that, he turned back to
his conversation.

"I was at Château-Thierry, Mr. Woollcott," I said to his
back. "And I just wanted you to know how much your
stories in *Stars and Stripes* meant to all of us. I'm sorry to
have intruded." Then I turned and began to walk away.

"Wait!"

I stopped. I turned around again, very slowly.

"*You* were at Château-Thierry?"

"Yes, sir."

"First Marines?"

"Yes, sir."

"Sit down."

I knew that Woollcott, who had an acerbic tongue for
just about everyone, held a soft spot in his heart for combat
veterans, especially Marines. This was probably due to the
fact that his own military career, during which he saw no
combat except as a *Stars and Stripes* correspondent far behind the lines or after the fact, made him feel less of a man.
Earlier in the war, he had emptied the bedpans of men who
had been in combat. And since he suffered from a dimin-
ished or possibly ambiguous sexuality—Ernest Hemingway

referred to him as a "fat capon"—this would trouble him all the more intensely, as though he had never really proven his own manhood. Therefore, acceptance by a combat veteran would, at the very least, make his day.

A chair magically appeared behind me and I sat. From then on, I could always say that I had sat at the Algonquin Round Table.

"You Marines did quite a job," Aleck said.

"They told us to hold the bridges and we did," I replied simply.

"Hah!" Broun ejaculated. "This man must be a journalist. Concise and effective. 'They told us to hold the bridges and we did.' I like it! Are you a writer, Mr.—?"

"Surrey, John Surrey. No, sir." Well, yeah, but children's books, eighty years in the future. That would cut no ice in this crowd.

"An editor, then? You must be an editor."

"Who's an editor?" a short, dapper man with a large nose and small mustache wanted to know as he pulled out a chair next to Broun.

"Mr. Surrey here. He has just impressed me with his brevity and clarity of expression."

The dapper little man regarded me critically. "Not an editor," he said.

I noticed that I wasn't introduced. Of course, perhaps I didn't have to be. The man who had just sat down was, at the time, the most famous member of the Round Table (as opposed to Woollcott, who was the most famous Member of the Round Table, a subtle yet vast difference) and the least known today. But in his heyday, Franklin Pierce Adams, or F. P. A., as he was known, was the most widely read and quoted columnist in the country. All anyone remembers about him today is his poem, "Tinker to Evers to Chance," and even then, almost no one can recall the author.

"Not an editor," Broun agreed. "What do you do, Mr. Surrey?"

No sense lying to these people, I thought. I *had* been a Marine, and I *had* been in combat; I had merely fudged the where and the when, so I hadn't really lied about that. "I'm a travel agent," I said.

"Oh, yeah?" Kaufman called from across the table. "Can you get me a good out-of-town opening?"

I had no quick or incisively witty answer ready, so I was glad when Woollcott said, "We're going to the south of France this summer, Harpo and Alice and I. Any suggestions?"

"Learn French," Ross said.

"Harold, are you trying to initiate clever conversation again? Go lie down, you look all in."

"Frog wheelchairs," F. P. A. said. "Bring 'em with you and sell 'em, you'll make a fortune."

"Just what did you mean by that?" Ross demanded of Woollcott.

"It's way over your head, Harold," Aleck replied patronizingly. "That's why I was a sergeant and you never rose above private."

"And a couple of fine soldiers you were," said F. P. A., who had been their captain. "We could have won the war without you."

"You mean '*couldn't* have won the war.'"

"No, I don't."

"Ease off," Ross fumed. "Don't think I'm not incoherent."

Woollcott and Adams glanced at each other and magnanimously decided to let that one pass. Ross's upstart magazine was beginning to do quite well, and there would soon be more than enough work for everyone.

"I should be home writing," Sherwood said. "I'm gonna have to crack a safe to pay my bills this month."

"Don't put all your yeggs in one basket," Kaufman remarked over his horn-rims.

"Oh! I've been hit with repartee," cried Sherwood.

"Which repartee is that," F. P. A. wanted to know, "Democrat or Republican?"

"Birthday."

"Whose?"

"Lincoln's?"

"Then take him to the theatre."

"Nah," said Broun. "He'd die on opening night."

"John Wilkes Booth," Connelly murmured.

"Sounds like a tennis match," F. P. A. said. "John Wilkes Booth, 7–5, 6–2."

"Yankees wilk Red Sox on Ruth's homer in ninth," rejoined Broun.

"Four scored seven years ago," Connelly said.

"Woollcott wasn't one of them," said MacArthur, his attention momentarily diverted from Althea.

"Can we get off this Lincoln train of thought?" Ross complained. "I need this like a hole in the head."

Once again, Ross was oblivious to his own remark. I laughed heartily with Woollcott and Adams, which was a mistake, because they both stopped abruptly.

"And what do *you* think of all this, Mr. Surrey?" Woollcott asked me pointedly.

Everyone at the table shut up—it was like one of those old E. F. Hutton commercials. Althea looked pained.

"Uh . . . I'm just sitting here, dreaming of a longitude without platitude," I said.

Woollcott and Adams both paused and then gave me a nod of approval, while I tried hard not to sweat with relief.

"This man is a genius," Woollcott declared. "Oh, all right, at least he's smarter than Ross. You must have gone to Hamilton College, Mr. Surrey," he added, referring proudly to his own alma mater.

Woollcott was assuming that I was a lot younger than he; actually, we were about the same age, although I looked a good ten years his junior.

"Afraid not," I said. "Cal State."

"California? When did they start building schools out there?"

I was about to answer when I saw Terry enter the Rose Room, looking about him in hurried concern. I was about to wave him over when I saw a short pixie of a man behind him, flawlessly imitating his posture and every movement.

Terry, who had never been ambushed in his life, felt a presence behind him and turned quickly. His jaw dropped in shocked surprise and he soundlessly mouthed the word *fuck*.

Again the small man aped his every gesture, including his astounded, silent expletive. Still unable to speak, Terry's jaw firmed into a broad grin and he stuck out his hand for his imitator to shake. The pixie accepted the hand and shook it profusely, holding on to it far longer than was expected, shaking Terry's arm off, while mutely giving Terry all sorts of salutations. After a while, Terry gingerly tried to extricate his hand, but Harpo Marx wouldn't let him go. Instead he pulled Terry into a passionate embrace, kissing the air near his face, and finally jumping into a leglock around Terry's waist, which toppled them both onto the floor. Even then Harpo refused to let up. He was all over Terry like an affectionate puppy. Even without the fright wig, stovepipe hat, and ragamuffin coat, Harpo was still very much Harpo.

Frank Case, who had heard the massive thump as the two of them fell, had hurried in from the Pergola Room to see what was the matter. Upon finding the culprit to be Harpo, he raised his eyes skyward and beat a hasty retreat.

"Harpo! You juvenile delinquent," Woollcott called. "Leave that poor fellow alone before he gets mad and kills you. Then what would I do for a croquet partner?"

"John," Terry called from where he was still lying on the floor, "Levitan split!"

"Where'd he go?" I said, rising quickly.

"Cotton Club. But that isn't all."

"What do you mean?" I walked over to him, grabbing Althea as I went.

"Two guys jumped in a cab and went after him. I heard them say it—" he laughed as I helped him up—"they actually said, 'Follow that cab!' "

"Who were they?"

"I didn't get a good look at them. I heard him give instructions to the cabbie, and then I turned around to get you. I only got a passing glimpse of two guys."

I nodded. "Of course. Why should you expect anyone to be following him? Okay, let's go."

And then, for a reason that eludes me to this day, I turned to the assemblage at the Round Table and shouted, "Cotton Club!"

Each member turned to the other and then, as one, they stood. "Cotton Club!" They roared it as if it were a battle cry, except for Harpo, who whistled it. He grabbed a palm frond and waved it in front of him like a drum major's baton.

"I liked that," Althea whispered to me, " 'a longitude without platitude.' Was that yours?"

"Nope. An Englishman named Christopher Fry will write those words about twenty years from now, in a play called *The Lady's Not for Burning.*"

"Strange title."

"Beautiful play. You'd love it. In fact, you'd probably kill to play the lead."

Her response was interrupted by MacArthur, who grabbed her elbow and marched her on ahead to the taxi rank. A taxi had been secured by Harpo, who simply opened the front door and crawled right onto the driver's lap. The stunned cabbie could do nothing, not even complain. I was beginning to understand the effect Harpo Marx had upon people; generally they were too shocked to do anything.

There were only seven of us in the taxi. Sherwood, who was too tall to fit anywhere, had begged off. Kaufman, a

somewhat neurotic fellow who hated being touched, took
one look at the crowded taxi, blanched, and slammed the
door shut from the outside.

Harpo blared the horn and whistled impatiently. The cabbie sat back and moaned, envisioning his cab wrapped
around a lamppost. From his vantage point on the cabbie's
lap, Harpo had difficulty getting leverage on the clutch, and
the car wheezed and stuttered away from the curb.

"*With* the traffic, Harpo," Woollcott said, "this is no
time to be iconoclastic."

Harpo whistled and made an accompanying facial expression that said either "don't worry" or "screw off."

"Now I lay me down to sleep . . ." began Ross.

"Well," said Broun as Harpo careened around a bread
truck, "in the immortal words of the Bard, 'WE'RE ALL
GONNA DIE!!!' Damn it, Harpo, there's a brake, use it!"

"Mr. MacArthur," Althea said evenly, "your hands."

"Are those mine?" MacArthur replied innocently.

In Manhattan, the traffic lights are sequential. The signals
change at, say, Forty-second, then Forty-third, Forty-fourth,
and so on. Therefore, to make every light, your speed had
to increase almost exponentially. As we made our way further uptown, the traffic thinned out considerably, and Harpo
began racing the lights.

"Uh . . . Harpo," said Woollcott, "there are other cars
on the road, you know."

The cabbie groaned, and I could see his complexion becoming more and more ashen the faster we went.

"Harpo," Broun warned in a ragged voice, "look out
for that TRUUUCCK!" We narrowly missed a stalled out
furniture truck. Very narrowly. I heard the cab driver gag
dangerously.

"So, tell me," MacArthur said to Althea, "how long are
you in town?"

"Hopefully, long enough to meet Helen Hayes," she replied.

At the mention of his wife's name, MacArthur removed his arm from around Althea's shoulder and folded his hands in his lap. "Rather clear tonight," he said. "I don't think it'll rain, do you?"

TEN

8–9 MARCH 1926—HARLEM

HARLEM, IN 1926, WAS RIGHT IN THE MIDDLE OF WHAT was referred to as a Renaissance, a place where men and women known under the umbrella title of the "New Negro" were enjoying a cultural rebirth. Flush from the inflated wages of World War I, Harlem was a middle-class neighborhood. The poorer side of Harlem, although in existence, did not become dominant until the Depression.

Originally a white resort, the area bounded on the south side by 96th Street and on the north by 155th was the one place in America where black people could truly express themselves and without fear. Black theatre, music, and literature flourished; pride in one's heritage, achievements, and possibilities became the order of the day for a once enslaved and downtrodden people.

However, it was still the twenties—not exactly the golden era of civil rights. And even the Cotton Club on Lenox Avenue and 143rd Street—the very center of Harlem—was restricted. While the performers were black, the audiences were white. Some blacks were allowed in as guests, but they had to be light-skinned, extremely well-groomed, and they had to conduct themselves far above reproach.

The prosperity of the twenties had given rise to a new pastime for the well-off called *slumming*. White people were awfully curious about this "New Negro" they'd heard so much about, and here they could actually see him close up—although, not *too* close.

There were two levels of seating in the Cotton Club, the lower of which was closer to the stage and required either a reservation, a monstrous bribe to the maître d', or a reputation. Actually, we didn't need any of the above, because we had something better—Harpo.

After spilling out of the cab in front of the Cotton Club—and lavishly tipping our hapless and palpitating driver—Harpo led us inside, snatched a towel from the arm of a waiter, and personally seated us at the best table in the house. There had been a Reserved sign on the sparkling white cloth, which Harpo immediately cast over his shoulder into someone's soup. It was a tribute to his own fame—and fearlessness—that we were not immediately ejected. In fact, Owney Madden, the English-born mobster who ran the Cotton Club, sent us a bottle of champagne.

The Club sold no hard liquor, although it did provide setups. Hard liquor could be procured at a ludicrously marked-up price from the doorman, but most people simply brought their own. Beer and champagne were available, however, as well as a standard steak house menu that also included a few Mexican and Italian items.

I spied Levitan and his date at a table on the upper level. As her back was to me, I couldn't tell who she was, but Mitch saw me and made an almost psychotic face that begged me to keep my distance, and he made a sharp hand motion that was something between a wave-off and a flip-off.

"Where're those two guys who were following Mitch?" I asked Terry, who was studying a menu.

''They're outside. Judging from their suits, they couldn't afford the water in here.''

The waiters at the Cotton Club performed their duties with a brisk elegance. The place had class, which was exactly the effect it was going for. I asked our waiter if Mr. Calloway was playing this evening, and if so to relay him my compliments. Usually when you do that, the waiter says he'll try, although you both know he'll do nothing of the kind. However, five minutes after giving the waiter my message, another complimentary bottle appeared on our table. ''Mr. Calloway said he's glad you could make it, Mr. Surrey,'' the waiter told me.

There was a chorus of scantily clad, light-skinned black women dancing on the stage to an African drumbeat. Levitan was in plain view. I was at a table in the Cotton Club with the most famous members of the Algonquin Round Table. Everything was perfect, so I decided to relax and have a couple of drinks.

However, it was just when I was at my most contented that a darkly handsome young man with a powerful build and hooded brown eyes approached our table. Actually, he approached Althea. I had to admit that I admired his moxie, but not at my expense.

''Excuse me, miss,'' he said, ''have I had the pleasure of making your acquaintance at an earlier date?''

''Who writes this guy's dialogue,'' I said a little too loudly to Terry, ''Damon Runyon?''

The young man flashed me a dangerous glance. I half-expected him to say, *Are you talkin' to me?* ''Have we met before?'' he said to Althea.

''I don't think that's possible,'' she replied, and turned back to me. I looked around the table for help, but all the Algonquinites—even Harpo—were exaggeratedly involved elsewhere.

''Thanks for stopping by,'' I said to him in polite dismissal. Terry, I noticed, was rolling his eyes and shaking his head at me.

He tapped Althea on the shoulder. "Sorry to intrude," he said, "but I found you too beautiful to pass up. Why don't you join me at my table?"

"Look, pal," I said, standing up and facing him, pleased to find that I towered over him by a good four inches, "the lady is with me. Now blow."

I was taught in the Marines, and later at the Police Academy, that facing down someone by having a staring contest is the surest way to the hospital. You don't glare into someone's eyes; if they make a move, you won't see it. Instead you look at their nose; that way, they *think* you're looking into their eyes, but you can actually see their whole body and catch them before they move. That was why I was able to grab the hamlike fist that snaked out in a split second just before it made contact with my solar plexus. I caught the fist in my hand, feeling its considerable power, and twisted it downward into a wristlock. I was fully intent upon breaking it, when I felt the tensed body of my opponent suddenly relax. I didn't have far to look for the source of my would-be assailant's sudden lack of resistance: The compact bulk of Owney Madden had come between us.

"All right, Ben," Madden said calmly, "that's enough. Now, go away and leave these nice people alone. No trouble in my place, you know that."

Ben, whoever he was, turned to me and said, "See you later, chump."

"I can hardly wait," I replied. Ben turned roughly and stalked away.

"I'm real sorry about all this," Madden said. "But you've made an enemy there, I'm afraid."

"I've made an enemy? I didn't do anything."

"Yeah, well, Ben Siegel don't see things that way. He's a hot-tempered kid. He's got a good heart, but he'll go off over nothin'."

"That was Bugsy Siegel?"

"Shhh! Jesus!" Madden winced. I had forgotten the lesson I had learned at the hands of Bugs Moran; it wasn't a popular or proud nickname. "Anyway, you're safe in here. Nobody does nothin' to nobody in my place."

"I appreciate that, Mr. Madden."

"Yeah, well, I'd watch myself on the way out, I was you."

"I'll be careful," I replied. I returned to my seat and immediately decided that an impending brawl with Bugsy Siegel was not going to ruin my night. Besides, I was sitting with a few of the keenest minds of the era, and I was determined to find out their take on the period I was now visiting.

"We're living in an interesting time," I said to Woollcott. He looked at me suspiciously, first gauging to see whether my statement merited a snide crack. But then he saw that I was serious.

"It's the war," he replied. "Until recently, most of this country was rural, the products of small towns with small minds and a single standard of conduct. You're born there, live there, die there. Step out of line and you're the talk of the church ice cream social. All of a sudden, Elmer goes off to war. He meets all kinds of men from all kinds of places. At first, he's mortified at the way some people behave. But then, he gets used to it, finds out it isn't so bad, being a New York Jew, or a Chicago Pole, or a German from Cincinnati. They're all nice guys. Then he comes home and hears the same old drivel from Pappy and the Reverend Zeke, and he thinks, 'What the hell do they know?'

"Remember that song we all heard going over on the boat? 'How Ya Gonna Keep'm Down at the Farm, After They've Seen Paree'? Well, it turned out to be true . . . in spades." He looked around him in mock-embarrassment. "You should pardon the expression," he added.

"It's also Prohibition," Broun chimed in. "What a joke our Noble Experiment is shaping up to be. Fifty million Americans who've never committed a single misdemeanor are now lawbreakers." He took a long quaff of champagne. "Myself included. All at once our legal system, the glue that holds our society together, is under suspicion. People break one law, it's a simple matter to break another."

"Don't forget automobiles," came a voice with a slight Russian accent. I looked around in surprise; Harpo was *talking*.

"Hard to forget automobiles when you're around, Harpo," said Broun.

Harpo shrugged. "The automobile is to this generation what the steam engine was to the Industrial Revolution. It affects our lives, our careers, and"—he stepped briefly back into character with a leer at a pretty girl at a nearby table—"our sexual habits. You don't have to sit in the parlor with her mom and pop anymore, bored to death. You can take a ride in the country and get laid."

"If you ask me," said F. P. A., "this whole decade is an accident. Hah! I like that: the *Accidental Decade*. God, I'm a genius. It never should have happened. But you have the war, the automobile, the movement of the general population into the cities, millions of veterans who've had a glimpse of the world out there, and above all, Prohibition. People are drinking more because it's illegal. When you drink, you lose your inhibitions; you lose your inhibitions, you do things you've never done before, would never do under ordinary circumstances." He looked meaningfully at Harpo. "That *most* people would never do under ordinary circumstances," he amended. "And from this virtually impossible concatenation of events, we have the era we now live in. What were the odds of all the events that brought us here happening when they did? Zero. But they did happen, and here we are."

"There are also immigrants," MacArthur said, finally getting the message that he wasn't going to get anywhere with Althea. "Up until the turn of the century, this country was mostly one sort of people. Now you have other nationalities joining in, bringing their own traditions, values, and even humor. I think the twenties will go down as an era when this country woke up. And what do you think, Mr. Surrey?''

''I think all of you are right,'' I said. ''But there's one other thing. We've become a world power. We've just won a World War. The United States has become a nation to be reckoned with, and I think that has added to our national pride and identity. We're all of us just beginning to flex our muscles, not just as a country, but as a society. It's not only that there's a big world out there, it's a world we can *rule* if we choose to do so.''

''Why would we want to?'' Woollcott wondered aloud.

''Exactly.''

We all looked about smugly, satisfied with our individual pronouncements. So smug was I at that moment, that I almost missed Mitchell I. Levitan's exit out the front door.

''Oh, shit!'' I groaned. ''Terry, let's go.'' I stood up, grabbed Althea, and reached into my pocket and tossed a hundred onto the table. ''Gentlemen, it's been an eye-opener. Enjoy yourselves, on me. See you tomorrow.'' Before any of them could move, I was halfway to the door with Althea in tow and Terry fast behind me.

Levitan's cab was already history, but we were just able to catch the instructions of his two shadows to their own driver; back to the Algonquin.

''Pretty good line of bullcrap in there, John,'' Terry said approvingly. ''History 101 at Cal State?''

''History 403, American Between the Wars,'' I replied. ''I got an A, of course.''

''Of course. You—'' Terry moved before I even noticed a threat. One moment he was talking to me; the next moment he had Bugsy Siegel against the wall, holding a .45 to the back of his head. He patted Siegel down quickly and relieved him of a .38 caliber revolver and a stiletto.

''You want to go downtown, Benjy?'' he asked Siegel, showing him the police captain's badge.

"I got no beef with you," he said to Terry. "This is between me and that wise guy over there."

"Well, you'll just have to forget it, won't you?"

"All right," Bugsy sighed, pulling a fat money clip from his pocket. "How much?"

Terry's expression hardened. "You haven't got that much. Now scram."

"Whatsa matter," Siegel called to me, "little nancy-boy needs his cop friend to fight his battles?"

"John," Terry whispered sharply, "let me tase this prick and let's get outta here."

"No good," I whispered back. "When he wakes up, he'll just come looking for me. I have to end it now."

"Well?" Siegel demanded.

"Okay," I said. "Fists, bottles, knives, what?"

"Whatever," he replied.

"This is all quite silly," Althea fumed.

"Honey," I said, "we're not dealing with a massive intellect here. It has to be done."

She rolled her eyes and kissed me. "Mr. Siegel? It's been a pleasure. I hope all of your affairs are in order."

"I'll see you again, babe," he replied. "And keep tomorrow night open; you're about to step way up in class."

Terry walked over to Siegel and put a hand on his shoulder. He whispered something, but all I could hear was Yiddish. Siegel blanched but quickly recovered. "I'll be ready," he said to Terry.

Terry laughed. "No, you won't, kid. No one ever is."

"What'd you say to him?" I asked Terry.

"Nothing. Just that if anything happens to you, I'll kill him."

"I'm touched," I said, meaning it.

"This is ridiculous!" Althea exploded. "Let's go, Terry. John, I'll be waiting with iodine and spirits of ammonia."

"What, no ipecac?" I kissed her, and then Terry ushered her into a cab.

"Remember," he called out the window, "the guy can box."

"Get outta here," I said. I tapped the fender of the cab and it slid away from the curb.

I turned to Siegel. "Well," I said, "alone at last."

Siegel had taken off his jacket and was shadowboxing. Terry was right; judging from his sparring, he was a boxer, and a good one.

However, I had learned self-defense under the tutelage of Master Gunnery Sergeant Emil Deevon USMC, a fellow reputed to have single-handedly cleaned out an entire barful of Australian SAS guys one night in the Philippines. Gunny Deevon took his instructing seriously and guaranteed results.

"If you live through my class, Brucies"—Deevon was *most* politically incorrect—"and you lose a hand-to-hand, I will personally fly my black ass to Arlington, shove your weepin' mama and papa outta my way, whip out Mr. Happy and piss all over your Brucie-boy grave."

Everything Deevon taught me came in handy later on the streets of L.A. When he was killed in an ambush in Somalia, I flew back to Arlington for his funeral. I was surrounded by hundreds of Marines who were torn between grief at his death and hysterical laughter at the memory of his high-pitched yelp and imaginative insults.

So, in respect to the Gunny's memory, I said, "Ready to die, Brucie-boy?"

"I'm shakin'," Siegel sneered, throwing a right hook at my face. I stepped back quickly to avoid the full impact of the blow. It still hurt, however.

Siegel was clearly enjoying himself. He threw a few good combinations and faked me out a couple of times with some expert feints. His sleepy eyes were wide and mocking, like those of a kid easily winning a one-on-one basketball game. I didn't fight back, though. I just let him try to hit me.

"I must say," I remarked as I ducked a roundhouse left,

"that I really love Vegas. You're gonna do a great job there, Ben."

"What the hell are you talkin' about?" he grunted, catching my shoulder with a right cross.

"Las Vegas, Nevada. Don't worry, you'll find out." I blocked a left. "Watch out for Virginia Hill, though."

"Fuckin' nut," he said, and came after me with a lethal combination. I took two in the face, which swayed me a little, and then I caught him over my hip and threw him to the ground.

"What the hell was that?" he demanded.

"What the hell was what, Benny? We're in an alley in Harlem, Ben, not a school yard." I remembered Gunny Deevon's opinion of fair fights. "Fair! Marines don't fight fair! You know who fights fair? *Dead* motherfuckers fight fair. Which do you wanna be?"

"Come on, Ben, get up." I danced around him. He got up and charged me, the poor dumb-ass. I kicked his legs out from under him and chopped the back of his neck. He was down, but not out, and rose slowly, seething with anger. In my head, Gunny Deevon screamed, "Press it home, Brucie, press it home!"

As Siegel got to his feet, I gave him the Deevon Special, a roundhouse kick that again swept his legs out from under him, this time following up with a flying boot to the jaw. I grabbed his hand and twisted his arm, pressing my shoe against his Adam's apple.

"We all done now, Ben?"

He struggled and I increased pressure on his arm and his neck. Then he relaxed.

"Yeah," he breathed heavily, "we're done."

I helped him to his feet. "You can sure scrap," he said with grudging admiration. "Where'd you learn that?"

"The Marines. Later on, the cops."

"You're a cop?"

"As far as you know," I replied.

"Then how come those two cops was followin' you?"

"How do you know they were cops?"

Siegel looked at me as if I were simple. "Okay," I said. "They wasn't locals, though."

"Really," I said, becoming interested. "What gives you that idea?"

"They had apple-knocker faces. And they sounded like apple-knockers, not New York, anyway. The big tip-off was they didn't know *me*. Every flatfoot in town knows me," he added proudly.

"Anything else?"

"They were sissies," he sneered.

"You mean . . ." I searched for the politically incorrect 1920s terminology, "they were . . . fairies?"

"Nah. They were just, you know, *sissies*. I gave 'em some crap before you got out here and they didn't give it back, like you did. I said, 'What're *you* lookin' at, bonehead,' and they just kind of backed off."

"Well, I appreciate your assistance, Ben."

"You wanna get a drink?"

"Thanks, but I'm in a hurry."

"I get it." He grinned. "That broad. I don't blame ya."

"Few people do," I replied.

9 MARCH 1926—THE ALGONQUIN

Althea and Terry met me in the Algonquin lobby. "Where is he?" I asked impatiently.

"In his room," Terry said. "And not alone."

"I'm glad. Where're Chang and Eng?"

"Outside, near the alley."

"I have it on good authority that they're on the job."

"Not locals," Terry said.

"That's what Bugsy said."

"Oh, you're pals now?" Althea scoffed. "Men! I may vomit."

"How'd that go?" Terry asked. "You don't have a scratch."

"You were right," I said. "He can box. He just can't fight. Let's take 'em down."

"Who, the boys outside? Okay, how do you want to do it?"

"This is ridiculous!" Althea erupted. "No more fighting. All you've done since you've been here is get your head beaten in. *I'll* bring them in."

"Althea . . ."

She turned and faced me. "Don't take this the wrong way, John, but you're getting to be quite a bore. You're beginning to take things entirely too seriously."

"But—" What else could I say?

"We've got a job to do, fine. But you'd better start learning how to relax. When we first met, you used to take such pleasure in everything you did. You enjoyed the good and understood that you couldn't change most of the bad. But now you've got this superior attitude—as if *your* era was just oh so perfect." She threw her hands up to her face and affected a whiny, effeminate voice. " *'Oh, the twenties are so awful! Oh, everybody's so mean! Oh, everybody smokes and doesn't have a stick up his ass like we do in 2007! Oh, people eat things because they taste good and do things because they feel good!'* You'd better"—she looked at Terry for help—"what's the term?"

"Lighten up?" Terry offered.

"Yes. Lighten up."

"I guess I'm not getting laid tonight," I whispered loud enough for only Althea to hear. It was a stupid thing to say, though, and with anyone else it would have meant trouble.

"No, you'll still get laid," she said, as if to a teenager who was afraid of being grounded. "Why should I punish myself just because you're being a pompous jerk? Now stop being a sourpuss. You *loved* 1940, and the world was falling apart. You were going to stay there and fight in

World War II—or was that another man I was sleeping with at the time? I refuse to believe that the twenties are any worse, even for a twenty-first-century tight-ass like you.''

We followed her outside at a discreet distance. Our two friends were standing in the alley next to the hotel, looking cold and uncomfortable. I couldn't help but pity them. I had done my share of stakeouts and knew from experience how miserable they could be.

Althea motioned us back and turned into the alley.

"You boys must be tired," I heard her say.

"Uh . . . you must be mistaken," I heard one voice croak. She had obviously caught them both by surprise.

"Mistaken?" she replied. "You're not tired?"

"No, ma'am," said the other. "I mean . . . yes, ma'am, we are tired, but no, ma'am, you must be looking for someone else."

"Why do you say that?"

"Ma'am, please . . ."

"Look," she said firmly, "you've been following us all night. Now, you can come inside and get warm and we can all sit down over coffee and a sandwich and talk this out. Or—we can run you all over town, making sure you never get anywhere near a bathroom for the next twelve hours."

"Oh, God, a bathroom!" moaned one of them.

"Got 'em," I said to Terry.

"I know just how they feel," he replied. "Boy, do I ever." The two were obviously new at stakeouts; otherwise, they'd have known about empty milk cartons and the proper use of cover in alleys.

Althea came out of the alley, arm in arm with our two shadows. "Now, that wasn't so difficult, was it?" she asked me with a smirk.

Terry produced his captain's shield. "All right, gentlemen, break out some ID right now."

I regarded the two of them critically. They were both young, blond, fresh-faced, and terrified. "You can frisk them," I told Terry, "but they won't be heeled."

"What makes you so sure?"

"They're Feds. They won't be allowed to carry for another eight years."

" 'Walters, Robert C.,' " Terry read, " 'Evans, Tyler D.,
Bureau of Investigation.' FBI, huh?"

"Just BI, for now, Ter. How badly do you need to go
to the can, Robert C.?" I asked Walters, the more frightened one.

"Pretty badly." He looked at Evans, who rolled his eyes.

"Why were you following us?"

"We weren't following you," Walters replied, standing
with his legs crossed.

"All right, then. Why were you following Mitchell?"

"Who's that?" Evans asked, trying to sound innocent.

"One more word out of turn and I run you in," Terry
said, affecting his best pissed-off flatfoot tone. "You're in
my jurisdiction now, farm-boy."

"I'm not a farm-boy," Evans replied indignantly. "I
went to Dartmouth."

"Shut *up*," Terry snapped. He looked at Walters. "Answer the question."

"Uh, I forgot what it was," he said, embarrassed.

"Why are you following Mitch?"

"Oh, is that his name?"

Terry removed a sap from his pocket and caressed it.

"No, really," Walters insisted, "I didn't know his
name."

"Terry," Althea piped up.

"Yes?"

"Don't you think the proper thing to do, before you hurt
these poor boys, is to let them use the john?"

Terry considered that for a moment. "No. Sorry," he
said finally. "They'll be more inclined to talk now, when
they're highly motivated. What were your orders?"

"I don't know what you're talking about," Evans said.

"Somebody told you to follow Mitch," Terry said pa-
tiently. "Who was it?"

"Nobody."

"Are you guys assigned here, in the New York Bureau?" I asked.

"No, Washington," Walters replied. Evans almost punched him.

"I guess that answers my question," Terry said. "What'd Hoover tell you?"

"Who?" Evans asked.

"Little guy, looks like a pissed-off owl?"

Walters guffawed. Evans *did* punch him that time. I motioned to Terry to take Evans back into the alley. I figured that Walters wanted to talk, if for no other reason than to be released to use the john.

"This won't take long, Robert C.," I said. "It's up to you."

"But Evans—"

"I'll deal with Evans. Tell me exactly how your day went, the day you saw Hoover and he sent you to New York."

Althea took out a cigarette and lit it for him. "Thank you," he said. You could tell that he was a little nervous around a girl as attractive as Althea. I instinctively decided to use this, but, as usual, she was a step ahead of me. She took his arm and leaned in closely.

"Got a girl, Robert C.?" she asked.

"Well, yeah," he said, not comprehending the change of subject. "I mean, there's a girl I like, but she doesn't know I'm alive."

"I don't see how," Althea replied sweetly. "You're a very attractive man." He was, too. He just wasn't overly bright.

"Well, I try to talk to her, but she just doesn't seem interested."

"Why do you like her?" Althea asked.

"Well, gee, she's the prettiest—"

"What else?"

"What do you mean?"

"What does she like? What does she care about? What's her favorite thing to do?"

"Uh . . . I don't know."

"Don't you think you ought to find out?"

Robert C. creased his forehead. "I don't get you."

"She's a pretty girl, Robert. Don't you think she knows this by now? If you come drooling after her because she's pretty, what makes you any different from anyone else who tries to date her?"

"You mean I should find out more about her? See what we have in common?"

"Very good, Robert. Try approaching her as a person, not just a creature who happens to be beautiful. Otherwise, why should she care about you—not if you don't care about her."

"Wow! I never thought of it like that."

"Good. And now that we have your problem squared away, why don't you help us with our problem."

"But Mr. Hoover—he'd fire me in a second."

"I'll take care of Mr. Hoover," I said.

"Yeah, sure. Listen, nobody takes care of Mr. Hoover—he takes care of everybody else."

"Trust me," Althea said, adding flirtatiously, "you do trust me, don't you?"

"Well, yeah," he said, melting. Whoever the object of Robert's affection was in D.C., she'd never be quite the epitome of perfection she had been before his meeting Althea.

"Mr. Hoover called you into his office," she prompted.

"Yeah, and he gave us this guy's name and description and told us that he was a suspected communist agitator, and we were to tail him and report on his activities."

I tried not to laugh. Mitchell, one of the richest men in California, son of *the* richest man in California, a communist. What a joke. But then, so was Hoover. He spent his career looking for communists under the bed and never uncovered one single plot. Meanwhile, organized crime flourished.

"What do you think brought Mitchell to his attention?" Althea asked.

"I don't know. Oh—he did say 'a contact in New Orleans,' if that'll help you at all."

I sighed with relief. "You have no idea," I said. "Thank you." I turned to Althea. "We've got it," I said.

"Are you sure?" she asked.

"Positive."

"Okay." She winked at Walters and patted his shoulder. "Okay, Terry," she called into the alley, "might as well forget it. We can't get a damned thing out of this guy."

Terry led Evans out of the alley. "You want me to talk to him?" he said.

"No, it's no use," I said, giving Terry a wink. "He won't say a word."

"Well, that's okay," Terry replied smugly. "Agent Evans here has been singing like a canary."

"He has?" Walters was shocked.

"Shut up, Bob," growled Evans.

"I won't say a word, Tyler," Walters assured him. "I promise."

Evans looked miserable. "Don't take it so hard," Terry said.

"You won't tattle on your partner, will you?" Althea asked Robert C. with a wink.

Walters, enthralled by Althea, winked back. "Not a word," he said. "After all, he is my partner."

We released a lighthearted Walters and downcast Evans to the custody of the lobby restroom attendant and went up to Mitchell's suite of rooms. There was a soft but insistent knocking sound—like a headboard against a wall.

Althea rapped on the door.

"Go away," a ragged female voice called.

"Sorry, but it's important," I said.

"Well, so is this," the woman argued, and then whispered urgently, but loudly enough for us to hear, "don't stop *now*, for Christ's sake!"

"I can't concentrate," I heard Mitchell growl, "I'm losing it!"

"Will this help?" the woman asked.

Apparently, "this" did help. The rapping sound quickened and there was soon a vocal crescendo from both partners. Terry grinned and looked up at the ceiling. Althea chuckled and knocked on the door again.

"Can't we smoke a cigarette first?" the woman's aggrieved voice called.

"We'll only be a moment," I said. We heard light footsteps approaching the door.

"If this is what the next century is like," her grumpy voice said, "you can damn well keep it."

The door opened, revealing a small dark woman clad only in Mitchell's bathrobe. She was smoking a cigarette in a long holder and wearing a sleepy, sated look on her face.

"Mitchell, your friends from the future are here," she called.

"I'll be right out," came Mitchell's voice from the bathroom.

"Well, your timing stinks," she said, "but you *are* considerate. I'm Dorothy Parker. Who the hell are you?"

ELEVEN

9 MARCH 1926—THE ALGONQUIN HOTEL, NEW YORK CITY

MRS. PARKER SIZED UP ALTHEA AND DECIDED TO LIKE HER. "So, you're from the next century, honey? How long have I got?"

"I wouldn't know, Mrs. Parker," Althea replied. "You see, although I was in 2007 briefly, I'm really from 1940, and you're still very much alive."

"Well, now I'm confused," Mrs. Parker said.

Althea took my hand. "John and I met when he visited 1940," she explained. "Nature took its course, and here I am."

"How romantic. What about it, John, am I still alive?"

Dorothy Parker died in 1967. There was no reason for her to know this, however. "Of course you are, Mrs. Parker."

"Liar, liar, pants on fire," she scoffed. "God, who in hell would want to live that long, anyway?" She brushed a loose wisp of brunette hair from her face. I could see a faded scar on her wrist as she did so. She saw me looking and gave me a wry smile, as if she'd caught me glancing at her cleavage and was pleased by the compliment.

"Every girl should try it once," she said. "After you get over the embarrassment of botching it, it's quite liberating. You never take men quite as seriously ever again."

After a silence that made everyone except Mrs. Parker feel awkward, Althea said, "I love your work, Mrs. Parker. I wish you'd do more of it."

"So does my landlord, dear."

"I'll take care of your landlord, and anybody else," Mitchell declared as he entered the room and sat on the arm of her chair. "Your money problems are over." She patted his leg.

"You're sweet, darling, but if you turn out to be good for me, I'll have to get rid of you."

"What are your plans?" I asked Mitchell.

"I think I'd like to take Dottie on a little trip. Maybe Atlantic City? Would you like that?"

She yawned expansively. "Wherever you'd like, sweetie. I'm yours—for now."

"That's good enough," Mitchell declared, but it was bravado and we all knew it.

"I'm going to take a bath," Mrs. Parker announced. "Don't get up." With that, she swept out of the room. Mitchell stared after her possessively.

"Well, Mitch," Terry said, "you've found your girl."

"That's right," he snapped defensively.

"Relax, Mitchell," I said. "She's a fine woman, and a great writer. Believe me, it's not hard to understand the attraction."

"Why would it be?" he demanded.

"It wouldn't," I replied hastily. "I just can't understand . . . why her? Why Dorothy Parker?"

"Because she makes him feel needed, John," Althea said impatiently. "Christ, it's so simple!"

"I know all that," I said, a little more peevishly than I had intended. "But what was it about her in particular?"

"Shut up, John," Mitchell said tiredly. "I like her. She's funny, and bright, and beautiful, and vulnerable. She's not some boyfriend-faced trophy-wife candidate who wouldn't give me the time of day if I wasn't a studio head worth over a bill—"

"I'm sorry." I laughed. " 'Boyfriend-faced'?"

"I came up with that in high school. You know, a girl who looks like she has a boyfriend, so don't even bother. Or if she doesn't have a boyfriend, don't bother anyway because it's not going to be you."

I nodded. "It works. I like it. *Boyfriend-faced*." But I also felt badly for Mitchell. Here was a guy who had been exposed to so much rejection that he had even come up with his own vocabulary on the subject.

"Was I boyfriend-faced?" Althea asked me.

"Nope." Mitchell replied before I could answer. "Some women, even if they have boyfriends, aren't."

"Why, thank you, Mitchell."

"He's right," I said. The mutual attraction between us had been electric from the git-go.

"You can't be boyfriend-faced on the screen," Mitchell said, comfortable in his area of expertise. "If you make yourself seem inaccessible, the audience won't care about you. That's what they mean when they talk about chemistry between stars of a picture." He stopped talking suddenly, embarrassed at having exposed so much of himself. I decided a subject change was in order.

"We've found Harry," I said.

Mitchell's jaw dropped. "What?"

"We've found your grampa," I said. "He's waiting tables at—"

"Rudley's," he cut me off. "I know."

"Don't you want to see him?"

"Well, yes. No—I don't know. I haven't been able to bring myself to do it yet. I was thirteen when he died, John. He was my best friend in all the world. He was the only one who gave a damn about me. I go see him now, he won't know me from Adam.''

"You'd be surprised," I told him. "I saw my grampa, and my dad and uncle, in 1957. It was great! And the funny thing was, my grampa *did* know me.''

"Maybe," he said. He turned to me suddenly. "How'd you know about Harry?" he said accusingly.

"*I* knew him," Althea said, instinctively covering for me. "I knew your grandfather in Hollywood in the thirties. When I heard your name, I made the connection and mentioned it to John, and he checked it out.''

"What was he like? In the thirties, I mean. I only knew him after the world had beaten the crap out of him.''

"You'd've been proud of him, Mitch. He had a lot of friends. Everyone said he was going places. I'm sure you must have seen the pictures he wrote.''

"Well, sure. Then he blows it all, goes off to Spain.''

"He did what he believed in, Mitch.''

"I'M AN IDIOT!" I shouted.

"No argument there," Althea said. "But why?''

"I've just had an epiphany," I said. Everything had just fallen into place at that moment. Now I knew it all.

"Jesus, Mitch," I said. "I thought I was good at this stuff, but man, you really had me going.''

"What're you talking about?" he demanded.

"You've been yanking our chains. This whole trip. 'I want to see if I can do it on my own.' I was right; you weren't lying, you just weren't telling us everything.''

"I don't know what you—''

"Mitch. This isn't about you. It's not even about Dottie. It's about Harry, isn't it?''

"I never said—''

"Sure, you've always liked Dottie—" I glanced over my shoulder at the closed bedroom door and lowered my voice. "And you never trusted any of the lookers who came after you once you made it. Hey, who can blame you? Reach your level of success and you're nothing but a walking checkbook. And where were all those babes when you were in high school? Dottie's a girl of substance, she's never heard of you, likes you for who you are. All that is to the good, Mitchell. But there's one piece of the puzzle that doesn't fit.''

"Oh," he asked heavily, "what?"

"J. Edgar Hoover. Why're you bugging him? Are you nuts? Why ask for trouble?''

"Dottie has socialist leanings," he said. "And she was for racial equality long before anyone—''

"I know, I know," I said impatiently. "She left her estate, what there was of it, to the NAACP. Everybody knows that. But Hoover never bothered her, at least no more than anyone else. It was her own self-destructive tendencies that were the reason why she didn't become as great as she should have been.''

"So," he remonstrated, "maybe I could help."

"Mitch," I said, keeping my voice low, "you could get her off the booze, screw her into la-la land, get her into aerobics, make her live up to her fullest potential. Maybe that'd make her happy. Go ahead. But that wouldn't make *you* happy, not completely.''

"Why not?" he asked tightly.

"Because she's a bonus of this trip. Not the real reason why you're here.''

"And why *am* I here?''

I looked around smugly. "Harry.''

"What could I do for Harry?''

"Mitchell. Grampa Harry was a communist.''

"So *what*?''

"Hey, don't get me wrong, Mitch. It's not a dirty word to me. It's an airy-fairy political theory that proved itself unworkable in the real world. But tell that to idealistic kids *now*. Here in 1926. Kids whose parents are being exploited in sweatshops and factories and coal mines. Getting paid shit wages, no regard to their personal safety, no medical benefits or disability. No protection from their bosses, no government oversight agencies. None of these kids today are aware that, as we speak, Joe Stalin is systematically starving or freezing one third of his nation to death. Or that he is going to decimate his own army in a massive purge. Nope, to these kids, Karl Marx's promised utopia is still a possibility.

"Harry was a card-carrying communist, wasn't he?"

"Yeah."

"He went to Spain to fight for Loyalists. But when he got back, and he saw that Stalin had signed a nonaggression pact with Hitler, he quit in disgust, didn't he?"

Mitch nodded miserably.

"But it didn't matter. This country's always been slightly paranoid about Reds. He tried to join the Air Force, but they found out that he had been a communist, and that disqualified him from Officer's Candidate School, right?

"So, Mitch, he tried to get to England to join the RAF, but the FBI turns him back at the Canadian border, like it did with a lot of kids back then, right? So he goes to China, shapes up at General Chennault's office. The general doesn't give a damn about some youthful indiscretion. He needs pilots, and Harry is not only a good one, he's been in combat. Not only in combat, but in those shitty Russian Poliakarpov biplanes that were turned into mincemeat by Messerschmitt 109s. And he *survived*.

"So he joins the Flying Tigers and is later absorbed into the regular U.S. Army Air Force. He has a good war. Mitchell, he was top-heavy with medals. I saw them in your office at home. Silver Star, DFC, Air Force Cross, you name it. I mean, I thought *my* grampa was a kick-ass pilot, thirty-two missions in a B-24. But Harry? Makes John Wayne—a close personal friend by the way, so I don't say this lightly—makes John Wayne look like a pussy."

"So what are you driving at, John? My grandfather was a war hero, and I'm proud of him." He paused and stared at me, fuming. "And so what if he was a Red, a lot of poor people were. And you're right, he did quit after Stalin and Hitler signed the treaty in 1939. He hated them forever after that. Screw you, John, I'm proud of him.''

"Hey, Mitch, guess what? I admire him, too. He was not only a hero, and he not only had the courage of his convictions, but he was man enough to admit it when he was wrong. Unfortunately, that's not where it ended.''

"Oh? Where did it end, John?''

"You would think that a young man as brilliant as Harry, who had had what used to be referred to as a 'good war,' you would think that upon his return, he would have the world by the balls. Major Harry Levitan, USAAF, hero of the CBI. And he cuts quite a figure in that uniform. Who could resist him?

"Well, Hollywood, for one. 'Had a good war, Harry baby, but, uh, what have you done for me lately?' But Harry's got balls. 'Fine,' he says, 'I'll show you.' And by God, he does. He goes back to New York, where he takes as his wife a lovely young woman—your grandma, by the way. She works, and he has some savings and mustering-out pay, plus he's in the 52-20 Club—all the GIs who got twenty bucks a week for a year after demobilization. For the next three years he works on his big war novel, during which time, your dad is born. He's almost done when the Russians decide to blockade Berlin and we in turn decide to supply our former enemies by air. Everyone who can still fly gets recalled. Including Harry. For the next six months, he flies C-47's from Wiesbaden to Templehof Airdrome and back again. Bo-ring, except for the odd game of chicken with a Yak fighter. But necessary to restrain the Russian horde. He gets another medal, plus a promise that he won't ever have to wear khaki again, and he returns home and finishes his book. It's a tougher sell than he thought it would be. The war's been over for four years, people are tired of it, and anyway, Norman Mailer said it all in *The Naked and the Dead*. But he persists, and sure enough, it gets published.

"Mitch, the book is a towering achievement. 'Not since

A Farewell to Arms . . . not since *All Quiet on the Western Front* . . . not since *The Red Badge of Courage* . . .' Well, you get my meaning.''

I poured myself a glass of water and looked around me. Althea seemed ready to spit in my eye. Terry was giving me his standard "you putz" face. And Mitch was looking out of the window, although I knew damn well he was listening.

I continued. "The book sells a ton. And Harry is loving it. He's dickering for a new contract with his publisher; his agent is squeezing Hollywood by the nuts on a downhill pull for the movie dough. The future? Harry Levitan is going places. What does he have to worry about?

"Well, he's right. He is going places. But not where he thinks. Because across the world, in his old wartime stomping grounds, the Chinese also decide to go places. They take one good look at the Yalu River in Korea, and ask, Why did the Chinese cross the Yalu? To get to the other side, of course. And as for Harry, well, the Air Force wasn't being entirely truthful when they told him he was through with his military service obligations. They send him to Washington, give him a pair of silver oak leaves, and ask him everything he can remember about China. 'Sure,' Harry thinks, 'what the hell. I've got my bestseller under my belt, they want me for a year, screw it, I'll write my next book at night, by the light of the Capitol Rotunda.'

"Once again, Harry does his bit. Washington's a nice town, he sports a high enough rank to enjoy it, his year passes quickly. He comes back home, full of piss and vinegar, and ready to resume his budding career.

" 'Uh . . . there's just one thing,' his agent tells him, 'I can't sell your book.' 'What the hell do you mean,' Harry wants to know. 'It's a goddamn bestseller, a million copies in print, more on the way. What the fuck do they want?'

" 'Well, it's like this,' his agent tells him. 'They're startin' to get a little nervous about commies. Seems there's this fruitcake rummy senator from Wisconsin, and he's been crackin' down on communists in the movies . . .'

" 'Wait just a goddamn minute,' Harry says. 'I've served with distinction three separate times, for Christ's sake. China, the Berlin Airlift, Korea . . . I'm *still* in uniform. I'm a friggin' *colonel* in the Air Force Reserve, and they doubt *my* loyalty?'

"Well, Mitch, you know what happened. Poor Harry got blacklisted, and it just took the wind out of his sails. His publisher dropped him, then his agent—you know agents better than anybody, they should all be put down at birth—his agent stopped returning his calls. He had enough money from his book sales to live comfortably until the Red Scare was over and Joe McCarthy was sent off to some loony bin to drool all over himself, but by then he just couldn't or wouldn't write anymore. He took a job out here at Cal State Long Beach, teaching creative writing to kids who really couldn't give less of a shit, and until you were born, he didn't care too much about anything himself."

Mitch was biting back tears. I felt pretty rotten, but I had done what I had to do. Getting to the bottom of things isn't always pretty.

"My dad hated him," Mitch finally said through a lump in his throat. "I mean, he loved him, but he hated what he became. That's why my dad went into business. He wanted to get as far away from the arts as he could. He saw what happened to my grandfather, how miserable and broken he was. That's why he never read a book in his life except in school. And that's why he made himself so rich. He didn't want anyone to be able to touch him, to bring him down like they did my grandfather."

"That's also why your dad became the ultimate capitalist," I mused. "So what do you want to do, Mitch?"

"I *know* what I'm going to do," he declared. "You can either help me or not."

"We'll help you, Mitch," Althea said. "Whatever you want."

"Thank you," he said.

"Where do you want to start?" Terry asked him.

"I want a good night's sleep," Mitchell said. "In the morning, I want to get up, eat a good room service breakfast. Then I want to just take a walk with Dottie. And then . . ."

"And then?"

"I want to go to Rudley's for a cup of coffee."

Mrs. Parker had a deadline to meet, so Mitchell put her in a taxi when we met him back at the Algonquin in the morning. Althea and I had also been tired and slept late. We were becoming snippy with each other. We both knew it, and even acknowledged it with promises to treat each other with more sensitivity, but our exaggerated politeness betrayed the tension in the air. It was the first night we had ever spent together without making love, and its significance escaped neither of us.

Terry had also begged off. He had been going on even less sleep, and still hadn't had time off to recover from his rugged mission in the Old West. Time travel can be quite exhausting, and I had discovered almost immediately that when you travel in time, you need more rest and better nutrition than usual. A long rest after a mission is also required. Your body and mind both need to adjust and readjust. Even though Terry seemed like a rock—and acted like one—he was just as human as the rest of us.

"Do you really think this is a good idea?" Mitch asked as we crossed Broadway.

"You don't have to do anything you don't want to do," I replied. "We can turn around right now and go back to the hotel, or over to a speakeasy, or anything else. Believe me."

He stopped for a moment. "No, I'll go."

It was just after lunch hour, and the place was almost empty. A young waiter took our order as I sniffed the donut-shortening smell appreciatively.

"Think Harry is here today?" Mitch asked.

"I'm sure of it," I said.

"What makes you so sure?"

"You just ordered a cup of coffee from him."

Mitch swivelled his head around to look at Harry, who was walking away from him.

"You'll catch him when he returns with our order," I said.

"Why didn't you say something?" he asked aggrievedly.

"I wanted to see if *you'd* say something first," I replied.

Mitchell drummed his fingers on the table nervously until Harry returned. I sat back comfortably and waited. I had seen this all before.

Harry returned with our coffee and sinkers. Mitchell stared at him. There *was* a family resemblance, but it was more of a general, almost unplaceable sort of relationship. My own grandfather and I had looked like brothers. Mitchell and his grandfather had the same build; both were tall, lean, and wiry, with a certain grace and natural coordination that was more common in smaller men. But Mitchell was a rougher, less attractive approximation of his young grandfather, and also lacked his self-assured intensity. Mitchell, at twenty-eight, looked barely postadolescent, while his grandfather, at sixteen, seemed fully grown and mature. However, this could be attributed to the circumstances of their growth. Mitch had been a millionaire's son who had wanted for nothing. Harry had been helping to support his family since grade school.

Harry caught Mitchell staring at him. "Was there anything else?" he asked.

Mitch couldn't speak. He tried to, but nothing came out.

"Are you all right, sir?" Harry asked.

"He's okay," Althea said. "He had a bit of a fright outside—a bus almost hit him."

"He seemed all right before," Harry replied.

"Delayed post-traumatic shock syndrome," I said. "It happens all the time. Not to him, I mean. In general."

"Well, okay." Harry sounded unconvinced. "Let me

know if he needs anything.'' He walked back to the kitchen.

"Mitch? You okay?"

Mitch wiped his forehead with a napkin. "I don't know what happened. The words just wouldn't come."

"That happens sometimes," I lied. I had never seen it before. Most people couldn't wait to talk to long-dead relatives, and almost always established a connection within minutes, even if they never revealed their identity.

"He'll never believe me," Mitch said.

"Of course he won't," Althea said. "Why would he?"

"You believed John when you met him."

"Not right away," she said, with a significant glance at me. "I did fall in love with him right away, though, and that made me a little more patient with him than I would have been with anyone else."

"It won't work," Mitch sighed.

"What won't work?"

"If I tell him, 'Harry, don't join the Reds, stay away from them, they'll make you pay for it later,' he'll tell me to take a hike. Look at him."

Harry was stacking cups and saucers, and he endowed even that simple task with a certain authority. Here was a young man who did everything well, whether it took an inherent or acquired skill, and his presence, even at that young age, was commanding. His fellow workers kept him at a distance that was respectful, not contemptuous.

"You're right," I told him. "He won't listen to you."

"What do I do?" Mitchell agonized.

"Mitchell, sometimes you can't do anything. Sure, I've gone back and changed history—but I couldn't make anybody do just anything. Certainly not a guy like Harry. You're right; look at him. He's been working all his life, and even though he's poor, he's in control. He's staying in school, and next year he'll go to City College, right on schedule. He'll have short stories published in the *New Yorker* before he's twenty. His good friend and fellow Rudley's alumnus, Moss Hart, will help him get an off-Broadway play produced that'll bring him to the attention of Hollywood. And while he's doing that, he'll be taking flying lessons at Roosevelt Field. Are you going to get him to deviate from that course? Is anyone? You know how poor your great-grandparents are, right now Harry thinks that communism is the answer. Are you going to convince him otherwise? I don't think so, Mitch.''

"But I've got to do something!"

"Do you like being alive, Mitchell?"

"I don't get you."

"Mitchell, you're a great man. I don't know if you're aware of this or not. But a lot of people depend on you. Not just for the jobs you create, but for the joy and satisfaction your artistry gives people. Think of the wonderful stories forgotten for decades that you've rescued from obscurity and turned into treasures beloved the world over. We can't do without you, Mitch.''

I turned to Althea. "*The Spectacles*, for Christ's sake. Who would have thought that *Edgar Allan Poe*, of all people, could write such a charming romantic comedy?" I turned back to Mitch. "Only *you*, Mitch. Maybe the only guy in the whole industry who knows that what's on his bookshelves is his real wealth. We need you, old buddy. This whole friggin' planet is becoming illiterate, and you're one of the only people left to keep us honest.''

"But Harry—"

"*You* are Harry's biggest creation, Mitch. Stop thinking of yourself as some twerp who was a geek in high school! It's gone way beyond that. People like your father—a nice guy, a decent man, I'm sure—but what is he going to leave behind? Money? You've already earned more money than you could ever dream of spending; you don't need his. And your reputation precedes you, Mitch—you don't give a shit about money, anyway. You don't lean on people just to prove you're the boss, you don't abuse your power over those who couldn't possibly afford to stand up to you. You don't screw your artists out of their fair share. You don't even demand sexual favors. You are a kind and generous man at the very pinnacle of a cruel and selfish business. Why, it's unheard of! But all that is secondary. The pleasure your movies have brought people like *me*, Mitch, you can't put a price on that. When I sit down with my popcorn and Milk Duds to watch a Mitchell I. Levitan production, I never know whether it'll make me laugh, or feel sad or pissed off—but I do know I'll walk out of there having gotten more than my ten bucks worth. The chances you take on unknown actors and writers and directors—folks who'd still be flipping burgers today if not for you—who spread the Mitchell I. Levitan gospel all over the world. I'll tell you what, Mitch. *You* look at Harry over there. And then think of the grandfather who raised you, who passed down to you an insatiable lust for nothing more than the chance to tell a good story—you go and tell that man what you've become and what you've accomplished. Tell him what your gift means to billions of people just like *me*. Do you think he'll want to change any of that? Do you?''

Mitchell looked down at his coffee. ''I don't know,'' he said miserably.

''Well, I do,'' I said. ''I'm not telling you not to try. Go ahead. But you know what can happen . . .''

He looked up suddenly. ''What? What can happen?''

I pushed my hands apart to mime a small explosion. ''Poof.''

'' 'Poof'? What the hell is 'poof'?''

''You,'' I said. ''You go poof. You disappear, you've never existed. That's why I asked you if you enjoy being alive.''

''What do you mean? You've changed history, you just said so.''

''That's right. I have. I've saved lives. Mitch, you know literature. Well, my meat is history, and I did what I had to do. But I'm still here. Everyone I know of, even slightly, is still here. Let's say you do get Harry to change his mind.

Let's say he doesn't join the Reds. What happens? He gets into OCS, becomes an Air Force pilot before we get into the war. He tried to join up in 1940. Let's say it takes a year for him to earn his wings—that brings us to 1941. Where do you think he'll be stationed?''

"I don't know. I'm not real familiar with—"

"Yeah, well, I am. There's a really good chance that he'll be assigned to the Philippines. That was our biggest overseas base just before the war started.''

Mitch closed his eyes. "Oh, shit," he breathed.

"Oh, yeah, Mitch, you got that right. You want to see your grandfather on the Bataan Death March? Or maybe, just maybe, he might be stationed at Hickam Field—right near Pearl Harbor. Now, you know Harry. He wouldn't be cowering in some foxhole when the bombs start falling. He'd be trying his damnedest to get a P-40 into the air.''

Mitch looked pained. He was obviously envisioning the same thing I was: Harry's plane being blown up by enemy fire before it even got off the runway.

We both turned to look at the young man hard at work behind the counter. It was all clear, we could both see it happening. We could even hear him yelling at his crew chief to start the goddamn plane as bombs exploded and bullets zinged all around him.

"So, Mitch," I said after a long pause, "what's the end result? He dies, and you never get born. The world has to go on without one single Mitchell I. Levitan film. All those rich, productive careers you've made possible, forget them. It's back to 'You want fries with that?' or 'I'm sorry, ma'am, but that video was due yesterday, I'll have to charge you extra.' ''

Mitch turned to Althea, who had been listening in a pregnant silence throughout my discourse. "What about you?" he asked her. "How do you feel about it?''

"I'm alive, Mitchell," she said softly. "That's not so bad when you consider the alternative. But, Mitchell, that doesn't apply. It was all over for me—finished. John snatched me back from the abyss. Anyway, it's too early to tell. I've only been, well, *alive again* for a few weeks."

Mitchell drew himself up in a last show of bravado. "You can't prove any of this," he declared. "Even if, God forbid, something did happen to Harry, I'm here now, aren't I? You're full of crap, John. I can't just disappear."

I sighed. I was hoping I wouldn't have to do what I did next. But Mitch left me no choice. "Okay, Mitch. Let me be blunt. A few months ago, I had to testify before the Senate Intelligence Committee. They had their doubts, just like you. So I had to give them proof."

"What kind of proof?" he asked nervously.

"Proof that changing your history doesn't affect everyone's life—it just affects *your* life." I reached into my coat and pulled out my .45, just enough for him to see the butt. "I'm gonna shoot Harry right now," I said matter-of-factly.

Althea put her hand to her cheek. "John, no!"

"I'm no Terry," I said, "but I can drop him easily from this distance. One shot." I withdrew the gun fully and held it under the table.

"John—" Mitch cried, "don't!"

"The hell with you, Mitch, my mind is made up."

Mitch grabbed his stomach. "I feel ... strange ... I'm ..."

I pulled back the hammer on the single-action weapon.

He began hyperventilating. "You're disappearing, Mitch. In another few seconds, Harry'll be gone and so will you."

He slumped in his chair. "All right ... John ... I be—"

"You believe me?"

"I ..."

"Okay," I said crisply, and slowly released the hammer. "Just kidding. I'm not a murderer, for God's sake, what's wrong with you?" I placed the gun back into my wristband. "Anyway, these bullets aren't lethal, they're only charged."

Mitch began to slowly recover. Althea put her arm around his shoulder and began rubbing his neck. "Mitch? Mitch, come back, you're all right." She looked at me with distaste. "Sometimes you go too far, John. You can be a real asshole."

"Mitch?" I followed his head movements until he was looking into my eyes. "I apologize for doing that, Mitch. But I had to. I won't let the world do without you, and I'll do whatever it takes to keep you here. Mitch? Mitch! Are you with me?"

"I'm a . . . I think . . ."

"Mitch? Are you mad at me?"

"Wow!" he said, smiling weakly. "That was un-fucking-believable! I almost just . . . vaporized right there! Jesus! Can you do that whenever you want?" he asked in wonder.

"I never want to," I said. "It's a last resort. But you left me no choice. Mitch, Harry made his own choices. Maybe his life didn't work out completely, maybe he did suffer a lot. But he never stopped being his own man, making his own choices. Sometimes, sacrifices have to be made. And I think that if Harry knew the whole story, he'd gladly make that sacrifice."

"All right, John," Mitchell sighed. "You've convinced me. Don't buy back the car." He took a bill out of his pocket and slid it under his plate. "Let's get out of here."

"You sure?"

"There's nothing else I can do here," he said, taking command. He got to his feet, a little unsteadily at first but then with growing confidence.

We stood on Broadway trying to flag down a taxi, when Harry Levitan came running out of the coffee shop.

"Hey! Hey, mister!"

Mitch turned around. "Me?"

"Yeah, you. Hey, pal, you made a mistake."

"What do you mean?" There was a smile on Mitch's face. He was plainly enjoying the brief exchange.

Harry held up a hundred-dollar bill. "You left this under your plate. Your bill was only sixty-five cents."

"Keep it," Mitch said.

Harry shook his head. "I don't think so, pal. You want to be a real sport, just gimme a buck and we'll call it square."

"Go on, keep it." Mitch grinned. "It's okay."

"Not with me, it isn't." He placed the bill in Mitch's breast pocket. He peered suspiciously at Mitchell's face. "Say, don't I know you from somewhere?"

Mitchell lit up. "I don't think so. But you never know." He gave Harry a five. "Here. This is for being a man of honor. Don't bother giving it back, because I won't take it."

Harry took the bill. "Okay, you sold me. Take it easy." He turned back toward the restaurant.

"Hey," Mitch called.

"Yeah?"

"You seem like a pretty smart guy. You don't plan on waiting tables for the rest of your life, do you? What do you really want to do?"

Harry looked down at his feet. "I want to be a writer," he said. "But I'm not expecting miracles."

"Yeah?" Mitch said. "Well, do me a favor."

"What's that?"

"Never give up. I mean, no matter how long it takes— even thirty years from now, don't give up."

"Why would I give up?"

"Just promise me. Remember the nut who overtipped you in Rudley's way back in 1926 told you, *never give up.*"

"Okay." Harry gave Althea and me a "this guy's engine is down a quart" sort of look.

"Shake on it," Mitch said.

Harry shrugged. "Okay, mister."

"Never give up," Mitch repeated.

"Never give up," Harry said.

"Thanks," Mitch said. "I feel much better."

TWELVE

GETTING A CAB TURNED OUT TO BE AN IMPOSSIBILITY, SO we walked up Broadway for a while. I was still feeling rotten about the scare I had thrown into Mitch, and I told him so.

"Forget it," Mitch said. "It was awesome! Can I use it in a movie?"

"Be my guest. You know, Mitch, you still might have managed to change history just a bit."

"I did?"

"Sure. You never know what sort of power the right words can have." I thought of what I had said to my own grandfather in 1957, and how he was able to endure when my uncle Jack was shot down and taken prisoner in Vietnam.

"Maybe," he said dubiously, and then brightened. "But he made the connection. He recognized me! Well, not me, but he saw *something* familiar. Does it always happen like that?"

"Yes," I said. "Almost."

"He was quite a kid, wasn't he?"

"You should be very proud."

"I am proud, believe me."

"Then you're about done here?"

He considered that for a moment. "There's still Dottie. And . . . one other thing."

"What's that?"

"Hoover. I've got a thing or two I want to tell him."

"Mitch . . ."

"Just bear with me on this, okay?"

"You'd better be real careful," I warned him.

"Don't worry about it."

"I'm paid to worry about it."

"Well, forget about it for now." He strolled breezily up Sixth Avenue for a while. "You know, you really don't know your friend very well, John," he said, abruptly changing the subject. "I'm surprised at you. I thought you'd be more perceptive than that."

"What are you talking about?"

"Your buddy Terry."

"What's the matter with Terry?"

"He's a man with a plan. He's here for a reason, too."

"He is?"

Mitch looked at me mockingly. "Duh. Look, John, the most important thing Harry taught me about dramatic writing was that everyone in a certain scene has to want something. They have to be there for a reason. Even if they're just bit players, they still need subtext to do a convincing job. Well, Terry isn't here just to take in the sights."

"Althea?" I said.

"In the words of our marvelously literate friend here. . . 'duh.' "

I didn't know what to make of it, but I waved down a cab and the three of us piled in. The Plaza was only ten blocks away, but we tipped the irate cabbie exorbitantly. When we got to the Plaza, I rang Terry's room. He was surprised to hear from me, but he said he was on his way down and would meet us in the lobby.

"You're a good detective, John," he said as he greeted us.

"Actually, Mitch and Althea are the smart ones. I had no idea that you were planning anything."

"That's why I came along," he said. "In addition to keeping you from breaking your neck, that is." He gave Althea and Mitch an apologetic grin. "Nothing personal, and Althea, you know I love you, but would you and Mitch mind awfully if just John came with me?"

"Of course not, Terry," Althea said, giving him an understanding peck on the cheek. "Too many cooks, and all that. Just be careful."

"Who do you think I am," he chuckled, "John?"

BROOKLYN

We climbed up the subway stairs into the sunlight. The train, which Terry referred to as simply "the Four," had taken us on an interminable ride under the East River to Court Street, which Terry informed me was "downtown" Brooklyn near the City Hall.

"I thought the City Hall was in Manhattan," I said.

"It is," Terry explained. "But until the turn of the last century, Brooklyn was a separate city. In fact, the fourth largest city in America. Most Brooklynites still think of it that way."

"You mind telling me what we're doing here?"

"Just another block." We came to a low awning beneath a green sign that read "Luncheonette." It was flanked by two logos, one for Coca-Cola and the other for Breyer's Ice Cream.

"Oh," I said. "I get it now."

"Good for you, John." In front of the store was a low metal case on which the day's newspapers were neatly stacked. Above that was a service window. We went inside.

The place was long and narrow, mostly taken up by a lunch counter.

"Soda fountain smell." Terry sniffed beatifically. "God, I miss that."

There was a young couple behind the counter, going over an account book. We sat down at the counter and they both looked up.

"They're so *young*," Terry whispered.

Terry's grandparents were both small, as he had said. But his grandfather's upper body, as a result of years of hauling ice, was massive. His grandmother looked older than her thirty years, and had a slight hunch from years of sewing shirt buttons in bad lighting, but she was still a vibrant woman upon whom the years had not yet taken their toll.

A tear plunked straight from Terry's eye onto the countertop. He ignored it, and acted as though it hadn't happened.

"*Nu*, gentlemen, and what can I do for you today?" Terry's grandfather asked.

"Two vanilla egg creams, please," Terry said evenly.

"Ready even before Jack Robinson could say Jack Robinson," Mr. Rappaport replied.

Terry smiled, as if he had heard his grandfather say this before. Often.

"What's an egg cream?" I asked. "Not what it sounds like, I hope?"

"West Coast barbarian." Terry shook his head. Two egg creams appeared in front of us, and Terry immediately ordered two more.

"Why are you ordering another one already?" I asked him.

"You'll see."

I put my lips to the straw, and when I took them away again, my glass was empty. I had never tasted anything so sweet yet wonderfully refreshing.

"See?" Terry said smugly.

"Wow! That was amazing!"

"Ready for another?"

"Oh, yeah," I answered. "Terry, are you sure it's today?"

His expression hardened. "I'm sure. You could set your watch by those bastards."

Sure enough, Terry's grandparents were counting out the contents of the cash register. They gave each other worried glances, then shrugged in resignation. They placed the money back in the drawer, withholding a single ten-dollar bill.

Terry looked up at the Coca-Cola wall clock. "Any minute now," he said. He looked out the window and a black police cruiser slid in next to the curb. One officer got out and gave instructions to the driver, who nodded and put the car into neutral.

The cop was not as big as family folklore had led Terry to believe, but he must have looked gigantic to Terry's diminutive grandparents. He was heavyset with a ruddy face and a wide insincere smile. Terry had been right, the uniform did make the difference. It was a heavy wool tunic, double-breasted with brass buttons polished to a high sheen, and a tight hook collar. The eight-pointed cap had the broad gold band worn by sergeants and above. Completing the ensemble was a blindingly polished gold sergeant's shield, which Terry later informed me was the largest of any rank in the department.

The cop entered the place like a movie star at a premiere. "Well, top o' the day to you, Mr. and Mrs. Rappaport. How's business been treatin' you on this fine day?"

I couldn't believe it; he actually had an Irish accent. But he was no stereotype. He was the real thing, and there was no mistaking the menace just beneath the surface of his hearty greeting.

"Very nice, Sergeant," Mrs. Rappaport replied, joining the charade. "And how's by your family?"

"In the pink, and for sure the kiddies appreciate your generosity with them jawbreakers and candy bars."

"What can I get for you, Sergeant?"

"It's me downfall, Mrs. R., but a couple packs of Old Golds for the filthy habit, if you please."

He handed her a dollar bill. She gave him his order already prepared: two packs of cigarettes secured by a rubber band. Between the two packs a bit of green was evident.

"Many thanks, Mrs. R.," the sergeant said, pocketing his smokes and his payoff.

"Wait, Sergeant, your change." She counted out four quarters and handed them over. The sergeant touched his fingers to his cap and turned to leave.

"Sergeant!" The sergeant looked back into the store, whipping his head around as if he had just been insulted and some poor fool was about to learn a painful lesson in manners.

"Over here," Terry called in his most authoritative voice. Terry jerked his head at me, and I moved down to the next stool.

The sergeant gave Terry a wide-eyed, dangerous glare. Mr. and Mrs. Rappaport had no idea what was going on, but whatever it was scared the hell out of them. They suddenly became very interested in their account ledgers.

Terry took out his captain's badge and held it under the counter so that only the sergeant could see it. Terry motioned sharply for the sergeant to take the seat between us.

The sergeant's expression changed in an instant to one of fear. In the flash of a badge, the hunter became the hunted. He sat heavily between us, and I could see that both his wool uniform and Terry were making him sweat profusely.

Still, he was a professional, and he was not stupid. "And how may I be of service, Captain?"

Terry leaned back. "Sarge, I think we have a slight problem here."

"Oh? And what might that be?"

"Ah, you know how it is downtown, right, Lieutenant?"

The sergeant looked at me and then at Terry. Outranked and outflanked. I almost felt sorry for him.

"Right, Cap," I replied. "Very disorganized."

"I know you have to make the pad, Sarge," Terry said. "Believe me, I know. I was a sergeant in the Two-One, Jesus, what a colossal screwup. The lieutenant gives you the sheet, says, make the pickup, ten from this guy, eight from this one, fifteen from the other. All that work, for what? A carrying charge of a buck a stop?"

But the sergeant wasn't giving anything away. "If you say so," he replied carefully.

"Well, I say so. Anyhow, lieutenants are always such lazy sons a bitches—nothing personal there, John—*most* of 'em, you report every week, who's moved, who's gone outta business, who's making more dough than you thought, who's got friends downtown. Lieutenant's supposed to keep track of that, make changes on the pad, keep it current. Do you follow?"

"I follow."

"Here's the problem, Sarge. Looks like your lieutenant was soldiering on the job, and now our asses are in a sling. Turns out these nice people here, well, they got connections. *Big* connections."

The sergeant jerked a thumb at the Rappaports. "Them people? Who the hell do they know? They're just a couple a little ki—"

"Let me ask you something, Sarge," Terry interrupted him curtly. "How big do *you* think they are? Think hard. Somebody sent a *captain* and a *lieutenant* to this little hole-in-the-wall to tell the bagman—you—that they're off the pad. Now just how important do *you* think their friend is?"

The sergeant paled. "Jasus," he whispered. "Jasus, Mary, and Joseph!" He drew the cigarettes and ten-dollar bill out of his pocket and handed them under the counter to Terry. Then he cleared his throat. "My mistake, Captain. What the hell, it happens, don't it?"

"Absolutely, Sergeant," Terry said loudly. He removed

the ten-spot from between the two packs and handed the cigarettes back to the sergeant. "Keep 'em," he said. "On me." And then, he added significantly, *"This time."*

The sergeant refused them, spreading his white-gloved hands in front of his face. "Awful habit, Captain," he said. "You're doing me a favor." He stood up and began to retreat with a small bit of dignity. "Good seeing you, sir."

"Same here," Terry said, "oh, and sergeant?"

"Sir?"

"These people will continue to receive the same caring and courteous service, won't they? I mean, if anything were to happen here, I know you'll take it *personally*, just as . . . well, a lot of people, including myself."

The sergeant looked wounded. "Why, of course, Captain! Protecting the good people of this fine city, that's what we're paid for, ain't it?"

After the sergeant left, Mr. Rappaport approached us tentatively. "Excuse me, sir," he said to Terry. "No disrespect intended, but we don't want no trouble."

"Don't worry," Terry said. "The last thing you're ever going to get is trouble." He slid the cigarettes and the ten-spot across the counter. Mr. Rappaport looked horrified, as if the little package were a tiny poisonous snake.

"Please . . . the sergeant, he takes care of us . . ."

"That's his job, sir." Terry stood up. "I promise you, you'll never have to pay another nickel. Just remember, you have friends."

Walking back to the subway, I asked Terry if he felt any different.

"How do you mean?" he asked.

"Do you think you changed anything?"

He shrugged. "Probably not much. That sergeant must have been transferred or promoted or retired sooner or later, and I guess a new guy came in and started shaking them down again. At least they got a little breathing room. But I don't *feel* any different."

And that was when Terry came up with the theory—or

theorem—that once it was reported back to Cornelia, completely revolutionized time travel as we knew it.

"I guess I'll have to ask you, when we get back, if you've noticed any changes. After all, you're my *hinge*."

I tripped on the curb. "Your what?"

"My hinge. Look, John, I'm just a dumb cop, whether it's for you or for the good old NYPD. I don't know a hell of a lot about anything else. But I have seen a thing or two working at Timeshare, and one of them is, you're right—when you change your own history, you don't necessarily change the world, just your own world."

"Go on."

"Well, somebody whose world *hasn't* changed is not going to notice the difference. Sometimes, you don't see it yourself. The person who knows the difference between the two, in my layman's term, is the *hinge*, the hinge between the two . . . fates, if you will."

We walked down the steps into the subway. "John, remember when you went back into 1940, and you met Althea, and Bogie, and Duke Wayne?"

"I'd need more than a good case of amnesia to forget that."

"Okay, do you remember meeting Ian Fleming and William Stephenson—Intrepid?"

"Quite."

"You told them what was going to happen. It didn't change the general course of history, but you did save more lives, didn't you? I mean, Fleming and Stephenson could only convince so many people."

"I remember," I said.

"What was in the history books—before you went back?"

"There were 335,000 British and French troops evacuated at Dunkirk. The head of RAF Fighter Command, Dowding, held back twenty-five squadrons in anticipation of the impending Battle of Britain."

"Do you—" A train thundered by on the opposite track,

interrupting his question. "And after you got back?"

"There were 440,000 troops rescued at Dunkirk. Dowding held back thirty-eight squadrons, and fighter command lost seven percent fewer pilots."

"Does anyone know this besides you? I mean, the history books all say—"

"I know what the history books say. I also know what I know."

"Bravo. Because you're the hinge. Closer to home, John, when you visited your grandfather and father and uncle in 1957, what happened?"

"I don't know. I mean, I don't re—"

"I do, John. You didn't exactly come right out and tell him that your uncle Jack was going to be shot down in Vietnam, you didn't tell him that he was going to be missing for six years."

"No. I just said, 'He's okay. Remember, he's okay, no matter what happens. He's going to be an admiral.' "

The train pulled up and we boarded, It wasn't crowded, but Terry and both I stood, hanging on to those peculiar straps.

"You came back, and the first thing you said was, 'I gotta call my grampa Joe. He's ninety years old today.' "

I stared at him in alarm. "What're you getting at?"

"I think you know, John," he said.

"But, Terry, I remember a whole life with Grampa Joe, fishing, ball games, teaching me to fly, just the way he is. You've met him, Terry, you know what terrific guy—"

"And that's wonderful, John. I'm not knocking it. I'm just telling you, that's not what happened the first time around."

"What did happen?"

He looked down at the floor. "When Jack's A-6 went down over Nam, and he went MIA-presumed-dead, it killed your grandpa. He started aging fast, got a little better when Jack got home, but by then it was a little too late."

"I told you this?"

"Yes, John. When we first became friends, remember how we used to sneak back to 1977 and party? Go to Hermosa Beach, someplace like Beach Bum Burt's or the Red Onion? Meet up with a couple of disco queens, get half a bag on and just relax, without any 2007 bullshit, which we both hate? You used to talk about him all the time, how much you missed him."

I swayed, and not from the motion of the train. Terry sat me gently on a nearby vacant seat.

"It's starting to come back," I said. "Jesus, I lived in a world without Grandpa Joe."

"Well, it's better now, isn't it?"

I breathed a sigh of relief. "It's like a bad dream, you know, when you're a kid, the way you always have a nightmare about your parents dying, and then you wake up and hear them snoring upstairs. But you still jump out of bed and run up there to make sure."

"Been there," Terry said. "Done that."

"So . . . you're my . . . hinge."

"Yeah, and I guess you're mine."

"Do you feel any different?"

"Not really. I guess we won't know anything until we get back to '07."

I ruminated for the rest of the trip. It occurred to me how we as a society pretty much dump on our grandparents, shove them out of the way and bring them out only for family holidays, but given the opportunity to go back in time, it's overwhelmingly their youth that we wish to see above everything else. Not our parents, because we always view them as being around forty, an age at which we ourselves arrive so soon that it takes our breath away. Envisioning our parents as younger doesn't require such an imaginative leap.

But our grandparents are already older when we first know them. And when we do see their photographs taken in middle age, they don't look all that different. Their hair is a little darker, their faces have fewer wrinkles. But we look at them as grandparents-to-be, selfishly believing that their true purpose in life begins only at our births. That's why seeing them in their salad days has always been such an attraction. In a strange way, we are given a preview of the full circle of our own lives.

"Let's get off here," Terry said, when the train pulled in at Wall Street.

"How come?"

"I just want to see something."

We went up the stairs and into a bright sunlight pouring in between the Stock Exchange and the Federal Reserve Building. "I love these buildings," Terry said. "I always have."

It was early afternoon and the streets were pretty crowded with businessmen and secretaries. I half-expected to see F. Scott Fitzgerald observing the crowds and taking notes.

Terry pointed eastward. "Over there, Exchange Pl— damn it, I forgot. It wasn't built until 1931."

"What?"

"Twenty Exchange Place. Beautiful Art Deco building. God, I love that place. My dad worked there for thirty years."

I stopped. In fact, I took a step backward, right into a guy in a dark blue suit and straw hat. "Sorry," I said.

"I beg your pardon," he replied, showing big, yellow Woodrow Wilson teeth.

"You all right?" Terry asked.

"Your father worked *where*?"

"I just told you. Twenty Ex—"

"What did he do?"

"He was—well, he is, but he does consulting now that he's retired—he's a corporation lawyer. I told you that a million times, for Christ's sake. In fact, he did some merger work with Mitchell I. Levitan's father back in the eighties."

"You mean, he wasn't a cop?"

Terry spread out his hands as if he were talking to a

brick wall. "Well, yeah, for a few years, while he was in law school. You know all that."

"Uh, actually, Terry, no, I don't."

Terry leaned back against the wall of the Stock Exchange and began to laugh. He tried to talk, then laughed some more.

"Okay," he said. "Give it to me straight, Hinge-boy."

The odd thing was that although the circumstances of his youth had altered considerably, Terry's own ambitions remained remarkably unchanged. Before our visit, he had grown up in Riverdale, a pleasant middle-class neighborhood at the northern tip of the Bronx. It was a happy if uneventful childhood, punctuated by milestones in his father's rise to high command in the police department. He had attended a pretty rough public high school called De Witt Clinton. His parents would have preferred that he had chosen college over the Army, but he informed them that he was planning to join the police department after his enlistment was up, and would educate himself on the Army's and the NYPD's dime. They saw brighter things for him, but they also knew he had his own mind, and besides, his father had enjoyed a stellar police career himself.

That was the Hinge-boy version. Terry remembered, vaguely, an early childhood in Riverdale. Chief among those memories were his father studying his lawbooks at the kitchen table, his gun belt and tunic draped over the back of the chair. And then, when Terry was around five years old, his father began wearing three-piece suits instead of a uniform and carrying a briefcase instead of a gun. He later learned that his father had graduated second in his law school class, and was immediately recruited by a top Wall Street firm.

By the time Terry was set to enter junior high school, the family had moved to an elegant town house in the East Sixties, and he was enrolled at the Dalton School, an exclusive private academy. He distinctly recalled summering in the Hamptons and wintering in the Virgin Islands.

His most vivid memory was his parents' extreme displeasure when he announced that he was joining the Army right out of Dalton.

"It was the only bad time I can remember about growing up," Terry said. "I mean, people went to Harvard or Yale from Dalton, not Fort Benning. It just wasn't done. I wasn't even going to West Point, which would have given them *some* slight consolation. I was just gonna be a dumb-ass grunt of a buck private like your average ridge-runner. My parents hit the roof and stayed up there till I left for intake at Fort Hamilton in Brooklyn. It was the longest month of my life."

But Terry had the course of his life well laid out. He would join the Army and go Airborne, and from there, the Department. He would get his college degree while still a patrolman, and hopefully make detective during that time. His parents, although they were never happy about the direction in which he had taken his life, became proud of him nonetheless. The cream of New York society—slightly bemused that one of their own wasn't even an officer, but a mere buck *sergeant*—attended his welcome-home party when he returned from Desert Storm, bedecked with medals and gleaming paratrooper's wings. With a singleness of purpose typically his own, Terry had accomplished every goal he had set for himself.

"I always wanted to be a cop," he said. "From the first time I looked up at that gigantic guy in blue and realized it was my own dad, that was it. And I never changed my mind. I thought I'd outgrow it, even tried to free myself of it, but I never could."

Remarkably, the rest of his life saw little deviation from its original course. I suppose that when you have a strong enough desire to do something, nothing can stand in your way. Especially if you're a guy like Terry.

"Amazing," Terry said, after I gave him the pre-1926-visit history of his life. "I seem to remember that my grandparents were able to put aside some money every week for years. They put it in the bank and never touched it until my dad was ready for college. It helped pay his way through Columbia.''

I chuckled. "Columbia? Your dad was an Ivy Leaguer, huh?''

"You've got to be kidding,'' he said.

"Nope.''

"Where?''

"CCNY,'' I replied. "Remember how you told me that tuition was free back then?''

"Just incredible. I guess that ten bucks a week we took back from that goniff sergeant really made a difference, didn't it?''

"Just a little.''

"It's really something, this time travel thing. I really ought to give it a try sometime. *Hinge-boy.*''

THIRTEEN

10 MARCH 1926—THE ALGONQUIN HOTEL

HINGE-BOY AND TERRY ARRIVED BACK AT MITCHELL'S room to find him packing. Actually, Althea was doing the packing. She reminded me of a young mother getting her son ready to go off to sleep-away camp.

"These socks go where?" she asked Mitchell.

"In the little pouch on the side," Mitch said, adding, "awesome, man!"

"What's awesome?" I asked.

"*Althea Rowland,* for God's sake, is doing my packing!"

"Sort of like Michelle Pfeiffer doing your laundry, huh, Mitch?" Terry asked.

"These're dirty," Althea said, holding up some shirts. "Okay if I just stuff 'em in here with the socks? You can send them out when you get to the hotel in Washington."

"Washington?" I asked.

"I have a meeting there," Mitch said.

"A meeting? Hello, Mitch, we're not in Century City. What's this all about?"

He picked up a small tape recorder from the nightstand.

"Mitch," I chided him, "you were distinctly told not to bring anything like that back with you."

He shrugged. "So sue me," he said.

"Mitch, you're a very high-maintenance customer, you know that?"

"Yeah, well, the customer's always right. Gimme a break, John. Here, listen."

The tape hissed for second and a voice said, "I'm very busy right now, if you don't mind."

"Nah, that's Lindbergh," he said, hitting the fast-forward.

"You're right," I exclaimed, "he *does* sound a bit like Judge Ito!"

"Okay, here it is."

OPERATOR: "BUREAU OF INVESTIGATION, HOW MAY I DIRECT YOUR CALL?"

MITCH: "DIRECTOR'S OFFICE, PLEASE."

OPERATOR: "ONE MOMENT PLEASE."

WILSON: "DIRECTOR'S OFFICE, SPECIAL AGENT WILSON SPEAKING."

MITCH: "THE DIRECTOR, PLEASE."

WILSON: "MAY I ASK WHO'S CALLING?"

MITCH: "NO."

WILSON: "THEN I CAN'T HELP YOU, SIR."

MITCH: "JUST ASK THE DIRECTOR IF HE KNOWS WHAT IT MEANS TO MISS NEW ORLEANS."

WILSON: "I DON'T THINK THE DIRECTOR—"

MITCH: "THAT'S NOT YOUR PROBLEM, SPECIAL AGENT WILSON. HOWEVER, IF I DON'T GET TO SPEAK TO MR. HOOVER WITHIN THE NEXT TEN SECONDS, IT WILL CERTAINLY BECOME YOUR PROBLEM."

"Hey, Mitch," I said admiringly. "I didn't know you could be such a hard-ass."

"I run a film studio," he replied. "I can be a prick when I have to."

WILSON: "CAN I HAVE THAT MESSAGE AGAIN?"

MITCH: " 'DO YOU KNOW WHAT IT MEANS TO MISS NEW ORLEANS?' "

WILSON: "JUST A MOMENT, PLEASE."

ON HOLD

"How long does he keep you waiting?" I asked.

"You'll see."

ON HOLD

WILSON: "UH, SIR? MR. HOOVER IS A LITTLE TIED-UP—"

MITCH: "WILSON, JUST TELL THAT OWL-FACED FUCK TO PICK UP THE PHONE."

WILSON: "WHOEVER YOU ARE, MISTER, I JUST HOPE FOR YOUR SAKE THAT YOU'RE PRETTY GODDAMNED IMPORTANT."

"Whoa, Mitch." I applauded.

HOOVER: "DIRECTOR SPEAKING."

MITCH: "JEDGAR . . . BUBELEH . . . LET'S DO LUNCH!"

HOOVER: "WHO THE HELL IS THIS?"

MITCH: "I'VE BEEN TO NEW ORLEANS, HOOVE-STER. LET'S HAVE A TALK."

HOOVER: "WHAT ABOUT?"

MITCH: "OH . . . THE FRENCH QUARTER . . . AN-TOINE'S . . . HUEY LONG . . . NEW ORLEANS IS A GREAT TOWN, AND I THINK WE HAVE LOTS TO TALK ABOUT."

HOOVER: "I DON'T KNOW WHAT YOU'RE TALK-ING ABOUT AND I'M A VERY BUSY—"

MITCH: "YOU'RE NOT THAT BUSY, HOOVE. AND YOU KNOW DAMN WELL WHAT I'M TALKING ABOUT. UNLESS YOU DOUBT THE *NEW YORK TIMES* MIGHT BE A LITTLE MORE INTERESTED IN WHAT—"

HOOVER: "OKAY. WHERE AND WHEN?"

MITCH: "OH, LET'S MAKE IT DRAMATIC. (EF-

FEMINATE VOICE) YOU SEE, WHAT WE'RE GOING FOR HERE, EDGAR, IS A SORT OF CINEMA-VERITÉ, THAT'S NOT TO SAY A FILM-NOIR TYPE OF QUALITY. (REGULAR VOICE) SO, LET'S MAKE IT THE LINCOLN MEMORIAL, TOMORROW AT MIDNIGHT.''

HOOVER: (PAUSE) "ALL RIGHT."

MITCH: "AND, HOOVEMEISTER?"

HOOVER: "YEAH."

MITCH: "COME ALONE."

HOOVER: "YEAH." (HANGS UP)

MITCH: "SURE YOU WILL."

"What are your plans, Mitch?" I asked after a long silence.

"I just wanna talk to him. That's all."

"You know he won't be alone."

"I'm aware of that." He clapped his hands together and rubbed them gleefully. "But I won't be alone, either. I have you guys, don't I? You can handle a few 1926 wussy-boys, can't you?"

I looked at Terry, who nodded. "I suppose we have no choice, John."

Althea gave me a dangerous glare that said, don't even *dream* of leaving me out of this caper. "Okay, we'll figure out how to proceed when we get to Washington. Anybody has any ideas, we'll talk about it then. Mitch, what about Dottie?"

He shrugged. "Dottie is Dottie. I don't think it's going to work out."

I was flabbergasted; after all, he had wanted her so badly.

"I may not be Mr. Romance, John," Mitch said, "but I don't walk right into getting hurt if I don't have to. And I don't have to. She likes her life. She needs drama, maybe even melodrama, for better or worse. It's just the way she is. I care for her a lot, but I have a funny feeling she'd take too much out of me. And anyway, she told me there's no way in hell she'd come back to '07 with me."

This was not what I had expected. I was prepared for a major depression on his part if Dorothy Parker didn't work out.

Mitchell read my thoughts. "I may not know much about women, John, but I know enough to back off when a woman's going to be bad for me."

"Aren't you hurt?"

"Hell, yes, I'm hurt. But I'll get over it."

"And what if she comes around after all?"

He brightened. "Well, then the situation would be drastically altered, wouldn't it?"

I punched him on the shoulder, a gesture of surrender. "Like I said, Mitch, it never really was Dottie, was it? It was for Harry all along."

"True," he said. "But if it turns out that Dottie was just protecting herself from getting hurt, we may have another passenger when we go home."

11 MARCH 1926—WASHINGTON, D.C.— THE WILLARD HOTEL

The Civil War was not my area of historical expertise, but I had studied it enough to know two things: 1) I could have never taken up arms against my fellow Americans, rebellious or not; and 2) I was impressed to a fare-thee-well by the history that dwelt within the walls of the Willard Hotel.

I doubt there was ever a Civil War novel written that didn't mention the Willard in some aspect or other. The class lodging in Washington before it was surpassed by the Mayflower, it was one of the first hotels on the continent to boast indoor plumbing and central heating. Even during the Civil War, if you could afford it, rooms with toilets and showers were available.

These conveniences were considerably updated by 1926, but there was still a hushed sense of history. Everyone who was anyone in American history of a certain era had stayed here.

But I didn't have much time to enjoy my surroundings. My client, whose very safety was in my hands, was off to meet with a dangerous and desperate character.

Relations between Althea and me were by now some-what strained. I put it down to nerves, but I was smart enough to know that I'd better not annoy her by being overprotective, no matter how much it hurt. I therefore bought my way back into her temporarily good graces when I laid out our plan of action.

"You and Althea will be strolling arm in arm in front of the Memorial," I began.

Mitch looked at Althea and smiled. "No-o-o problem," he sang.

"I appreciate your vote of confidence, John," she said, slightly surprised.

"It'll just work better. Hoover'll expect you to be alone. I want the element of surprise on our side, not his."

"Nothing personal, Althea," Terry said, "and don't get mad at me, but, John, are you sure you want her on the front line?"

"No, I don't. But it's the best way. And if Hoover puts her in any danger at all, I'll kill him."

"Thank you, I'm sure," Althea said, rolling her eyes. "Really, John, could you for once dispense with this . . . Terry?"

"Macho bullshit?" he offered.

"The very thing."

I ignored it. "Terry, you and I will be providing flank security. He's going to have other guys at his back, and we'll have to take them out first."

" 'Take them out?' " Althea asked.

"Tase them," I replied. "Not hurt them."

"I'm glad to hear it."

"We'll keep the area clear for you, Mitch," I continued,

"but don't expect anything to come of it. Hoover was never a man to reason with."

"I'll take care of Hoover," he said dismissively. "You know, I wish we had a dog."

"A dog? What for?"

"It'd just look better if we were walking a dog."

"Don't worry, Mitch," Althea said. "I'll be there."

"You're no dog."

"And thank goodness," she replied.

LINCOLN MEMORIAL

Through Terry's night-vision binoculars, I could see Mitch and Althea strolling in front of the steps of the Memorial. They appeared to be talking earnestly, but I wondered if Althea was just mumbling "rhubarb-rhubarb-rhubarb," an old movie-extra trick to make it look like you were actually having a conversation in the background of the shot.

The bushes rustled and Terry crawled up next to me.

"Okay, do you see them?" he asked.

"I count three," I said.

"Show me."

I handed Terry the binoculars. "One, at the top of the steps, keeps looking at his watch. Two, the drunk on the bench they keep passing. He looked sober enough before they got here. Three, in the Ford near the grass over there. How'm I doing?"

"Good, but you missed one. Over by the Reflecting Pool, but I got him already. I checked his ID: that was Mitch's phone pal, Wilson."

"How do you want to play this?"

"You get the guy in the Ford. Then I want to take out the guy on top of the steps at exactly the same time you get the 'drunk.' "

The guy in the Model T was already asleep. He was

snoring fitfully, his mouth wide open. He barely flinched when I shot him in the arm with my Taser.

Mitch and Althea saw us coming but had been briefed in advance not to take any notice. Terry climbed the top of the stairs to the monument, taking a pack of cigarettes from his pocket.

"Excuse me, do you have a light?" he asked as he approached the agent. My drunk's head shot up, but I tased him immediately. Terry's man took a step forward but was dropped in another instant by Terry's charged .45. I pulled the "drunk" off the bench and settled him into the bushes then took his place on the bench. Terry took up the station of the agent he had rendered unconscious.

This had all happened within a few seconds. We were still twenty minutes early, but we were sure that Hoover hadn't the wit to show up before then while he had men already staking the place out. To be truthful, neither Terry nor I had much respect for Hoover's ability as a street cop; in all honesty, we doubted he had much courage.

All was in readiness. We all began to feel a little on edge as zero hour approached. Mitch and Althea's practiced stroll became a bit less natural, I began to drift in and out of my newly assumed drunk character, and Terry's patrol became a bit more impatient.

Hoover was late. We had staked out the Lincoln Memorial for more than an hour, and Hoover was at least forty-five minutes overdue.

Finally, Terry signalled us all to join him at the top of the steps.

"What do you think?" I asked him.

"Let's blow it off," Terry said decisively. "He's not coming."

"Or else, he smells a rat."

"Oh, yes, I certainly do smell a rat," a voice came from behind us. "A big, fat rat."

We turned and saw J. Edgar Hoover holding us at gunpoint.

"How'd he get the drop on us?" Terry wondered aloud.

"Never mind that," Hoover barked. "Hands up!"

We all complied, except for Terry, who held his more out to the side.

"Which one of you called me today?" Hoover demanded.

"Nobody say anything," I said sharply. "Not a word." With the information Mitch possessed, he could destroy Hoover, and the Bureau Director knew it. There was absolutely nothing to stop him from putting a few holes in Mitch to keep him quiet.

"Mr. Hoover," Althea cooed in the style of a Southern belle, "you look just the way you look—in the papers, I mean." She smiled at him flirtatiously.

"Shut up, bitch," he snapped.

The snub-nosed .38 in Hoover's hand was the only thing between him and my beating him senseless right then and there. I turned to Althea, wanting to comfort her, but I saw that she had only cocked an eyebrow and twitched her lips in a smile of new understanding.

"My word," she continued in her Scarlett O'Hara voice. "Ah sometimes seem to forget that some men just aren't the marryin' kind."

"Shut her up," Hoover demanded.

She put a hand over her breast. "Mah stars, what a sad day fo' American womanhood."

He tried to ignore her. "Now somebody tell me what all this is—"

"Mr. Hoover," Althea O'Hara interrupted, "tell me it's just me, personally. A big—well, a strong man like you, gettin' rid a all them awful communists, I just can't believe it. Why, any woman in the country would just dream—"

"Shut her up or I will," Hoover shouted.

"Tell me, Mr. Hoover," Althea persisted, her voice dropping to a confidential tone, "jes' betwixt us girls, do you like the skinny the-ay-ter types, or the big ath-a-letic—"

With a strange gurgling noise in his throat, Hoover

charged at Althea, the gun held high like a club. He was about to pistol-whip her across the face when he stopped suddenly, a confused look crossing his features. He fell to the ground, so hard that he bounced.

Terry's .45 caliber stun gun was smoking.

"Nice job, Althea," he said admiringly.

She spread her hands. "Am I good? I ask you, am I good or what?"

A wave of relief washed over me. "You were baiting him," I said. "You probed and you found a weakness, then you exploited it." Jesus, I thought, not for the first time, what a woman! Was there anything she *couldn't* do?

"We need a nice long vacation, you and I," I told her.

She kissed me. "Thanks, John, for not interfering and letting me run with it."

"I never horn in on a great performance," I said. "Let's—oh, shit." In our relief and self-congratulations, we had forgotten about Mitch. He had straddled the unconscious Hoover and was slapping his face.

"Wake up! Wake up, you pig-eyed sack a shit!"

In the other hand, he held Hoover's gun.

"Wake up, you prick! I want you to see it coming!"

"Mitch! What're you doing!" I shouted.

"Stay back! Stay back or I'll blow his head off right now! I mean it, John. Terry, don't move."

"What're your plans, Mitch?" Terry asked calmly.

"I want to kill this son of a bitch! All the lives he ruined, including Harry's. And for what? For nothing! For almost fifty years this bastard held the country hostage, *presidents* were afraid to fire him. Everybody was a communist spy to this creep. And did he once, ever, uncover a single communist plot? Once? Never! Oh, but he had the goods on everybody. And in the meantime, gangsters knew he was gay and held it over him. Did he resign, like a man of honor? No! He let then have their way!"

"Mitch," I said calmly. "You're not going to kill him. I can't let you do it."

"Oh, because he's a cop? You guys all stick together, is that it?"

"No, Mitch. This guy's no cop. He doesn't even belong in America, as far as I'm concerned. He'd be more at home in Nazi Germany or Soviet Russia. It's not for moral reasons. I can't let you kill him because it wouldn't make a difference."

"How do you know?"

"It's not always the man, Mitch. Sometimes, it's just the climate of the era. There's always somebody else, another power-mad lunatic, ready to step in and do exactly the same thing."

"Bull-shit!" Mitch exclaimed. "What if somebody killed Hitler? Would it still be the same? Would it even have happened?"

"It wouldn't be the same, Mitch," Terry said quietly. "It'd be worse."

"How could it be worse?"

"Because it was."

THE WILLARD HOTEL

Hoover was gagged, with his hands bound by plastic handcuffs. Mitch, who was drinking a scotch on the rocks to calm himself down, dipped into his glass, picked up a piece of cracked ice, and flicked it at Hoover. There was murder in Hoover's eyes.

"Shut up," Mitch snapped at Hoover. "Now, John, what Terry said before, was that true? Or did you just say that to get me off of him?"

"It was true," Terry said quietly. "How much do you remember, John?"

I thought hard. "I just remember being in Munich, in our room of that Gasthaus near the Marienplatz. You had a Browning Mark II Safari Rifle, .308 semiauto with a Swarovski scope. I was spotting for you with a pair of Zeiss binoculars. We were just about to do it when—''

"Cornelia barged in," Terry said. "She was the hinge."

"When was this?" Althea wanted to know.

"Right after we rescued you from 1940," I said. "Remember, Doc Harvey insisted that they put you in the hospital overnight? That's when we went off and did it."

"I don't understand," Mitch said. "You were gonna kill Hitler?"

"Of course we were," Terry said. "And, apparently, we did."

"Mitch," I said, "isn't that the first question anyone asks about time travel? *If you could do it, wouldn't you go back and kill Hitler? Whatever the consequences?* Well, that's something Terry and I had been asking ourselves ever since we first started this gig."

"I had no idea," Althea said.

"Nobody did. Except Cornelia. Hell, it was easy. When we came to get you, the Zoom Room was moved lock, stock, and barrel to the London suburbs. We zoomed back to 1923, and from there getting to Munich was no problem."

"1923?" Mitch asked. "Why 1923?"

"The Putsch," Terry explained. "The Nazis tried to take over the city government. They thought the cops would back them up. Instead, the police fired on them. They weren't big enough then, I guess. Anyway, when the shooting started, that's when we made our move. In all the confusion, no one would know where our bullets came from."

"Man, it was perfect," I continued. "Adolf was right there, standing in the back, of course. He looked like such a putz, a nobody. Like the kind of guy, if you sat next to him in the movies, you could muscle the armrest away from him and not worry about it."

"I had the semiauto because I needed to be sure with two quick shots," Terry remarked. "I was using hollow-points that I reloaded myself. Not so great for accuracy, but it was only a couple hundred yards.''

''Terry owned him'' I said. ''I scanned the crowd, and when I found him, I froze for a second. But only a second. I gave Terry his coordinates, and this I remember, Terry said something in Yiddish—''

''I did? That I don't remember.''

''You probably thought you were only thinking it, but it came out. Then you said, 'You're *mine*, you monster.' ''

''There's a million swear words in the world,'' Terry said with a bewildered look on his face, ''but 'monster' was the only fitting word I could come up with. There just wasn't an obscenity that was strong enough.''

''So what happened, for God's sake?'' Mitch demanded.

Terry and I looked at each other. ''I got him,'' Terry said softly. ''There's a part of me that remembers, two quick shots.''

''What were you thinking?''

''You want the truth? I mean. I would have thought that I'd've said something vengeful and profound. Something for the ages. But my first thought was, 'Nice grouping.' '' He looked at us apologetically.

''It was,'' I said, covering for him. ''Two shots in a circle the size of a nickel. Of course, with what was left of Adolf's head—''

''We can well imagine *that*, John,'' Althea said. ''But he was dead?''

''It's all hazy,'' I said. ''I have to really concentrate to remember it. Because what is much more clear is Cornelia stopping us.''

''Why would she do that?'' Mitch wondered.

''Ernst Gerhardt.''

''Who the hell is Ernst Gerhardt?''

''As it stands now, nobody. A failed actor who was a minor SS official. But he was the new front man they came up with. All the smart guys, like Strasser, and the dangerous guys, like Roehm, all backed him up. They came to power the same way they did originally. Gerhardt was the same kind of guy as Hitler. He didn't have his animal charisma, but he had more charm. The difference was that he didn't bump off all his friends in 1934, on the Night of the Long Knives, like Hitler did. But worst of all, Gerhardt was smart enough to let the military fight its own war. Without Hitler's meddling, like when he made Guderian halt his tanks at Dunkirk, the British and the French were completely defeated. There *was* no 'Miracle of Dunkirk.' ''

Althea's eyes were wet. ''You mean, the British surrendered?''

''They had nothing left to fight with, which means that the Nazis held on to North Africa. As for the Russian front, they probed it, staying close to their supply line. There was no 'hold or die' order; Stalingrad never happened.''

''What about the . . . Holocaust?''

''Worse,'' Terry said. ''There was no SS, and without Hitler, Himmler was just a mid-level officer in the SA. But Roehm proved every bit as bloodthirsty.''

I looked at Althea. We had thus far kept all that from her, but she didn't like the sound of any of it.

''More than bloodthirsty,'' Terry said, ''because America never got into the war to stop him.''

''What about the Japanese?''

''Gerhardt believed that the Pact of Steel should be more than just useless words on paper, and he established a much closer working relationship with the Japanese. Unlike Hitler, he really didn't care all that much about the racial issue. He just wanted the power. He asked the Japanese not to involve America in the war—that time would come, and when it did, the Japanese could attack from the Pacific and the Germans could invade on the Atlantic side. So there was no Pearl Harbor. The Japanese instead turned eastward, and *did* eventually link up with the Germans in India.''

''When did America get into the war?''

''We'll never know,'' I said. ''Because Cornelia, being

the hinge, found out exactly where it went sour—or more sour, anyway—and made us give it up.''

Terry and I were silent for a minute. We were exhausted.

''Drink,'' I said.

''Drink,'' said Terry.

Mitch poured us both a couple of healthy ones. ''This is all quite fascinating,'' Mitch said, ''and certainly worth a movie, but where does that leave us with him?'' He jerked a thumb toward Hoover.

''He's going to go on,'' I said tiredly. ''He's going to abuse his power, and he's going to hurt people. He'll create one of the finest investigative organizations in the world, and for that you have to give him credit. But there's no point in taking him out. Someone else'll just step into his''—I looked down at Hoover's feet—''surprisingly small shoes.''

''But what about Harry?''

''You can try,'' I warned him. ''But he's awfully mad at you. He might take it out on Harry.''

''Oh, Christ,'' Mitch sighed miserably. ''What the hell, it's worth a try. Hoover! Hoover, you listening?''

''MMMMFG! MMMFFG!'' Hoover screamed against his gag.

''I was gonna take that off,'' Mitch said, ''but you just blew that.'' He stopped and put a hand to his forehead, as if in deep thought. ''And speaking of *blowing* . . .''

''MMMMMMFG! MMMMMFG!''

''Hey, Hoove, we're all liberals here. At least, when it comes to that. We're all very enlightened, don't-ask/don't-tell and all that. But it's funny, you of all people, in addition to your many other character flaws, are also homophobic.'' He turned to me. ''You may be the boss historian around here, John, but I did my homework on this guy. He and Clyde''—he turned to Hoover—''that's Clyde Tolson, Hoove. As in 'Someday, my prince will come.' Well, in your case, in about two more years.

''Anyway, Jedgar and Clyde were the worst fag-bashers

imaginable. They even used to bust gay bars. And when they got that kind of dirt on somebody, watch out! It's kind of a self-hating thing, isn't it?''

"Must be," I replied. "I think your average headshrinker would have a picnic with this guy's neurosis."

Mitch drew a flimsy piece of paper from his pocket. "See this, Mr. Hoover? This is an incident report from the New Orleans Police Department. It cost me a great deal of time and money, but was it ever worth it."

"MMMMMMFG!"

"Shut up. I'm doing the talking here. The charge is 'lewd public behavior,' but what it basically translates into is that the cops caught you soliciting a male prostitute."

"MMMMFG!"

"All right, Hoove, I'll take off the gag." He nodded to Terry, who drew out his .45, which Hoover thought was a real gun. "If you make one single sound, I'll have him blast you. Okay? Blink once for yes."

Hoover blinked. Mitch removed the gag.

"That was a setup," Hoover rasped. "It's a fake!"

"Edgar, if it had been a girl, it would be a setup. But you solicited the guy. You approached *him*."

"How do I know that isn't a forgery?"

I took the copy of the report out of my pocket, the one that Chief Blaine had gotten for me. "Because I have a copy of it, too. Also, courtesy of the NOPD."

"Edgar," Mitch said, almost kindly, "nobody has a problem with your being a homosexual. God bless ya, that's your lifestyle."

"I'm not a f—"

"Fine. Whatever. Our problem with you is that you are not fit to hold the office with which you have been entrusted. But there's nothing we can do about that. We can't even tell you not to go after commies or not to spy on just about everybody who catches your attention. But what I can tell you is that this incident report will go out

to every single newpaper in America if you do one thing
to Har—''

"Mitch?'' I became worried. Mitch had stopped talking
and sat down, facing away from Hoover. "Mitch, are you
okay?''

"I can't do it.''

"It's okay, Mitch,'' Althea said. "You don't have to.''

"If I tell him to stay away from Har—Grampa, you
know what'll happen. He'll be all over him like . . . Jesus,
I can't even come up with a good simile. He's crazy. And
worse, he's scared and crazy.''

"Scared, crazy, and powerful,'' Terry amended.

"What do you want to do, Mitch?'' I asked.

"It's not what I want to do. It's what I have to do.''

"Let it go?''

"Let it go.''

Terry put his arm across Mitch's shoulder. "Welcome to
the club,'' he said.

The question now, of course, was what to do with Hoover.
We had the son of a bitch; we weren't going to kill, damage, or blackmail him. But we also couldn't just shove him
in a closet—you should pardon the expression—and leave
him there, as tempting an idea as that was.

"I've got to do *something* to the no-good bastard,''
Mitch said, regarding our prisoner, who was gagged once
again. "I have to ruin his whole week. It's not much of a
revenge, compared to what he's going to do to people, but
it'll at least be something. I nccd closure, can you understand that?''

"What about—'' Terry began.

"I appreciate it Terry,'' Mitch interrupted, "but this is
my party. I want to think it up.''

"Do what you have to do, Mitch,'' Terry replied approvingly.

"What we need here,'' Mitch said, "is a little poetic
justice.''

"How about we dump him in the men's room of the nearest gay bar?" Terry asked.

Mitch shook his head. "No good. Knowing this creep, he'd take it out on them. I don't want a bunch of innocent gay guys getting hurt."

Hoover struggled against his bonds.

"Look at his mug," Mitch said with an ironic smile. "He's all red in the fa—yes!"

"Yes, what?"

"Is this the only phone in the place? Go pick up the extension." Mitch dialed the hotel operator. "Operator, get me the Russian Embassy—all right, the Soviet Union, whatever. Just ring it for me? Thank you."

"Embassy of the Union of Soviet Socialist Republics," a heavily accented female voice answered. "Good morning."

"Good morning," Mitch greeted heartily. "This is Special Agent Wilson of the Bureau of Investigation. Which one of you commies is in charge of spies?"

"I beg your pardon, Mr. Wilson, I am not . . . mmm-wah . . . familiar with your agency."

Mitch held the speaker part of the phone over his chest. "Ever notice," he said to me, "how Russians always make that 'mmmmweeah' sound when they're stumped for an English word? Only Russians, nobody else." He spoke back into the phone. "Bureau of Investigation. It's not so famous right now, but when we change it to the *FBI*, it'll scare everyone shitless. Especially you guys."

"Pliz, Mr. . . . mmm . . . Wilson, pliz state the nature of your call. I know of no 'Bureau of Investigation.'"

"Yeah, sure, like you never heard of borscht. Just put the head spy on the phone, ma'am. I'm sure *he's* heard of us."

There was a short wait before the phone was picked up again. "Mr. Wilson?" a male voice with almost no accent at all came on the phone. "I am Iosif Antonov, Cultural Attaché. How may I be of assistance?"

"Iosif. That's Russky for Joseph, right?"

"If you like."

"So, Joey, you're the cultural attaché. That's head spook, right?"

"I beg your pardon, Mr. Wilson."

"Spy. You're the spy guy, right?" Mitch was having a great old time for himself.

"The Soviet Union has no spies, Mr. Wilson. Certainly not in America."

Mitch laughed. "Yeah, and I'm the man in the moon. Listen, Joe, seriously, we've got one a your spies here."

Hoover shrieked into his gag.

"Not one of ours, Mr. Wilson."

"I don't know, Joey. He's got that kinda thick head, fat butt, belly-over-the-belt thing working there. Looks Russian to me."

"None of that makes him a spy, Mr. Wilson," Antonov replied, offended.

"Joe. Help me out, okay? I'm trying to do the right thing here. We've got our own problems, you've got your own problems. I don't need this crap right now. If he's one of yours, I'm offering you the chance to take him home. No strings."

"I'm sorry, Mr. Wilson, what means 'no strings'?"

"You don't have to give us anything in return."

"I find that hard to believe, Mr. Wilson. Your director, Mr. Hoover, is a well-known anticommunist—"

"Yeah, but he's feeling mellow today." He looked over at an almost apoplectic Hoover. "Believe me, Joe, Hoover has full knowledge of what I'm doing."

"MMMMMMMMMPPPH!" Hoover roared.

"How did you apprehend this man, Mr. Wilson?"

Mitch looked warily at Hoover. "Joe. My Russian is nonexistent. *Sprechen Sie Deutsch?*"

"*Ein biBchen,*" he replied, surprised. "*Warum?*"

I grabbed a piece of hotel stationery and scribbled quickly.

"The walls have ears, Joey," Mitch said. I handed him the scrap of paper, which he read quickly. He glanced at me questioningly and I nodded.

"How did you apprehend him?" Antonov repeated.

"Er ist schwul," Mitch said, translating in a whisper, "he's gay."

"Ne!" exclaimed Antonov. *"Schwul? Ne! Du Schlaukopf!"*

"I'm not being a wise guy, Joe. *Sehr schwul,*" Mitch assured him.

Hoover was listening intently now. Fortunately, he didn't understand German.

"His . . . habits notwithstanding, Mr. Wilson, he's not one of ours."

"Joe, where's the harm? Just check his identification against your records, badaboom, and if he's clean, badabing, let him go."

"And if he is, as you say, one of ours, then we will have admitted to espionage in the United States. A clear admission of guilt to the very agency charged with the apprehension of spies."

"Hello! Joey! What is this, *Curious George*, here? Everybody knows you have spies. You're *Russia*, for Christ's sake. That's your *business.*" Mitch looked down at the paper I had given him. "Of course, what everyone *doesn't* know is that your Soviet Union is allowing the German Army to train on top secret bases right in your own backyard—in direct violation of the Versailles Treaty."

"That is a lie!" Antonov shouted.

"Then what are you bellowing about? Joe, just do me a favor? Then I'll owe you one. Fair enough? Unless you want photographs and documents proving the existence of a German military training on Russian soil? I wonder what the League of Nations would say about all that?"

"Then you must give me the documents, the photographs, and all negatives."

"Eeeeennnnt!" Mitch made a game-show buzzer sound. "I'm sorry, Joey, the correct answer is 'Thank you, Wilson, we'll pick up the son of a bitch in two hours.' "

There was a long pause. "Someday, Mr. Wilson," Antonov said evenly, "we must meet."

"Hey, I'm looking forward to it."

"As you say, Mr. Wilson, we'll 'pick up the son of a bitch in two hours.' "

"Love ya, Joe. And, Joey?"

"Yes, Mr. Wilson," Antonov said with obvious fatigue in his voice.

"Don't get purged." He hung up. "God, that was fun! How'd ya like that Antonov? Was he a pisser or what?"

"He seemed like a pretty good guy, considering the circumstances."

"I wonder whatever became of him," Mitch said.

"We can look it up when we get back," I said.

"Hoover!" Mitch shook him. "It's time to say good night. I hope you have nice visit at the Russian Embassy."

"MMMMMMMMMFG!"

"I know just how you feel," Mitch said, falsely comforting. "But you're going to screw up the lives of a lot of decent people. I just want you to experience the feeling."

He nodded at Terry, who zapped Hoover unconscious with his Taser.

"You must love your job," Mitch said to me.

"It has its moments," I replied.

We sat in the lobby watching the action from the vantage point of a comfortable lounge area hidden by palm fronds. Mitch had left word at the desk to send a Mr. Antonov right up to the suite.

Antonov was easy enough to spot. He was tall and slender, with high Slavic cheekbones and icy blue eyes. He moved like a man on a mission, followed by three loutish subordinates who couldn't have been more obvious if they wore name tags that said "Hello! I'm *Boris*!"

Mitch laughed to himself and leaned back with a good Cuban cigar. "Ah, the human comedy," he pronounced. "I couldn't dream of putting this in a movie, nobody'd believe it."

Five minutes later, the three dress extras returned to the lobby. Two of them were supporting the unconscious Hoover, who had an arm draped across each of their shoulders. The third man walked in front of them, occasionally turning back to Hoover with a scolding expression, to convey the idea that they were taking home a friend who had over-indulged himself.

"Hmmmm! Interesting," Mitch remarked. "Where's Antonov?"

Terry's hand suddenly snaked under his coat.

"Mr. Wilson?"

Antonov was standing behind us.

Terry allowed the butt of his .45 to peek from under his jacket.

Antonov threw up his hands in a nonthreatening gesture. Terry smiled tightly, just enough to let Antonov know he'd be a fool to try anything. Antonov, comprehending this instantly, nodded to Terry and took a seat next to Mitch.

"I'm Wilson. How are you, Joey?" The two shook hands.

"I had to meet you, Mr. Wilson," he said. He dipped his head in a courtly gesture to Althea.

"Can I offer you a cigar?" Mitch asked.

Antonov took out a gold cigarette case and lit up. "You can get good cigars anywhere," he told Mitchell. "Only in America can you get decent cigarettes."

"I know you're just dying for me to ask, Joey, so I will. How'd you know me?"

Antonov shook his head, one professional surprised by a deficiency in the other. "Why, the same way you knew me, Mr. Wilson. You were looking for me. I was looking for someone who would be looking for me."

Mitch blinked his eyes and waggled his head as if to

clear it. " 'The Headstrongs married the Armstrongs,' " he quoted to me. He faced Antonov. "What can I do for you?"

"Well, I want to thank you, personally," Antonov began. "But I am curious. Is there a coup d'etat going on at your agency?"

Mitch was about to answer, but I cut him off, sensing trouble. "Why do you ask?"

"And you are?"

"An associate."

Antonov glanced at me, then back at Mitch, trying to get a feel for where the true power rested. He settled on me.

"Very well. Why have you turned over the director of your agency to my embassy?"

"Because he's a hump," Mitch snapped.

Antonov had already discounted Mitch, but was probably a student of American slang. "What means 'hump'?"

"Just what it sounds like," I said. "Do you want the hump or not?"

"You have a term in America, something about a 'gift horse.' "

"Just scare him a little," Mitch said. "Give him some vodka, throw him down the stairs a few times. Yell in his face that he's going to talk, but don't ask him any questions. Make him pee all over himself."

Antonov smiled, the smile of a man who was in for the better end of a deal. "And why would I want to do your work for you?"

I started to reply, but Mitch waved me off. "Here's the problem, Joe. We're a young organization. Much like yours. And what we have is a conflict of objectives. Hoover thinks you guys are the problem. He thinks that you commies are gonna come in and change the national anthem to the *Internationale*."

"And you, Mr. Wilson?"

"Well, I think that's what you'd *like* to do. However, I believe you have two things working against you. One,

Americans themselves just don't like communists. We're a free people, Joey, we hate it when the government tells us what to do. We've fought wars over that. And unlike you, we were born free. We know what it means and we'd never give it up, not without a fight that you would lose even if you won. Secondly? Well, it'll take time, but your system just won't work.''

Antonov was taken aback. "As you Americans are so fond of saying, 'bullshit.' ''

"Not at all. You're all spying on each other. One in five—'' He looked to me for approval, and I nodded. "One in five of you is on the government rolls as some kind of operative. What country can afford that? Meanwhile, your natural resources go unharvested while your nation spends all of its budget on defense and internal security. Sooner or later, Joe, we're gonna beat you. Not on the battlefield, always a transitory victory at best, but in your wallet. We'll bankrupt you.''

Antonov nodded smugly. "Typical capitalist argument. The almighty dollar rules again.''

"And don't you forget it, Joe. People can't eat ideology. Anyway, our immediate problem is this: Hoover thinks you guys are the Great Satan. And, nothing personal, but we think you're simply schmucks, and anyway, you've got problems of your own. We think Hoover is wasting our time, and our mission. We want to catch crooks. He thinks it's a job for the local cops. I keep telling him, 'What if a crook leaves one jurisdiction to go to another? Who can catch him?' Look what the automobile has done for this country. You can rob a bank in, say, Chicago, and be in Philadelphia twenty-four hours later. The Chicago cops can't touch you and neither can the Philly cops.''

"A problem,'' Antonov commiserated. "But what am I supposed to do with your boss? And how may I benefit?''

"Commies may not be popular in this country, Joe, but nowhere is it illegal to be a member of the Communist Party. We frankly don't care what you do, as long as you don't hurt anybody. We'll leave you alone. The Communist Party will never amount to anything in America, so what do we give a shit? We've got crooks to catch."

Antonov stubbed out his cigarette in a floor ashtray. "You're so sure our system is no good. Why is it so popular in other countries?"

Mitch grunted disparagingly. "That's Europe. Most Americans came from Europe and are happy as hell to be out of there. Study the American character, Joey. Get out of Washington, get in your car and drive around this country. Visit the people and ask them. Don't argue Marx at polite cocktail parties. Visit small towns and farms and cities, and especially with the first generation citizens who get lumps in their throats when a breeze catches the flag and makes it wave." He jerked a thumb toward the door. "And that's why we've got to get rid of *him*. He loves America because it's his home, but he's an enemy of freedom, and without freedom, there is no America."

Antonov snorted derisively.

"I know, it sounds like patriotic, flag-waving tripe, but go see for yourself. One of these days, I wouldn't be surprised if you turned up at one of our embassies with a suitcase in your hand."

Antonov stood up. "I'll do what you ask, Mr. Wilson."

Mitch rose and stuck out his hand. "I appreciate it, Joey."

"But only because I can see that you are a good and decent man, doing the wrong thing for the right reasons." He smiled ruefully. "Why is it," he asked, "that so often I find more honor amongst my enemies than my friends?"

Mitch laughed. "Maybe you need new friends."

Antonov bowed to us. "Till we meet again," he said.

"It may be a while," I said.

"I have time," he replied.

"So do we," Mitch said. "So do we."

FOURTEEN

12 MARCH 1926—THE WILLARD HOTEL

ALTHEA AND I WERE IN BED. I HAD BETRAYED MY FELLOW
males and was oddly satisfied to be merely cuddling. The
fact was that after our meeting with Antonov, all four us
were so overcome by fatigue that we could barely keep our
eyes open.

"We'll have to be leaving soon, won't we?" Althea
asked with a deep yawn.

"I think so," I said, temporarily halting my fall into the
chasm of sleep. "Remember when we first met how tired
I became, seemingly out of nowhere?"

"You fell asleep on my couch, right in the middle of a
sentence."

"It's time travel. There's something about it that ener-
vates you."

"I think I know what it is," Althea said, snuggling up
against me. "Do you get more tired the further back you
go?"

I hadn't actually thought about that before, but on earlier
trips to periods that weren't so markedly different, such as

the late seventies, I had never experienced this level of exhaustion. "I think so," I said.

"It's probably because your mind has to work so much harder," she said. "Everywhere you go, even the smallest of things are different. It's a lot for your mind to constantly take in and adjust." She yawned again. "Makes me tired just to think about it."

There was a silence and soon I could hear her measured breathing. She was asleep. I closed my eyes and, as if my body were responding instantly to a command, I was asleep, too.

"Twenty-plus bandits heading two-three-zero. Angels fourteen. Squadrons 72, 78, and 249 A Flight, scramble."

I sat up in bed. Althea was asleep, but she was speaking in urgent but controlled tones. I had never heard her talk in her sleep before.

"No, sir."

She was speaking clearly, replaying a conversation that had taken place before, providing gaps in the places that I guessed were where she had received an answer.

"No, 78 Squadron is refueling . . . Wait, they can send up B Flight."

I shook her gently. Her eyes flickered open. "What?" she asked in a sleepy, almost childlike voice, a strange juxtaposition to the clear and loud tones of her dream.

"You were talking in your sleep," I said.

"I was? What about?"

"I guess you were at the Station Command Center. You were reporting on the disposition of planes during a raid I suppose."

"Oh." She rubbed an eye. "I go there a lot when I'm asleep."

I sat up in bed. "You miss it, don't you?"

She shook a cigarette from the pack on the night table and lit one. "I still feel like I'm AWOL. Sometimes I feel like I'm cutting school during exams. Or as if it's long past dinnertime, it's getting dark, and I'm still out playing."

"I know," I said.

"I know I've been a little . . . distant, recently. I know I've been a little rough on you. But it isn't you, John. It's me. I'm just not sure where I fit in anymore."

"You fit in fine with me."

"That's easy enough for you to say," she snapped. "You weren't dead." She patted my shoulder. "I'm sorry. I didn't mean for it to come out like that. It's just that sometimes I'm so damned . . . confused. And I hate that. I've never been confused about anything, least of all, the way I feel about you. And then I think about the war, and all those people still in the fight, and I feel like I'm playing hooky. Only everybody's dying and I'm safe."

I took a deep breath. "So, you want to go back, is that it?"

"Part of me does. The other part wants to be by your side. Have your children. You ever think about having kids?"

I shook my head. "When I was married, in my early twenties, sure I thought about it. I got divorced, but I figured I'd meet somebody else pretty soon. Then time went by and I never did get remarried. I stopped thinking about it. To tell you the truth, seeing people my age with kids all the time began to annoy me. I don't know why, it just got on my nerves. And then, when I got assigned to Juvey and saw all those mutilated kids and their mutilated lives, the last thing I wanted was to bring another child into the world. After a while, I figured I'd be a Henry Higgins type of bachelor, except that I'd get laid every now and then. And then somewhere far down the road, when it got so even I couldn't stand it anymore, I'd get married and start a family, later on in life. I was resigned to eventually becoming a white-hair/high-chair kind of dad."

Althea giggled. " 'White-hair/high-chair'?"

"Yeah, you know those older guys, still in good shape but let's face it, older. They have kids in their sixties and give them obscure names out of history or Greek mythology and nobody understands the wit of it, not even their wives. They marry some young trophy wife who they manage to convince themselves has more brains than she really does—and that the money means absolutely nothing, she'd love him just the same no matter what.''

"Jesus, John, that's a lot to look forward to," she said sarcastically.

"Well, I got used to being alone, and I liked the freedom. It wasn't until you came along that I decided to get involved without even thinking about that other stuff. I just knew I'd be happier and better off with you than without you."

"Are you still against having kids?"

"Not with you. Why, are you pregnant?"

"I'm surprised that I'm not, since I've been with you. Except for the last few nights, but that's just been nerves. I don't know, I just don't feel that things are fully resolved, John."

"Can we make a pact, before we fall asleep again?" I asked her.

"What kind of pact?"

"That we stick to the original pact. Whatever we decide, we do it together. Fair enough?" I stuck out my hand.

She shook my hand with mock solemnity. "Fair enough."

THE WHITE HOUSE

Mitch had gone to Union Station to meet Dottie Parker, who had agreed to come to Washington and stay the night. Terry was asleep, so flat-out exhausted that he could barely replace the phone on its hook when he hung up. Althea and I had decided to spend the day walking around Washington.

At Pennsylvania Avenue, we saw a long line stretching through the iron gates of the White House. I recalled that every day during the noon hour, Calvin Coolidge would throw open the doors to the Oval Office and invite anyone who felt like showing up to come in and shake his hand. Coolidge had often boasted that he could shake twelve hundred hands in less than half an hour.

We stood in line between a diminutive Japanese man and a mother and father with two spoiled kids.

"I couldn't imagine a president doing that today," I whispered to Althea. "Some wacko'd kill him."

I could tell from the Japanese man's change in posture that my words had captured his attention, so I lowered my voice. "I wonder if anyone's tried it yet."

"It is hard to believe," Althea agreed. "Even in 1940."

"I hafta go ta the bathroom," the little boy wailed.

"Wait till we get inside," the mother said.

"You think the President's gonna let some kid piss all over his favorite seat?" the father argued in a harsh whisper.

"Better than the floor," the mother said.

"I gotta pee," the kid insisted.

"You'll have to wait," the mother said. "The line's moving fast enough, it won't be too much longer."

"I gotta pee now!" the kid shrieked.

The kid's tantrum began to seriously annoy everyone standing on line nearby. Someone even grumbled, "Get that goddamn brat outta here."

The parents were probably from out of town, however, and had most likely been looking forward to this once-in-a-lifetime meeting with a President of the United States.

"Please be patient," the mother said, kneeling to her child. "I know you're uncomfortable, but your father and I admire your ability to try and get through this. Don't we, *dear*?"

"You tryin' that child psychology hooey *again*?" he asked aggrievedly. "It's newfangled horse crap. My old man—"

" 'Would belt you one in the chops, that was his psychology,' " she recited tiredly.

"I gotta go pee!" the kid wailed again.

"Please." The Japanese man had stepped out of line in front of us and approached the beleaguered parents. "May I be of service?"

The father eyed him suspiciously. "Whyn't you mind your own bus—"

The wife cut him off. "Do you have children?"

"Yes, of course." The man's accent was heavy, but his English was excellent. He knelt in front of the little boy. "How badly do you have to go?" he asked the little boy.

The boy looked at his mother, who nodded. "Sorta, y'know, like bad."

"All right," the man said softly. "Why don't you pee in your pants right now. You'll feel better."

"Are you fu—" the husband began, but the wife nudged him.

"Pee my pants?" the little boy asked incredulously.

"Of course. No one will laugh at you, I promise. Go ahead."

The boy made various facial contortions of effort. "I can't!"

"Try, young fellow."

"Can't!"

He stood up. "Keep trying." He returned to his place in line.

"Jesus," the father said in grudging admiration, "that little Nip sure knows his stuff."

The man turned back and bowed slightly, acknowledging the "compliment."

"Are you a psychologist?" I asked him.

He turned to me. "Nothing so lofty," he replied. "Just a sailor. On leave, travelling your great country," he added, gesturing at his civilian clothes.

Some kids walked by the line, carrying baseball gloves and bats.

"Such a wonderful game," the Japanese man sighed. "I wish it were baseball season instead of just spring training."

"Who do you like?" I asked conversationally.

He smiled. "I'm a Detroit fan, but I must admit, if Ruth is healthy this year, no one will stop the Yankees. That young fellow, Gehrig, those great pitchers, Hoyt, Jones—no, it'll be the Yankees this year."

The line was moving rapidly now, and we were inside the main entrance. A Secret Service agent escorted the little brat to the nearest john.

"Who is your choice?" the man asked me.

"I'm a National League man, myself, a Dodger fan. But this year I'd bet on the Cardinals. I think they'll win the Series."

"A powerful club." He nodded. "But fast, great speed on the bases. They'd have to score a lot of runs in the early innings, then their pitching would have to take over."

"They'll win," I said decisively.

His eyebrows shot up. "Are you a gambling man, sir?"

"Given the right thing to bet on."

"You'll take the Cards in six?"

"How much?"

"Twenty?"

"The Cards in seven," I recalled. "I'm confident, but not stupid."

"Done," he replied.

We had moved through the corridor quickly and were now just outside the Oval Office. Through the door I could see the President, Calvin Coolidge. He looked just like his photographs, but I noticed that his manner was far different than I had always been led to believe. I had expected a taciturn, humorless fellow, the one Alice Roosevelt Longworth had reportedly described as having been "weaned on a pickle." But the man the line was fast approaching was animated, with a charming smile and pleasant manner. It was almost hard to believe he was the same "Silent Cal" of legend.

I was about to introduce myself to the Japanese sailor, so I would at least know from whom I would be taking an easy twenty bucks, but it was his turn.

"Well," Coolidge greeted him. "One of our friends from the Orient. What brings you here, Mr.—"

"Yamamoto, Mr. President. Commander Isoroku Yamamoto, Imperial Japanese Navy."

I almost fell over when I heard *that*.

"Welcome, Commander. I hope our two great nations will forever share the peaceful relationship we now enjoy."

"It is my fervent hope," Yamamoto replied. He was suddenly struck with emotion. "I have travelled . . . your beautiful land . . . I love your country . . ."

Coolidge's smile froze, and their handshake stalled. The two men stood gripping hands, staring into each other's eyes as if they had suddenly shared a terrible secret.

Yamamoto broke contact first. He came to attention and gave the President a crisp bow of his head. "It has been an honor, Mr. President."

He turned and was ushered out of the Oval Office by a bewildered Secret Service agent, a young fellow who apparently knew he had just seen something important, but couldn't quite grasp what it was.

Coolidge stared after Yamamoto. "May God help you," he whispered.

The moment passed. There is nothing to distract a man from any tribulation like the sight of a beautiful woman, and when Coolidge saw Althea, he became himself in an instant.

"An American Beauty Rose," he greeted her. "Nothing in the world like the flower of a young American girl."

"I'm charmed, Mr. President," she replied. She put out her hand and Coolidge gave it a businesslike shake.

I stuck out my hand and Coolidge accepted it in his strong, dry, farmer's grip.

"You're an awfully lucky young fellow," he said to me.

"I always thought so, Mr. President, but now it's officially recognized by the United States Government," I replied.

We were ushered out quickly. Coolidge had taken up more time with Yamamoto than he usually allotted each person, so he was eager get the line moving again.

As we exited the White House, I searched in vain for Yamamoto. But he was gone.

"All right, John," Althea demanded. "Who was that guy?"

"Calvin Coolidge."

"Not him. The Japanese guy."

"Uh, nobody." I wasn't prepared to tell her about it just yet.

"Then why are you going nuts trying to find him?"

I thought, because he's the guy who masterminded the raid on Pearl Harbor, however reluctantly. I knew that Yamamoto had developed a great affinity for America and its people, but I was also aware that what he had found on his pilgrimage had scared the hell out of him; Japan would never be a match for the sheer industrial might of the United States. And that was why he would order the raid on Pearl Harbor: With victory an impossible dream, the best he could hope to do was hold us off until we could rebuild our navy.

I faced her. "Hey, the son of a bitch is gonna owe me twenty dollars. How the hell am I gonna collect?"

There was one last piece of business left in 1926, and Mitch was attending to her now. The classy thing would have been to let them alone, but I couldn't fight the perverse desire to be there. Oddly enough, Mitchell answered our knock and let us into his suite without comment.

Dottie Parker nodded to Althea and patted the seat cushion beside her.

"Come sit by me, dear, we have lots to talk about."

Althea sat next to her. I went over to the bar and stood near Mitch. The scene was almost comically clichéd; the guys near the bar and the ladies on the couch sharing girl-talk.

"You're the prettiest girl I've ever met who I haven't wanted to strangle," Dottie told Althea, "probably because my instincts tell me that there's quite a brain in that pretty head."

Althea became slightly Dorothy Parkerish in response. "We're not after the same man," she said, "so I won't have to kill you."

Dottie was impressed. "Oh, good for you, dear."

"How can I help?" Althea asked.

"Do I go back? Or is front—forward? I mean, the fella's not even married. What more could I ask?"

"Does she know everything?" Althea asked Mitch.

"Go ahead." He nodded.

"Dottie," Althea began, "Mitch isn't just a writer."

"Oh? He's just doing it until he can get that job he's always wanted, waiting tables?"

"No. He's a filmmaker. A very successful filmmaker."

Dottie narrowed her eyes at Mitch. "How successful?"

"His studio has made almost two billion dollars on his movies."

That hardly fazed Dottie. The figure was too incomprehensible in 1926. There were countries in that era not worth that much. "So, he's single, sweet, *and* rich?"

"Yes."

"Gotta dump him, then. Bye, Mitch." But she was kidding.

"That's not what you really want to know, is it?"

"I knew you had a brain. No, it isn't."

"You want to know if you'll like 2007, if you'll be happy there."

"And will I be?"

"Could you be happy in 1926?"

"Not so far." She smiled at Althea. "I guess that's my answer."

Mitch's face fell. "I guess that's that."

Althea stood up and nodded to me. We both went to the door. "If I don't see you again," Althea said, "I just want you to know how much I admire you."

"Get a new role model," Dottie replied, but then softened for the first time. "I'm sorry we couldn't become friends."

"We *are* friends," Althea said. "We just don't spend much time together."

We went out the door to give Mitch some privacy on his last sad night with the fleeting girl of his dreams.

FIFTEEN

14 MARCH 1926—CEDAR RAPIDS, IOWA—
ABOARD THE 20TH CENTURY

NONE OF US HAD SPOKEN MUCH SINCE LEAVING WASHING-
ton. Terry still hadn't recovered his energy and slept most
of the time. When he was awake, he was lethargic and
unable to maintain his end of a conversation. His mind
wandered and he would rise up without a word and shuffle
back to his drawing room for another nap.

"I'm worried about Terry," I told Althea. "I've never
seen him like this."

"We've all been under a great deal of strain," she replied. "We all need a lot of rest."

"Why has this trip been so different?" I wondered.
"Why has it taken so much out of us? Is it time travel?
Can the body and spirit only take just so much of it?"

"I think I know," she said. "There's something about
this trip that's been . . . personal. We've really gotten involved, perhaps more than we should."

I nodded. "You're right, of course. I've just never felt
so emotionally drained. Even when I was in 1940, maybe

because I was so happy, I never felt this out of sorts.''

"I hate to say it, John, and I think you'd hate me to say it, but I think you miss 2007. It's a terrible year, but it's your home.''

I stared out at the newly sown cornfields and harvested winter wheat. "Maybe I can only do so much of this, maybe I really need a break. I know I'm sending Terry on a long vacation, on the company. Anywhere he wants to go. For however long.''

"He's a wonderful friend,'' Althea said. "I'm glad he's my friend, too.''

"God, I'm hungry all of a sudden. Are you?''

"I'm going to be a blimp by the time we get off this train. All I do is eat like a pig and sleep around the clock.''

"I think our bodies have had it. We need a major rest, lots of exercise. Hey, let's go get Mitch. The guy hasn't left his drawing room since Washington, won't answer the door.''

"Well, he hasn't been starving himself,'' Althea replied. "I've seen the empty trays piled up outside his door.''

We walked through the club car. As we stepped outside between the cars, a freezing wind cut through our clothes and chilled our bones.

"We can't reach California too soon for me,'' I shouted above the clatter.

We came to Mitchell's door and I rapped on it. "Mitch! Mitch! Come on, Mitch, let's get you some dinner.''

"Go away!''

"Come on, Mitch, you can't stay in your room, moping like a little kid. Just for an hour, you can do it. You've got to stretch your legs.''

"Buzz off, John, I mean it!''

"Mitch, I know you're upset, but sitting alone feeling sorry for yourself won't help. It'll just make you feel worse.''

"John, I know you mean well. But leave me alone!''

"I won't leave you alone. I'm your friend and I care about you."

"If you're my friend you'll go away."

A porter turned sideways to pass us, diplomatically ignoring our situation.

"Have you got a passkey?" I whispered.

The porter shook his head. "I can't be doing that."

I took out a fifty-dollar bill. Then I removed my old Naval Intelligence ID that Uncle Jack had given me long ago.

"National Security," I said sternly.

The porter looked around carefully, snatched the fifty, and had his key in and out of the lock within seconds. He disappeared before we even knew the door was unlocked.

"That's it, Mitch," I called. "I'm coming in."

I shoved the door open and saw Mitch in bed, obviously naked under the covers. A pillow came flying at my head and I almost ducked. Then I remembered Althea was behind me, so I stood up straight and took it full in the face.

"In the future," Dorothy Parker snapped, "I hope you'll be a little more considerate of people who are getting properly laid. Your record in the past isn't all that hot."

"Sorry," I said, edging out of the room. I closed the door carefully. "Well, I guess old Dottie decided to give '07 a try," I told Althea.

"She doesn't give any more of a damn about '07 than I do," Althea replied. She smiled. "Good for you, Mitch," she whispered.

"She won't like '07, then?" I asked.

"Of course not."

"Why's she doing it, then?"

Althea shook her head at me. "Will you never learn, John? She's in love. Nothing's more important than that. Not even time."

7 APRIL 2007—TIMESHARE—LOS ANGELES

We got off the train in Los Angeles and went through the long process of retrieving our luggage and lavishly tipping all the train personnel who had treated us so well.

With the five of us standing in a tight circle, I turned to Dorothy Parker. "I have to ask you this, Mrs. Parker. Sorry, but it's procedure. Are you sure you want to do this?"

She turned to Mitch. "I have to quit smoking?"

"Well, in public," he replied.

"Drinking?"

"Definitely."

"Even though it's legal?"

"Until you can control it. You have a wonderful mind and I don't want you soaking it with booze."

"And I'll have to . . . exercise?" She made a moue of distaste.

"You'll love it. We've got machines that make it easy for you. You won't even know you're working out."

"And that's all you ask?"

"That's it."

"Let's go," she said.

"You're sure?" I asked her.

She nodded. "Its my hobby," she replied. "I collect brave new worlds."

I held up my Decacom. "Let's go home."

You would have thought that we were aboard a Cunard ship docking in New York Harbor. There were more people in the Zoom Room than I had ever seen in my career, and I wondered why Cornelia allowed it. All that was missing was the confetti.

Mitch held up Dottie's hand as if she had just won a championship fight. "Ladies and gentlemen of 2007," he announced, "may I proudly introduce Mrs. Dorothy Parker."

A ripple of applause began that soon gathered momentum and became a full-fledged ovation. Amid the high-technology layout, it brought to mind the reaction to a safe reentry at NASA Mission Control.

Dottie looked over at Althea and me with a puzzled expression on her face. "Was I that good?" she asked.

"Better," Althea replied.

Cornelia was staring at me with the same look as a school principal who had just caught a kid writing graffiti on a bathroom wall.

"How are you, John?" she asked me.

"I need a vacation. In fact, I was *on* vacation, remember? Oh, did Kirk get back okay?"

"He just landed at Van Nuys a minute ago. He's fine. So the girl turned out to be *Dorothy Parker*, for God's sake?"

I shrugged. "A man's gotta do . . ." I began.

"Whatever *I* tell him to do," she finished for me. "Anything significant?" she asked, wanting to know if I had anything urgent to tell her that couldn't wait for the official debriefing.

"Terry's made an important scientific discovery," I said. I looked over and saw Terry conversing with a technician. I breathed a sigh of relief that he seemed to have recovered since zooming back.

"Terry?" She was surprised. "Not that he's stupid, he's just not a scientist."

"Oh yeah?" I replied. "Ask him about the 'Rappaport Hinge.' I think you'll find it the most significant discovery since you invented this thing."

I left her wondering and walked over to Mitch. "Do we go home now?" he asked.

I shook my head. "Tomorrow. We have accommodations you'll find quite comfortable. But you have to debrief, and so do we."

"I have to call my office," he said. "How long have we been gone?"

I looked at the giant chronometer on the wall. "Five minutes," I said.

"That's all? It seems like months!"

"It was months. It's just that those months happened eighty years ago."

"John, tomorrow night, I want to have a party at my house."

"That's nice of you, Mitch, but I think we're all too tired for a big Hollywood—"

"No, not a full-of-crap bash," he said. "Just the five of us. The 1926 Kids."

"I'd like that," I said.

He looked at the ground. "I've spent my whole life busting my—I never had a lot of friends. And, of course now, who can I really trust?"

I put an arm on his shoulder. "We're your friends, Mitch. You go through an experience like this, you bond."

"Tomorrow night, then?"

"Sure."

Except for Terry's childhood, nothing had changed. Hoover had remained head of the FBI until his death in 1972, the Mafia had still flourished, and the Hollywood blacklist had still taken its toll. His kidnapping by the Russians was un-documented. It was almost as if we had never crossed paths.

And there was something else. Dorothy Parker had still died in 1967. Her work was unaffected, her failed marriages still the same as in the earlier record. Perhaps it was still too early to tell. She might still change her mind, and the option to go back remained an open invitation. It was all up to whether or not her relationship with Mitchell worked out.

Both Chief Blaine and Randy Dickinson had left urgent messages for me. I couldn't deal with that at the moment, even though the deadline for my return to active duty was fast approaching.

Even though Terry seemed better, Doc Harvey insisted that he, as well as Althea and myself, go on an extended leave of absence. He didn't have to tell us twice. We all made plans for the day after Mitch's party. Terry and one of his on-again, off-again girlfriends would go to Aruba. Althea and I debated whether or not to pick up our La Quinta vacation where we left off, or to go to someplace entirely different. We decided to loll around the apartment for a while until we came to a decision.

However, we were interrupted in mid-loll by our doorbell.

"Chief Blaine?"

"Hello, John. I hope I'm not intruding."

"Not at all, sir. Please come in."

He looked around the apartment appraisingly, and I saw him deflate almost imperceptibly. He was probably thinking that there was no way a mere lieutenant's salary would pay the freight for this place. And he was right.

"Althea, this is Chief Blaine of LAPD."

"I'm pleased to meet you, Chief."

Blaine looked at her, frowning. "Have we met before?" he asked as he shook her hand.

Althea and I shared a secret smile. "No, sir," she replied. "I'd've remembered. I'll leave you gentlemen alone."

"Lovely girl," he said, glancing after her. "But I'm sure I've seen her before." He shook it off. "You know why I've come."

"Can I get you a drink, Chief?"

"No, I'm fine."

"By the way, I loved the way you handled that protest rally."

He waved it off. "John, do you remember what we discussed at our last meeting?"

"Yes, sir. You told me you had found a way to rid the city of gangs once and for all."

"That's right. How do you suppose I would go about it?"

"I haven't a clue, Chief."

"You've heard of the RICO statutes, haven't you?"

"Of course, sir. Federal racketeering laws."

He pulled his chair closer to mine. "That's what Randy Dickinson and I intend to do. Any street gang that we can prove is making a profit by illegal means—drugs, guns, extortion—will be subject to arrest by federal authorities. The first thing we have to do is get the evidence—prove that every gang is making money through illegal means. Once we do that, we bring in the Feds and bust every damn one of them. We'll make it a crime just to belong to a gang."

I leaned back in my chair. For some reason, the chief's enthusiasm wasn't contagious.

"Well?" he asked.

I shrugged. "Where would I fit in?"

He smiled, a man with a royal flush showing his cards. "You'd be reactivated as a lieutenant, and summarily promoted to acting captain with all the pay and benefits, et cetera."

That struck me. Me, a *captain*? That magic rank, the police equivalent to a knighthood or, at the very least, a vice presidency?

"And what would I have to do in exchange for this honor?"

"You would supervise all intelligence-gathering on all the gangs in the city. You would determine whether or not we have enough evidence to prosecute successfully under the RICO statutes. And then, once that phase was completed, you would be the liaison to the Feds when we made the busts. Needless to say, if successful—and there's no reason why it shouldn't be—your rank would become permanent and your further career prospects, somewhat brighter."

But I had my doubts. "Chief, it's a great plan, and yes,

it can work, but there's one big problem that I can see. A lot of people aren't going to like the idea of bringing the Federal Government in to solve a local police problem. I know we're past the point of worrying about such niceties, but what do you think is going to happen when we bring these people to trial? I can see a shitload of lawsuits by the ACLU, insisting that we're violating the first, second, and probably fourteenth amendments.''

I thought he'd be angry with me for raining on his parade, but he simply gave me an approving nod. ''You're absolutely right, of course. I've already gotten this argument from Randy Dickinson, Commander Silvera, and the Department's legal advisor.''

''Then why are you going ahead with it?''

''Because it's a good gamble. If we can get enough evidence on each gang, nobody can sue us and win.''

''Does even the Federal Government have enough facilities to process 100,000 arrestees? I know for sure that we don't.''

''Of course not. We're not going to arrest everyone, just the top guys. Maybe five thousand head gangbangers. At least twenty percent will turn out to be illegal aliens, so we can deport them right away. Of the remaining four thousand, I'd bet you ten-to-one that at least half will be on probation or parole, so it's right back to the slam for them. It'll be a stretch, but we can prosecute the other two thousand with a little help from the Feds.''

''And what about the rest of the guys still out on the streets?''

''With no leadership, they'll fall apart. They'll get the message.''

I closed my eyes and thought deeply. It was an enormous plan, and he wanted me to ramrod it. I could see myself leading the charge, getting on national television, career revived, the rank of at least deputy chief somewhere in my future.

Then why couldn't I just grab it? Something was holding me back. Was it because, like Althea, I felt as if my life was unresolved?

"How long do I have to decide?"

The chief was taken aback. "What time is it?"

"Chief, I can't tell you now."

He stood up. He was disappointed, but he was also a fair man. "You have a month, John. That's the best I can do."

I walked him to the door. "I had dinner at Randy Dickinson's last night," he said.

I nodded. I had been right, Chief Dickinson did like him. Randy's wife, Martha, was a brilliant cook, good enough to make Escoffier seem like an amateur and Wolfgang Puck, a stumblebum. As such, dinner invitations to the Dickinson home were not regarded lightly. When Randy invited you to dinner, it was his way of rewarding you for earning his friendship.

"Is he the luckiest man alive, or what?" I replied.

"It was so good I almost forgot myself and asked for the check," he said.

"I'll call you soon. Chief."

"John," he said, "I know you have other things, but please give my offer serious consideration."

"I promise you that, Chief."

We were both silent as we drove to Mitch's house. I was pondering my conversation with the chief, and Althea was content to give me my space. But it was going to be a long night.

The party was anticlimactic. Even though there were only the five of us, Mitchell had set up his dining room for a giant feast. There was an orgy of iced shellfish, hollowed-out melons, cold cuts, prime rib, and sushi. But we were all too spent to really enjoy it. There was no conversation besides the usual compliments on the food and discussions of movies. At one point in the evening, Mitch offered Althea a three-picture deal worth almost twenty million, and all she could do was shrug and reply that she would give it some thought.

But despite everyone's lack of enthusiasm, the evening did prove that we were all true friends, not just some group thrown together in a crisis who were secretly relieved to be rid of each other once it had passed. The real fun would come later when we had the energy for it, and we all knew it. For now, we were just too damned tired.

Even though she was abstaining from liquor, Mrs. Parker fell asleep during dinner. It was understandable; her constitution was nowhere near as hearty as Althea's, and Althea was still in recovery.

She awoke momentarily as Mitch carried her gently up the stairs. I was following for safety's sake.

"Mitch," she whispered in a half-sleep.

"Yes, Dottie?"

"This'll all still be here when I wake up?"

"Yes, love."

"*You'll* still be here?"

"Of course."

"And you won't have turned into a prick, or have gotten married by then—which amounts to the same thing?"

He kissed her forehead. "Of course not. But if I did I'd give you a million dollars and send you back to 1926, so you really can't lose."

She yawned. "Only a million?" she asked, and then fell asleep.

We decided to call it an early night, but not before Mitch pulled me into the library.

"It's the damndest thing, John," he said. "Check this out!"

He showed me to the bookshelf where Harry's picture and medals were kept. There were four thick novels that hadn't been there before, all of them written by Harry Levitan. Two of them, I noted after inspecting the covers, had won the Pulitzer Prize and the National Book Award.

"You were right," he said excitedly, "I did make a difference." He flipped open one of the books to the dedication page.

"Look at this, John. 'To the nut who overtipped me in Rudley's in 1926. *Never give up.*' John, this is the first of the four, all of them big ones that probably took years to write. This one was released in 1956, his first book after the blacklist."

"Fantastic," I said. "Do you remember reading them?"

"Hell, no! I can't wait. And the movies I'll make with them!"

A tear ran down his cheek. "I owe you a lot, John."

"You did it yourself, Mitch."

"But I've got to give you something in return."

"Just keep making those movies, Mitch. Keep looking for those great stories, and taking chances on all those people who want to help you tell them."

He looked at me almost shyly. "John? What about *your* life? What I've seen already would make a hell of a story."

I clapped him on the shoulder. "You're probably right, old pal. There's just one small problem."

"What's that?"

I put on my nasal critic's voice. "The problem is, the script is still in development."

The night wasn't over yet, however. Althea and I both had an unusual desire to stop off for a drink on the way home from Mitch's party. Little did I know that one short beer would affect the course of our lives.

I figured Althea was probably a little homesick, so I drove to Santa Monica and stopped at a bar frequented by members of the surprisingly large British expatriate community in that city. It was a pub called Boz, after the pen name of Charles Dickens, and it was decorated according to the themes of his stories. There was a kitchen that served English fare, such as bangers and mash, Shepherd's pie, and fish and chips. The bar had all kinds of British beer and ale. At the piano, the entertainer led the enthusiastic crowd in British Music Hall songs like ''Tipperary,'' ''Bye-Bye Blackbird,'' and ''My Old Man Said Follow the Van.''

Everyone seemed pleasantly drunk, and there was a definite coziness to the atmosphere, enhanced by fake hoarfrost left over from Christmas covering the walls and ceilings. Not for the first time, I was amazed at the lack of a generation gap in British drinking establishments. Tattooed kids in leather grunge sang along to the old standards as lustily as matrons and retirees.

We were shown to a table near a mirrored wall. I paid the ten-dollar smoking fee for Althea and ordered us each a mug of John Courage. Her face was glowing as we sang along to ''Maybe It's Because I'm a Londoner.''

''I'm glad there are places like this in L.A.,'' she said.

''There has to be,'' I replied. ''There aren't any more Brits left in England. They're all on American television.''

It was a wonderful place, and we felt as if we had stepped into another era, something for which the two of us required more convincing than the average person. I was congratulating myself on my choice of watering holes when the piano began a soft intro. The entire place suddenly hushed, as if an anthem were about be played.

> ''There'll be bluebirds over
> the White Cliffs of Dover,
> To-morrow, just you wait and see.''

It might just as well have been an anthem. It was virtually the British theme song of World War II, and everyone joined in softly, including the younger people, whose *parents* weren't even born at the time. As maudlin as it might have seemed, it was a song that tugged at the heart and wouldn't let go. Even more than sixty years later.

> "There'll be love and laughter,
>   And peace ever after,
>   Tomorrow, when the world is free."

The tune had been written during the war, but long after Althea's departure from the era, so she had never heard it before. But the song worked its wistful magic. Although she didn't know the words, she hummed along solemnly.

> "The shepherd will tend his sheep,
>   The valley will bloom again,
>   And Jimmy will go to sleep,
>   In his own little room again."

That tore it. Althea put her drink down and buried her face in my shoulder, convulsing with noiseless sobs.

I felt a tap on my shoulder. I turned and saw a big bluff guy, holding a giant stein of Guinness, nodding with understanding. "Know just how she feels, mate," he said in a comforting manner. There was no real answer for that, so I simply nodded my thanks.

> "There'll be bluebirds over
>   The White Cliffs of Dover,
>   To-morrow, just . . . you . . . wait and see."

The song ended, and there was a palpable moment of reflection before the bar resumed its normal sound level. Althea disengaged from my arms and sat up straight, her eyes red, an embarrassed smile on her face.

"Do you want to go?" I asked gently.

She shook her head. "I'm fine." She still shuddered from time to time, but she was beginning to recover. At first, she had trouble meeting my eye, like an actress doing a weeping scene in the movies. But soon she began to stare at me, with love, but also with expectation.

A few days ago we had made a pact. We were both

people of honor, and keeping our word was the very essence of our beings. She had made her decision. Now the question was, would I keep my end of the bargain?

I took a good long look at the woman with whom I was determined to share the rest of my life. An extraordinarily pretty girl, a California kid, a British-American woman. An actress who had been a rising star during Hollywood's Golden Age. A transplant from more than half a century before. And through it all, a soldier, for whom the words *defeat, dishonor,* and *surrender* were the three most distasteful obscenities imaginable.

This girl was mine, but only because of an insanely freakish piece of luck, an impossible discovery that science had long ago ruled, at best, improbable. I had searched the span of years and, by an incredible turn of events, I had found her.

She knew me so well that she could tell that my thought processes were clicking away furiously, and she was content to wait until they were done. Part of that thought process was another long look at her. She wore a pair of 2007 designer jeans from Big Star and a Versace sweater, both of which I had bought her a few weeks before on Rodeo Drive. Her flowing brown hair had been cut and styled the day before at Christophe, and her skin was flavored by the latest perfume from Giorgio. To the casual observer, she was the epitome of the most stylish woman Beverly Hills could offer on that April night in 2007.

But that wasn't who I saw. Not even the actress, the girlfriend, or the fellow time traveller. The girl I saw was Section Officer Althea Rowland, Royal Air Force.

Then I looked in the mirror at my own reflection. I searched in vain for the police captain and could no longer find him; he had long ago left that world behind. I looked for the CEO of Timeshare, and he was there, but buried deep, to return at a much later date, if ever.

All I saw was John Surrey, first and foremost the soon-to-be husband of Section Officer Althea Rowland, and he was going to war.